Readers love the Love Can't series by KIM FIELDING

Love Can't Conquer

"Author Kim Fielding once again gives us a gorgeous story of love and healing—of quiet determination and strength and does so with the greatest of skill."

—Joyfully Jay

"I thought this story was quite beautiful, even in it's dark moments."

—Just Love: Queer Romance Reviews

"The story was gripping and emotional and I had a hard time putting it down…"

—Two Chicks Obsessed

Love Is Heartless

"*Love Is Heartless* is just a gorgeous story that has you hoping for that happy ever after right up to the end."

—The Novel Approach

"…this was another hit from the pen of Kim Fielding. This is why she is one of my solid go-to authors in the genre."

—The Blogger Girls

"Full of tons of emotion, two memorable and extremely charismatic characters, and a story line that will pull you in right from the beginning, this book is a gem and truly not to be missed."

—Diverse Reader

By KIM FIELDING

Alaska
Anyplace Else
Astounding!
Blyd and Pearce
The Border
Brute
Dear Ruth
Exit Through the Gift Shop
Get Lit
Grateful
A Great Miracle Happened There
Grown-up
Housekeeping
Motel. Pool.
Night Shift
Once Upon a Time in the Weird West
Pilgrimage
The Pillar
Rattlesnake
With Venona Keyes: Running Blind
Saint Martin's Day
Speechless • The Gig
The Tin Box
Venetian Masks
Violet's Present

BONES
Good Bones
Buried Bones
Bone Dry
The Gig

DREAMSPUN BEYOND
#8 – Ante Up

DREAMSPUN DESIRES
#56 – A Full Plate
STARS FROM PERIL
#67 – The Spy's Love Song
#82 – Redesigning Landry Bishop
#91 – Drawing the Prince

GOTHIKA
Stitch
Bones
Claw
Spirit
Contact

LOVE CAN'T
Love Can't Conquer
Love Is Heartless
Love Has No Direction

Published by DREAMSPINNER PRESS
www.dreamspinnerpress.com

LOVE HAS NO DIRECTION

KIM FIELDING

DREAMSPINNER PRESS

Published by
DREAMSPINNER PRESS

5032 Capital Circle SW, Suite 2, PMB# 279, Tallahassee, FL 32305-7886 USA
www.dreamspinnerpress.com

This is a work of fiction. Names, characters, places, and incidents either are the product of Kim Fielding imagination or are used fictitiously, and any resemblance to actual persons, living or dead, business establishments, events, or locales is entirely coincidental.

Love Has No Direction
© 2020 Kim Fielding

Cover Art
© 2020 Brooke Albrecht
http://brookealbrechtstudio.com
Cover content is for illustrative purposes only and any person depicted on the cover is a model.

All rights reserved. This book is licensed to the original purchaser only. Duplication or distribution via any means is illegal and a violation of international copyright law, subject to criminal prosecution and upon conviction, fines, and/or imprisonment. Any eBook format cannot be legally loaned or given to others. No part of this book may be reproduced or transmitted in any form or by any means, electronic or mechanical, including photocopying, recording, or by any information storage and retrieval system, without the written permission of the Publisher, except where permitted by law. To request permission and all other inquiries, contact Dreamspinner Press, 5032 Capital Circle SW, Suite 2, PMB# 279, Tallahassee, FL 32305-7886, USA, or www.dreamspinnerpress.com.

Trade Paperback ISBN: 978-1-64405-691-2
Digital ISBN: 978-1-64405-690-5
Library of Congress Control Number: 2019951817
Trade Paperback published January 2020
v. 1.0

Printed in the United States of America
∞
This paper meets the requirements of
ANSI/NISO Z39.48-1992 (Permanence of Paper).

Prologue

Portland, Oregon
November 2006

"Parker Hershel Levin, stop messing with your gadget and get your homework done."

"I *am*, Mom." Parker set the iPod on the desk. "I was just listening to music. It helps me with my essay."

"Then how come you've written only seven words? 'When I grow up, I want to.' Want to what? Waste your time fidgeting with gizmos? Live in your parents' basement because you couldn't pass ninth grade?"

"Mo-om," Parker grumbled as he bent over and rested his forehead on the desk. It smelled of pencil eraser and the Coke he'd spilled the previous week. At least he hadn't ruined the computer when he spilled—although on second thought, maybe that wouldn't have been so bad. Then he'd be handwriting his essay right now, meaning he could have more easily hidden the nearly blank page from his mother.

She mussed the hair on the back of his head. "C'mon, kiddo. Aside from teenagehood and homework in general, what's the cause of today's angst?"

Parker groaned. He wanted her to go away and leave him to wallow, but she wouldn't. Once Rhoda Levin decided to tackle an issue, she never let it go. She would have had this stupid essay written in five minutes flat.

"I'm supposed to talk about my career goals," he whined.

"And?"

"I don't have any." Ever since he was little, adults had asked him what he wanted to be when he grew up. Apart from a brief period when he was four and toyed with the idea of being a garbage man, he'd never had an answer.

His mother stared at him thoughtfully for a moment before nodding in agreement with whatever decision she'd reached. "Come for a drive."

"But my homework—"

"Isn't getting done anyway. C'mon."

His mother didn't often encourage him to neglect his duties, so Parker jumped at the rare opportunity. Abandoning the computer and iPod, he jammed his feet into tennis shoes, smoothed his hair in front of the bedroom mirror, and zipped up his hoodie. "Where are we going?"

"You'll see."

Eastbound traffic was light on Sunset Highway. Rush hour was over, and they were heading into downtown Portland rather than away. Parker looked through the window longingly as they traversed the city streets. He hated living in the burbs. Beaverton was so… boring. Mundane. Downtown was way more interesting. But although he was fully capable of getting there by bus, his parents didn't let him go very often. *You can hang out with your friends at home*, they said. *Or go to the movies. Or the mall.* Ugh. The mall. There weren't any vintage clothing stores there, or funky antique shops full of cool stuff he could imagine owning someday, when he had a house of his own.

This evening he didn't get to stay downtown either. His mom drove over the river to the east side of town, which was mildly interesting since he rarely visited there. The houses were way older than in his neighborhood, and they didn't all look the same. He imagined they might have hidden stairways, secret rooms, mysterious boxes tucked into the attic rafters. His parents' house didn't have an attic. Or a basement—thereby negating his mom's fear of him living underground should he fail ninth grade.

After a couple of miles, his mother pulled to the curb and turned off the engine. "Let's take a look," she said, opening her door.

Confused but curious, Parker left the car, pulled up his hood against the rain, and followed his mom along the sidewalk to a long two-story commercial building. A tattered awning protected them from the worst of the wet when his mom stopped in front of a big window.

"What do you think?" She gestured at the window.

He peered inside. It was hard to see much because there were no lights on, but he could make out a few old tables and chairs and a reception desk. "It's a dump."

"It's a dump *now*. But use your imagination. Gut the insides. Refinish that cool old wooden floor, paint the walls nice colors, hang some art. Along that far wall, put in a long counter with a glass display case for pastry. Have a shelf full of bright dishes and mugs. Add comfy chairs everywhere, cozy little tables. A sound system. Hmm, maybe even a little stage for live music? Yeah, I like that." Her eyes had gone all big and glittery, and she was smiling widely.

Parker put an arm around her shoulders. He was taller than her now, which was weird. "I have no clue what you're talking about, Mom."

"A coffeehouse. That's what I'm talking about."

"Starbucks?"

She snorted. "Not corporate. Quirky. Where people love to hang out. Where they can connect. It would be warm and welcoming, a peaceful haven for good people. And there would be really great coffee."

Parker squinted through the window. If he tried, he could almost picture the scene his mother was describing. It would be a pretty great place, actually. The kind of place where he'd hang out if he could. "Why are we doing pretend coffeehouses?"

"Because maybe someday it won't be pretend." She tucked a lock of hair behind his ear. "I'm going to show your dad this store when he gets home from Boise. If he likes it as much as I do, we're going to rent it."

"You're… what?" Parker often found adults hard to comprehend, but this was extra mystifying.

"Rent it. Then we'll fix it up—you'll be helping, kiddo—and open a coffeehouse here."

He removed his arm from her shoulders, took a step aside, and turned to stare. Nope, she didn't seem to be kidding. "Why?"

"You're shivering. Why do you insist on wearing that ratty old sweatshirt instead of the perfectly nice winter coat I bought you?" She sighed loudly. "Let's go back to the car."

No way he'd admit he was cold, but he followed her and got back into the passenger seat without complaint. She started the engine and cranked the heater, but she didn't shift out of Park. Instead she searched through her enormous purse until she found a couple of Werther's; she handed him one before unwrapping the other and popping it into her mouth. She always had hard candy. And Kleenex and pens and Tylenol and Chapstick and Band-Aids and hand sanitizer and Wet Wipes and rubber bands and paper clips and saltines or oyster crackers. Parker was fairly certain her purse was magic.

"When I was in tenth grade, they didn't make us write an essay about our career plans," she said. "Instead we had to take a test on a computer, which was a big deal because nobody had computers at home back then. The computer told us what we were supposed to be."

It would be nice if a computer made decisions on Parker's behalf so he didn't have to. "What did the computer tell you?"

"That I should be a lumber salesperson."

Parker almost coughed out the candy. "Lumber?"

"The software was sponsored by a wood products company, so everyone got something related to that. Forest ranger. Mill operator. Log truck driver."

Okay, maybe it was just as well the computers weren't in charge. "You didn't take their advice, huh?"

She didn't answer right away, seemingly focusing her interest on some dust on the dashboard. She wiped it away with a Kleenex. Parker picked at a loose thread on his hoodie hem.

"You know what I wanted to be?" Her voice sounded dreamy, almost as if she were talking to herself.

He shook his head. No idea.

"A talk show host. Like Johnny Carson. I don't think there were many women talk show hosts back then—no Ellen or Oprah yet—but that was my goal. Except instead of interviewing celebrities, I was going to have ordinary guests. You know—teachers, landscapers, grocery store clerks. And I was going to ask exactly the right questions to draw out fascinating stories from every one of them. I figured everyone has those stories, but hardly anyone gets to hear them." A heavy sigh. "Everyone told me my dream was ridiculous, so I got a business degree instead. Which is how I ended up in HR for an insurance company instead of making everyday people look remarkable on TV."

It had never occurred to Parker that his mom might hold any particular aspirations. She was simply his mom. She went to work, came home, and made sure he got to his orthodontist appointments and did his homework. She read the newspaper, complained about local politics, and snuck chocolate bars when she thought he wasn't looking. She volunteered at an animal shelter because she loved animals but Parker was allergic to everything. She insisted on family game nights, where she whooped Parker's and his dad's asses at *Trivial Pursuit* but always lost at Clue and Monopoly. She was a really great mother even though she sometimes embarrassed him, but Parker had never imagined she harbored unfulfilled hopes and dreams.

"Your job pays pretty well, though, right?"

She shrugged. "Sure. But it's soulless. I like some of the people I work with, but I hate the forms and the cubicles and the stupid beige walls. I hate wearing sensible professional clothes. And you know what else? Your dad isn't thrilled with his job either, dragged away constantly on business trips to Boise and Louisville and... where was the one before that?"

"Ohio somewhere."

"Right." She patted his knee. "He and I have been talking about this for a long time, actually. And now with that money Grandma left us last year, we can finally do it. We're going to quit our jobs and run a coffeehouse. I can wear whatever I want and paint the walls however I like, your dad gets to stay in town, and I think we'll both be a whole lot happier."

Parker rubbed his chin. He didn't have to shave yet, but he was hoping that would happen soon. And maybe he'd put on some muscle and add some breadth to his shoulders. He was tired of looking like a kid.

"That sounds great, Mom. Really cool. Do I get free drinks and stuff?"

She laughed. "Of course. And a paid job on weekends if you want it. You can save up for college. And buy yourself a new sweatshirt."

A job. He liked the idea of earning his own money, and working for his parents would maybe be better than fast food. "Okay."

"It's a plan, then, Gonzo?"

He tried not to wince at the nickname, a holdover from years ago when he'd had a thing for the Muppets. "It's a plan, Stan."

"Good. Also, there's a moral here. I'm a whole lot older than you, Parker, and I'm only now finding a career I really want to do—and one that's practical. So you shouldn't feel bad about not making up your mind at fourteen. But when you do get inspiration? Don't let anyone dismiss it. Don't wait until you're decrepit like me to do what gives you joy."

"You're not decrepit, Mom." Forty-five *was* pretty old, but he didn't say so.

She chuckled, put the car into Drive, and pulled into the street.

As they headed west, he waited until they'd almost reached the river before he cleared his throat. "Hey, Mom?"

"Yes, honey?"

It was easier to do this now, when she had to look at the road instead of him, when the pattering raindrops and swooshing windshield wipers made the car feel like a comfy little shelter. "Um… I need to tell you something."

She didn't push him to spit it out as they crossed the bridge or as they headed through downtown. She waited patiently; he loved that about her. She could hold on to ideas like a bulldog, but she didn't poke and pry when he didn't want her to. And she always let him get his thoughts in order before he spoke.

They merged onto the highway and went through the tunnel. When Parker was little, he'd sometimes ask his dad to honk the horn in there, and his dad would often do it. Tonight Parker didn't mention it to his mother, didn't say anything at all until they were passing the exit ramp for the zoo.

"Mom, I'm gay."

The world didn't end. A bolt of lightning didn't come from the sky and strike the car, a chasm didn't open before them on Sunset Highway, and he didn't drop dead. His mom didn't even crash the car, although she stole a quick glance his way and then took her hand off the wheel long enough to pat his knee. "Thank you for trusting me enough to tell me."

"You're not freaked out?"

"Not freaked out." Another quick glance. "I've had my suspicions for a while, actually. And if you think I'd love you any less over this, you don't know me very well, kiddo. Ditto with Dad, by the way."

His heart was still battering his chest, but at least he could breathe freely. It wasn't that he thought he'd be disowned or anything. His parents weren't bigots. But it still felt like a pretty big truth to drop on her. It had been weighing on him for a long time.

"Okay," he said.

"Gonzo, you're an amazing kid. You're smart and kind, and you always see the best in people. If I could wave a magic wand and change anything about you, I wouldn't change a single thing. I love you—*we* love you—exactly as you are."

"I'm practically perfect in every way?" he asked, trying out a small smile. He was fond of *Mary Poppins* when he was little, as well as all of the other old-school musical films for kids. No wonder his mother wasn't shocked at his announcement.

"Practically. Now if you'd only finish your homework…."

"Mom!"

Laughing, she took the exit for Highway 217. It was a long, tight curve, and when he'd been little and sitting in the back seat, he used to put out his arms and pretend he was an airplane banking. Too bad he was too old for that now.

Back on the straightaway, she made a tiny humming noise. "Is there anyone in particular? A certain boy?"

"Mo-om!" he exclaimed, louder this time, his cheeks flaming. In truth, he had a major crush on his friend Troy, and Troy had kinda sorta been hinting lately that he might have similar feelings about Parker. Parker had been too chicken to do anything about it, though. What if he was wrong and Troy was straight or not into him? Oh God.

"All right, all right. Just… it's not the easiest path, kiddo. Let me know if anyone flips you any shit."

He smiled; the cussing signaled she meant it. She hardly ever swore, and when she did, she was dead serious. Now that they were almost home, he changed the subject. "I still don't know what to write in that stupid essay."

"Make something up. It's not like twenty years from now your teacher's going to retroactively erase your grade if you're doing something else with your life."

That? That was brilliant. He had a great mom.

She got off the freeway and stopped at a red light. When she turned her head and smiled at him, she *meant* it. He could tell. She wasn't disappointed in him. Not at all. He felt warm and full inside, as if he'd been drinking hot chocolate. And even though he still had no clue what he wanted to be when he grew up, that was okay for now. He was only fourteen. And he was loved.

"What are you going to call the coffee shop?" he asked. "Rhoda's?"

"Boring."

"Levin's Café?"

"Yawn. Your father and I are currently in negotiations over the matter, but neither of us is really satisfied with the options."

"How about… P-Town? You know, like the nickname for Portland? Plus it sounds kinda hip. And, well, pee—'cause everyone's gonna be drinking a lot. Only you don't have to tell customers that part."

Ignoring the light, which had turned green, she threw back her head and laughed. "I love it! Thanks, Gonzo. P-Town it is!" And she hit the gas in a credible mom version of a burnout, leaving Parker shouting with delight.

Chapter One

Seattle, Washington
November 2018

PARKER SAT on the curb, leaning back against his suitcase and staring morosely at his phone's blank screen. At least it wasn't raining; he tried to be thankful for that rarity. He was cold, though, his fuchsia hoodie too light for the season. He could feel the stares of passing motorists as they wondered about the skinny guy with the bright orange hair, the red jeans, the suitcase, the trio of bulging cardboard boxes. He wanted to glare at them but didn't have the energy. Or maybe he was just too chicken.

So he kept his head down and shivered, and he didn't look up even when a car stopped in front of him and a door slammed. A moment later a pair of boots appeared in front of him. Familiar boots—purple Fluevogs. But he still kept his eyes on his phone.

A long, silent moment passed. Then… yep. There it was. The sigh. "You need a heavier coat, Parker."

"Mom." Nothing more—just that one warning word. Then he stood, tucked his phone into his back pocket, and braced himself for the hug. And the kiss, complete with lipstick marks on his cheek. If he were tortured, he might admit he was thankful for the hug and kiss, that they smoothed a few of the jagged edges inside him. That without them he might have fallen apart completely. But only if he were tortured.

His mother let go, and he stood for a second, allowing her to scowl at him. She wore yellow leggings, a black dress with gray boomerang shapes, and a fuzzy purple scarf. No coat, but then she'd spent the past four hours or so inside her car. Her hair was shorter than the last time he saw her, and although she was letting most of the natural gray show, she had a purple streak in front. Her eyes looked tired.

He had no idea what she saw as she gazed at him. Five feet eleven inches of disappointment, probably.

Parker bent and picked up the biggest box. Rhoda used the key fob to open the back of her modestly sized SUV, and he wrestled the box inside. She brought him the suitcase, then the other two boxes. Everything fit just fine; he didn't have much stuff.

He shut the hatch, they got into the car, and his mom pulled into the flow of traffic. They got all the way to Tacoma before either of them said a word.

"I'm going to need to pee," she said. "And eat. I missed lunch."

"Fine."

"Did you have lunch?"

"I'm not hungry."

Her only response was a humph.

Several miles later, he took a forward step. "I can drive, you know. If you're tired."

"I'm fine."

And that was it between them until she took an exit in Chehalis, where she filled the gas tank and then parked at the Burgerville. She left him in the SUV and went inside. He leaned his head against the window and pretended to be napping.

When she returned ten minutes later, she held a paper bag and two paper cups. She handed him one of the cups as soon as she got inside. "Chocolate," she announced. Then she dug in the bag and gave him a wrapped sandwich. "You don't have to eat it. But you can."

And, well, he *was* a little hungry now that he smelled the food. Plus there were no Burgervilles in Seattle, and he really liked their turkey burger and milkshakes. So he ate in silence while his mother did the same, and she didn't even blunt the edges of things by turning on the radio. He would have sold his soul for one of her NPR shows, the ones she liked to talk back to.

After the food was gone, Parker gathered the trash and threw it in a nearby can. On his return, he reclined the seat and closed his eyes, felt the wheels rolling beneath him as they left the parking lot and returned to the freeway. Tried not to feel his heart shatter a little more with every mile that passed.

She finally spoke up somewhere near the Mt. St. Helens signs. "I didn't like him anyway."

"Mom."

"He's flaky, and I don't think he treated you very well. When you two came down to visit, he kept interrupting every time you tried to say something."

Parker rolled his eyes and turned to look out the side window. His mother was right. Logan was terrible about letting Parker finish a sentence. And he was flaky even by Parker's standards.

"And even if he'd been a perfect gentleman—which he wasn't—dating a coworker is a bad idea."

Well, duh. Which Parker almost said, except he wasn't twelve anymore. And even though he'd needed rescuing by his mommy yet again, he was pretending to be an adult. He made a sour face instead.

The truth was, he'd known from the beginning that it was stupid to hook up with someone he worked with and even dumber to move in with him. Sure, some people could probably pull that off, but those were people who had better romance track records than he did. Parker's longest relationship had been four months, and that one lasted so long only because the guy in question was in Colorado for one of those months.

Parker had a tendency to jump right into idiocy, a tendency his mother had remarked on more than once. She didn't call it idiocy, of course. She just said Parker should try to be less impulsive. Same thing.

"Logan's really cute," he mumbled. "We had fun together."

Now it was his mother's turn to roll her eyes. Instead of replying, she swore at a BMW drifting into their lane. "Pay attention to the road, numbnuts!"

Despite the situation, Parker chuckled. "You've been spending time with Nevin, haven't you?"

Nevin was one of his mom's friends, a regular at P-Town. He cursed more than anyone Parker had ever met, and more colorfully, but he was also a really good cop. And he and his husband, Colin, were adorable together. Relationship goals, right?

"If Nevin were here," Parker's mom said, "I'd ask him to ticket that shit-for-brains. Although I suppose this wouldn't be in his jurisdiction."

It had occurred to Parker more than once that she would have made a great detective. She liked to investigate things, and her interrogation skills were excellent. As she demonstrated a moment later when she patted Parker's knee. "Tell me what happened with Logan, honey." Ah, so she was playing good cop for now.

"Ugh."

"Ugh?"

"The apartment was in his name 'cause he lived there first, right? So every month I gave him my half of the rent and utilities, and he paid it all. Only it turned out he hadn't been. And he'd been tearing up all the overdue notices, so I never saw them."

"What did he do with the money?"

Parker grunted. "He claims he invested it, but I doubt that. Oh, and he's been getting this really complicated tattoo all over his back." It was really good art, and it must have cost a fortune. But when Parker had asked how he afforded the ink, Logan said the artist was a friend who was giving him a huge discount.

"He was stealing from you."

"He…. Yeah. I guess so." Parker hadn't looked at it that way until now. "This morning the apartment manager showed up while Logan was at work. She said if we didn't pay the back and current rent, we'd be evicted." Deep in his heart, Parker hadn't been shocked to learn that Logan was avoiding the bills. It was exactly the kind of thing Logan would do.

"You confronted Logan over it?"

"Yeah. I was pissed off, Mom. So I went to work to talk to him about it, and we got in a huge fight, and that upset all the dogs, and our boss canned us both." Yes, it had been especially dumb for Parker to confront Logan so impulsively, and at the doggie day care. But at least he had the satisfaction of knowing that Logan was now unemployed too and would soon be homeless. Logan's family lived somewhere in Oklahoma—a location he claimed had no redeeming value—so if he had to resort to parental rescue, he was going to be stuck somewhere he hated.

"I'm sorry, Gonzo. You liked that job."

He had. Doggie day care might not have paid all that well, but it was a lot of fun. Beagles and golden retrievers never judged him or made him feel inadequate. They were thrilled if he rubbed their ears and tossed a few toys around.

Parker and his mom remained silent for a long time, until they reached the outskirts of Vancouver, Washington. "Thanks for coming to get me," he mumbled. "Even though I'm a screwup."

"I'll always retrieve you. And I love you even when you make mistakes. Do you think you'll stay in Portland for a while this time? I could use the help since I'm about to be down two baristas. Ptolemy's doing a postdoc, and Deni's expecting a baby any day now."

He didn't know whether she was truly desperate or just trying to make him feel better. "Sure, I can stick around for a bit." Back to living with his mother and working at P-Town. Neither of those was a fate worse than death, but dammit, he'd been doing them when he was sixteen. It would be nice to have made some advances in maturity and independence over the past decade. He pictured himself at ninety, tottering around the coffeehouse with his mom still giving him advice on how to be an adult. And oh yeah, he'd still be sleeping in his old twin bed. Completely and tragically single.

Ugh.

Maybe he should consider becoming a monk. The kind who locked himself in a cell and took a vow of silence. Did they still have that kind? The only ones Parker knew about for sure were the monks in Mount Angel who made fudge. Well, he could do that too, couldn't he? Spend his days in a long black robe, making candy and praying. Too bad he was an agnostic Jew.

He'd just have to find a secular way to get his act together.

RHODA PARKED the car in her driveway. This wasn't the house in Beaverton that Parker had grown up in. As soon as he graduated high school, his parents sold that house and bought this one instead. It was in Southeast Portland, much closer to P-Town, and had a lot more character than the one in the suburbs. Over a hundred years old, this bungalow boasted lots of interesting architectural details, with a modern kitchen and bathrooms.

She helped Parker schlep his stuff into the house and set the boxes on the living room floor. "Your room's not made up yet. I didn't have enough lead time with this crisis."

He scowled at her. "I am at least capable of making up a bed."

"Glad to hear it." She disappeared up the stairs, probably to change clothes. She had a whole suite up there—bedroom, sitting area, and huge bathroom. Hers alone, ever since Parker's father died. Parker had one of the ground-floor bedrooms; the other served as Rhoda's home office, and the bathroom sat across the hall.

He carried his suitcase into the bedroom, sat on the bed, and sighed, gazing at the painting of Bigfoot and a unicorn watching TV in the middle of a forest. One of Rhoda's friends had painted it for her as a gift, and she'd decided Parker's room was the perfect place for it. Which it was.

But despite the painting, and despite the fact that he'd inhabited this room off and on over the past eight years, it didn't quite feel like home. Not that he'd shared the apartment with Logan for very long. Not that Parker had lived *anywhere* for very long since he was a kid. In fact, cumulatively, he'd spent more of his adult years in this room than anywhere else. He landed here every time he fucked up. Yet it wasn't… it wasn't where his heart wanted to be. Of course, his heart hadn't told him where it *did* want to be, the stupid thing.

He stood, pulled off all the bedding, and wadded up the sheets for a later trip to the washing machine in the basement. A set of clean sheets waited in one of the drawers under the mattress. A captain's bed had been the coolest upgrade in the world after he outgrew his Thomas the Tank Engine toddler bed.

Parker had just finished making up the bed when Rhoda knocked on the open door. The scarf was gone, and she'd changed out of her purple boots and into a pair of kelly green clogs. "Everything okay?"

"Yeah, I'm cool."

"I'm heading to the shop for a couple of hours. Deni says it's busy. Want to join me?"

He shook his head. "I think I'll unpack and do laundry. And wallow. Want me to make us some dinner?"

She walked over and tucked a lock of hair behind his ear. "That'd be great. There's pasta, some chicken breasts, maybe—"

"I'll figure something out, Mom." He wasn't a great cook or anything, but he'd learned to make simple dinners when he was in high school and his parents worked long hours at P-Town.

"I know. I have confidence in you."

Ouch. She meant well, but it hurt anyway. "I'm really sorry I messed up again," he murmured.

"Oh, sweetheart. You have such an open and trusting heart. I'd hate for you to close it off. Just maybe… be a little more careful?"

He bent to kiss her cheek. "I'll try." And he would. But he wasn't optimistic about his success.

DECIDING TO make a good start of things, Parker woke up early the following morning, showered, and dressed. Making coffee seemed redundant when he was about to go work at P-Town, so he was yawning as Rhoda drove them the two and a half miles to work.

Conscious that their schedules wouldn't always mesh, he asked, "Do you still have my bicycle?"

"It's in the basement. But do you really want to ride in the cold and rain?"

"I won't melt."

"At least tell me you have a decent raincoat."

He chose not to answer.

As soon as Rhoda unlocked the café door, Parker got to work. While she readied the till and received deliveries of baked goods, he pulled chairs off tables, adjusted window shades, and filled containers with milk, sugar, and sliced lemons. He helped Rhoda fill the display case with goodies—pausing to eat a fantastic cherry-almond Danish. Then he wiped down the long glass countertop and made some pitchers of iced tea. These were all familiar tasks he'd been performing for years, and he and Rhoda had the timing down perfectly. The first pot of drip brew was ready exactly as she unlocked the door for their first customers.

"Parker! I didn't know you were back in town."

Parker tried not to cringe as he greeted the big man in the green uniform. "Hi, Jeremy. I just got here yesterday."

"Welcome back."

"Thanks."

Parker gave him a weak smile. There was nothing wrong with Jeremy Cox. Quite the opposite, in fact. He was an enormous hunk of gorgeousness, with bulging muscles, a square jaw, and tightly cropped light hair, and his park-ranger uniform only added to the vision. He looked like a movie superhero and acted like one too. As a matter of fact, back when Parker was a high-school senior, Jeremy was one of his first real crushes, an intense puppy love that had Parker stammering, swooning, and secretly drawing little hearts in his school notebooks. Jeremy was only a few years younger than Rhoda, so Parker realized even then how impossible the whole thing was, but that hadn't stopped him from dreaming. He'd outgrown the crush long ago—mostly—but was still embarrassed when Jeremy saw him repeatedly fail at life. And God, Parker would be mortified if anyone knew how he'd once felt.

"The usual?" Parker asked.

"Yep."

The usual was an oversize Americano, no milk, in a huge mug Rhoda kept just for Jeremy. "Anything to eat with that?"

"Nah. Qay's been bugging me to cut back on sugar and fat. *We're not getting any younger*, yada yada. I'll have a sensible, boring breakfast later."

Parker smiled at the fondness in Jeremy's expression when he mentioned his husband. "How's Qay doing? He started grad school, right?"

That made Jeremy beam. "Yeah. A few more years and he'll be Dr. Hill. He's doing great. Will you be here this afternoon? I'll tell him to stop by after class."

"I will, and please do."

It was inspiring to know that Qay was doing well. He'd spent most of his life embroiled in much bigger problems than Parker's— drug addiction, mental illness, minor brushes with the law. And he had a pretty horrific childhood, complete with parental abuse and rejection. But he managed to pull his life together, marry the amazing Jeremy Cox, and become an academic star. If he could do it, maybe there was hope for Parker. If only Parker didn't have to wait until his midforties to get there.

P-Town became busy almost immediately, but Deni and two other employees arrived to help handle the rush. Parker loved it when he had to hurry around at work—it made him feel competent and kept him from dwelling on his personal disasters. Some of the customers were regulars who recognized him from his previous P-Town gigs, and almost everyone was unusually pleasant because Rhoda had an uncanny knack of attracting good people. It was her superpower. Parker had no other explanation for it. She also managed to cultivate a varied customer base: rich, poor, queer, straight, old, young. People of every imaginable ethnic background. And yes, some of Rhoda's people were decidedly... eccentric, but that was cool too. Parker enjoyed them all.

"Hey, Gonzo. Take a lunch break."

Parker looked up from the sink full of dirty dishes. "Let me finish these first."

"Benny just clocked in—let him do them. You go find something substantial to eat and rest your feet for half an hour."

Parker didn't want a rest—too much opportunity to dwell on his shortcomings—but he'd never yet won an argument with his mother. He turned off the water and dried his hands on a towel. "Want me to get you something?"

"I brought some leftovers. Now go. Shoo."

A few minutes later he stood under the front awning, trying to decide what to have for lunch. The neighborhood offered several opportunities, many of them within his limited budget. A man in a denim jacket, his sandy-colored hair in a ponytail, strode toward the café door and nodded at him. Parker smiled back. The guy was handsome, and although he appeared preoccupied or worried, he was humming quietly to himself. After he entered the coffeehouse, Parker returned to ruminating.

He'd finally settled on the Thai place and had taken two steps in that direction when his phone rang. He didn't know the name, but he recognized the 206 area code.

"Hello?"

"Is this Parker Levin?"

"Yeah. Who's this?"

"I'm Detective Jocelyn Saito. Seattle Police Department. Mr. Levin, we have some questions to ask you."

Chapter Two

Wes usually liked the drive from southern Oregon to Portland. The first part had some nice forested mountains, and the straight shot up the Willamette Valley brought green fields and distant hills. Sure, traffic would get obnoxious as he neared Portland, but he generally didn't mind. He was rarely in a hurry, and the van's great sound system had been a worthwhile splurge.

Today was different, though. Gray skies refused to give up their moisture, and the road felt unusually bumpy under his tires. The van—he'd named it Morrison—grumbled loudly and fought his control like a balky mule. Every note of music jangled his nerves so badly that he finally turned it off. The real problem was what awaited him.

The furniture delivery would happen first, and that was fine. He'd unload the table-and-chairs set he'd so carefully crafted, and the store owner would give him a nice fat check. Usually after he unloaded the van, he'd take himself out for pizza because he couldn't get a decent pie anywhere near where he lived. He'd often visit his favorite hardware store and maybe pick up some antique fittings to incorporate into a future project. Then he'd almost always head over to Powell's and spend a couple of hours browsing the miles of bookshelves. By then rush hour traffic generally had abated, and he'd either start the drive home or find someone to hook up with. He used to go to bars for that, but lately he'd been using an app. When he finally returned to his comfortable, isolated home, he'd make preparations to begin another table or maybe a dresser or bookcase.

That was the customary plan. Today, though…. After dropping off the furniture, he'd be facing the ghosts of his past. He hated ghosts.

"They'll keep on haunting you if you don't face them." Frowning, he turned the music back on. It was better than giving himself smug advice.

Black Lightning Interiors occupied a former cracker factory near the edge of the Pearl District. The building's owners had retained as many of the original architectural details as possible when they converted the ground floor to retail space and the upper floors to lofts, but they had succumbed to practicality by installing showroom windows along the sidewalk. Wes parked in a loading zone in front of the building and smiled when he saw one of his pieces on display: a walnut-and-maple credenza with weathered steel legs. He texted Miri, the shop's owner, to let her know he'd arrived. A moment later she appeared, along with a couple of her employees.

"You haven't sold the credenza yet?" he asked after he shook her hand.

"We sold it the day you delivered it. But the buyers are remodeling their house, so we're keeping it on display until they're ready." She chuckled warmly. "I could have sold that thing about a hundred times over—I've had a lot of offers. I think I need to up the prices on your pieces."

Wes thought eight thousand bucks was already a hell of a lot of dough just to store a few dishes, but he wouldn't complain.

It took the four of them only a few minutes to get the table and chairs out of the van and into the store. Miri had already set up a spot where the lighting would accent the detailed wood inlays.

"Gorgeous," she said, stroking the gently arched back of a chair. "Really stunning work, Wes."

"Thanks. I appreciate you taking it on." He could have found buyers closer to home, but not at the prices Miri gave him. Besides, deliveries gave him an excuse to visit civilization every now and then.

"It's my pleasure. You know that."

They walked through the store together, pausing periodically as she pointed out items she knew he'd appreciate. Miri had excellent taste—hey, she carried his stuff!—and he always liked new inspiration. They finally arrived at her office, which was crowded with catalogs, magazines, and stacks of papers. "Coffee?" She gestured toward an espresso machine.

He shuddered as he remembered what he had to do next. "No, thanks. Drank too much on the drive up."

"It's a long haul for you. Must get boring." Miri pulled a checkbook out of her desk drawer and spoke as she wrote. "You know, you could increase your output tenfold—more than that—and I'd still sell everything you made."

"I'm doing as much as I can. Unless I start cutting corners and lowering quality, which I'm not going to do."

"Oh, I didn't mean to imply that. Not at all." She signed the check, tore it from the book, and recorded it in the register. "What I meant is maybe you could consider taking on some employees. People you could trust to be good craftsmen. Opening up a real workshop, maybe closer to Portland."

"I can't—"

"I've been thinking about this, Wes. I know we're talking about a lot of capital up front, but we can sit down with my accountant and work something out. Partnership, loan... whatever makes sense."

Shit. Most people would be ecstatically grateful for an offer like this. Miri was widely respected, not just in Portland, but throughout the West Coast. People came from LA to consult with her and see what she had to offer. But just thinking about her plan made his chest feel tight.

"I need to stay small for now," he said quietly.

Maybe he sounded stricken, because she frowned a bit but didn't push the matter. She handed over the check. "It's always a pleasure, Wes. I hope to see some more from you really soon."

"A couple of weeks. Probably." As usual, he didn't commit to a timeline or a specific project. At one point she'd urged him to let her know in advance what he was going to make—maybe even provide an idea book customers could leaf through—but he said no. It would stifle his creative process, he said. Which was only a partial lie.

Wes and Miri exchanged a few minutes of small talk before he said goodbye. He drove a few miles to the bank, where he deposited the check and withdrew a few hundred dollars in cash, which he tucked into his wallet. If he keeled over and died during his next errand, at least they'd find enough money on him to cover his cremation.

Yeah, that wasn't entirely a joke.

After seriously considering excuses to procrastinate, he drove across the Morrison Bridge and up Belmont. He kept going all the way to Mount Tabor, where he pulled into a parking lot, shut off the engine, and spent fifteen minutes calling himself names. He eventually resorted to his mental teddy bear, the one thing most likely to calm him when the world spun too fast. Checking to make sure the van windows were rolled up, Wes closed his eyes and began belting out "Sloop John B."

After he'd sung it three times, Wes felt good enough to start up the van again.

He was back on Belmont, where parking proved to be a challenge. He couldn't exactly squeeze Morrison into a tiny spot. He circled for nearly ten minutes before he finally parked, four blocks from his destination. A four-block walk that offered the likelihood of chickening out again.

"Nope," he said as he locked the van's door. "Be brave. Nobody's going to be shooting at you." Probably.

He hummed the Beach Boys quietly as he traveled the sidewalk.

Drawing close to his destination, he saw a man standing outside under the awning, looking thoughtful. And looking, in fact, like a human rainbow: orange hair, brilliant pink hoodie, yellow jeans, green sneakers. He was a literal bright spot in a gray landscape, and he was handsome too. Almost beautiful, really. And far too young for Wes, who was on the far side of his thirties. This kid looked like he was still in college. Nevertheless, his colorful presence soothed Wes's nerves a bit. Wes nodded at him while reaching for the door, and the kid smiled back. Oh yeah. Definitely beautiful.

Concentrating on that lovely face rather than on what was going to happen soon, Wes entered the coffee-and-cinnamon-scented warmth of P-Town. He ordered a decaf and an oatmeal raisin cookie from the very pregnant woman behind the counter and took his purchases to a small table at the back of the café. A good place to see everyone who entered without being spied right away.

There weren't many other customers at the moment. Most people had already eaten lunch, and it was still too early for late-afternoon caffeine needs. Billie Holiday sang through the speakers, colorful paintings hung on the walls, and his chair was comfy. He would have loved this place under other circumstances. He might have stayed for a couple of hours, sipping drinks and reading a book. But not today.

P-Town had never been his particular hangout when he lived in Portland, although a few coworkers favored the place and had occasionally brought Wes along. He was hoping they still came here—while at the same time fervently wishing they did not.

Suddenly the rainbow man burst into the café, phone in hand, his expression so stricken that Wes nearly leapt from his seat to offer help. But the kid rushed across the floor and disappeared through a door behind the counter, leaving Wes seated and rubbing his chin. The kid had looked content when he was standing outside a few minutes earlier. What could have happened in such a short time to distress him so deeply? Was there something Wes could do to help?

He almost laughed out loud at that last thought. He couldn't even help himself, aside from getting through the basic motions of life. What the hell could he possibly do for a stranger?

He dissected his cookie and tried not to look as if he were stalking someone, even though he sort of was.

A few customers wandered in: a white-bearded man in his late sixties, a pair of elderly ladies wearing matching cat-print sweatshirts, a young woman in a suit and carrying a laptop case. They bought drinks and food and sat at tables. The Billie Holiday album ended, and Etta James piped up instead.

Wes thought about a coffee table he might make out of reclaimed oak and a nice hunk of driftwood. He'd been considering a nautical theme, with the oak resembling a ship's profile and the driftwood, which would support and arch over the oak, shaped to suggest a sea monster. A little more over-the-top than his usual work, but it would be fun. Wes could almost feel the smooth wood grain under his fingers and the worn handle of the coping saw in his palm. He did most of his work outside, under a large plastic canopy he'd strung between branches, and the resident scrub jays seemed to enjoy watching and chattering at his progress. If Miri didn't want the sea-monster piece, maybe he could sell it elsewhere. He might even—

"What the fuck are you doing here?"

Startled from his reverie, Wes almost fell out of his chair. He found himself facing two scowling men: one of them short and wiry, wearing a tailored black suit and blackberry-colored shirt, the other man tall and muscular and in a green uniform.

Wes held up his hands and addressed the large man, who he knew was a better bet for reasonable conversation. "Hi. I was hoping I'd see you here. I wanted to—"

The smaller man took a step nearer. "You can get your miserable ass out of that fucking chair and drag yourself back to whatever shit-slicked hole you crawled out of." He looked as if he desperately wanted to pull his gun.

Yeah, this was going well.

Wes didn't lower his hands. "Please. If you could give me—just five minutes, okay? Then you never have to see me again. Please?" He knew he sounded pathetic and desperate, but then he *was* pathetic and desperate, so at least he was consistent.

"Now is not a good time." Jeremy Cox didn't swear at him, but his jaw looked tight and his hands were loosely fisted. Wes was a bit confused—Jeremy should have been wearing a blue uniform rather than green—but that wasn't the issue at the moment.

"I'm sorry. I live all the way down in Rogue Valley, though, so I can't really…." Shit. He rubbed his face hard. "I sort of really need to do this now. Please." Because if he left now, he'd never summon the courage to try again.

Nevin Ng, who had apparently worked his way up to detective in the ten years since Wes last saw him, snarled. "Go the fuck away, Wanker."

Before Wes could make an even more pitiful appeal, a woman in a coffee-cup-print dress sailed over. "Hey, what's going on? Parker's waiting for you, and he's falling apart."

Nevin looked uncharacteristically chagrined. "Sorry, Rhoda. We're just getting rid of this fuckface."

For the first time, she looked at Wes, a sharp assessment that probably missed very little. "He doesn't seem like he needs getting rid of."

"He fucking does. He's bad news. When he was in the bureau, he—"

"That was a decade ago!" Wes interrupted. "I'm not that guy anymore. That's why I'm here."

Nevin opened his mouth again, but the woman—Rhoda—held up her hand, and he remained silent. Which was a miracle in itself, because Wes didn't think anyone could get Nevin Ng to shut up and back down.

"Whatever old drama you three have is currently upstaged by my son's new drama. I don't think this man— What's your name?"

"Wes. Westley Anker."

"I don't think Wes is going to cause any trouble right now. Are you?"

Wes shook his head. "No, ma'am."

She sighed and took Nevin's arm. "You hear that? He ma'am'd me, so he can't possibly be a miscreant. He's going to sit here with his cold coffee—get a warm-up, Wes—and crumbled cookie, and you two are coming with me. You can yell at each other later."

Maybe Nevin would have argued, but she still held his arm. And then Jeremy gave his shoulder a gentle shove. "C'mon. Rhoda's right. We need to triage the emergencies."

Wes didn't feel like an emergency. Mostly he felt exhausted. Maybe he should switch to full-caffeine espresso.

Jeremy and Nevin glared at him once more before stomping away. They went through the same door the rainbow kid—Parker, Wes supposed—had gone through. Rhoda remained, hands on hips, staring at Wes. "Those are two of the best people in this city, so normally if they told me to get rid of someone, I'd listen. But I'm not getting an off vibe from you at all. So I'm going to give you this chance, and when they're done dealing with my son, the three of you can work out your problems."

"Thank you," Wes murmured, genuinely grateful.

"You're not going to make me regret this decision, are you?"

"God, I hope not."

His answer must have come out more fervently than he intended, because Rhoda laughed. "Yeah, I think I'm right about you. Sit tight, honey."

She walked away and joined everyone else on the other side of the door, and Wes sat tight. He didn't want to. His muscles twitched with the urge to run away—back to Morrison and then to the Rogue Valley. But this Rhoda woman apparently believed in him, so he stayed. Besides, he was dying to know what had gone wrong in Parker's life. He hoped it was nothing too awful. Someone that dazzling ought to be immune from disaster.

The other customers who'd been watching the entire little show got bored and turned their attention back to phones, laptops, and conversations. After popping a crumb-covered raisin into his mouth, Wes stood, grabbed his cup, and went in search of a refill.

Chapter Three

Parker was going to be sick. No, he'd already *been* sick, puking into the toilet in the tiny employee bathroom. But now, sitting in the kitchen, he feared he was going to be sick again. Even though his mom had given him a mug of strong ginger tea and a packet of saltines she unearthed from the depths of her purse.

"Just *breathe*," he ordered himself quietly. "Slowly. In and out." He'd taken a yoga class once, mostly because the guy he'd been dating was really into it. Shortly after the second class, Parker caught the guy cheating and they broke up. Parker quit going to yoga and remembered nothing but Mountain, Child's, and Corpse poses. But he learned one form of yogic breathing, so he practiced that now: long, slow inhales and exhales through his nose. Good for calming the nervous system, he'd been told.

Maybe those two classes hadn't been a total waste—or maybe the tea was to credit—but after a short time, the nausea subsided. It would have been replaced by tears if Jeremy and Nevin hadn't come bursting through the door like heroes in an action flick.

"What the fuck happened?" Nevin demanded immediately. His cussing was oddly soothing; it meant the world was spinning correctly on its axis. Jeremy knelt beside the chair and set a huge paw on Parker's shoulder, an action that also proved comforting. And then before Parker could gather words to answer, his mother joined them. Parker almost smiled. He would have bet on these three against the entire array of Marvel villains. Thanos would run screaming from this trio.

"How are you feeling?" Rhoda asked.

"Okay. Good tea." He lifted the mug weakly.

She came over and gave him a hug. He liked to think he was too old for comforting embraces from his mother. Except she was always warm and soft, she smelled like coffee and pastries, and when her arms were around him, he felt as if the world was a steadier place. He hugged her back, and if he sniffled a little in the process, nobody commented on it. After she pulled away, she handed him a Kleenex from the plastic packet in her purse.

He wiped his eyes and nose before looking at Nevin. "Someone from the Seattle police called me." His voice wavered only a little. "Detective Saito."

"Rhoda told us that much," said Jeremy quietly. "What was the call about?"

Apparently Rhoda hadn't shared details with Jeremy and Nevin, yet they'd still zoomed over to help Parker out. Which was pretty amazing, really. What if Seattle PD had decided Parker was a drug kingpin or serial killer? Parker's own friends had abandoned him under much less serious crises, yet here were his mom's friends, automatically on his side. God, he was so lucky to have his mother and her team! Yet a tiny bit of despair gnawed at him. He'd never *be* part of a team like that.

He blew his nose and took a deep breath. "It's my boyfriend, Logan. My ex. We broke up yesterday. And... this morning he died by suicide."

There. Got that out. That wasn't so hard, was it?

With a strangled noise, Parker made a dash for the employee bathroom.

When he returned, Rhoda handed him a can of 7UP, which is what she'd always given him when he was sick as a kid. P-Town didn't sell soft drinks, and he didn't know where she'd acquired it, but he was deeply appreciative.

He was also thankful that neither Nevin nor Jeremy looked judgy. They'd undoubtedly seen worse than one barfy guy. Nevin had been a cop for years, and Jeremy spent his career first in the police bureau and then as a park ranger. A lot of puking probably happened in Portland's parks.

"You okay to talk now?" Nevin asked. "Maybe you need something stronger than fizzy sugar water."

Jeremy rolled his eyes. "Booze doesn't solve problems."

"But it can temporarily make them less painful, Germy."

Their fond bickering helped settle Parker's stomach. "The 7UP is fine." To prove his point, he took a long swallow.

"Slowly now." Jeremy leaned back against the big sink and crossed his arms over his massive chest.

"The detective said that our building manager found Logan dead in our apartment—his apartment—this morning. He OD'd on something. I dunno what."

"Was Logan a heavy drug user?" Jeremy's expression was grim. Maybe he was thinking about how his husband, Qay, had struggled with addiction in the past.

"No, he didn't use at all. I mean, he smoked weed sometimes, but everybody does that." He shot Rhoda a guilty look even though weed was legal in Washington and Oregon, and even though Parker was old enough to make those kinds of decisions for himself. She just shook her head.

Nevin ignored all of that. "The grunts in Seattle don't think it was an accident?"

"He left a note. To me." Parker's stomach roiled again, but he remained seated. "That's why they called, they said. Just tying up loose ends, I guess."

"What'd the note say?"

"I don't know. She didn't tell me."

"Fuckwads," Nevin muttered. "So what did they ask you?"

"Where I am. His family contact info. I didn't know that—only that they're in Oklahoma. I told her maybe he had them in his phone. I didn't really tell her much else, and she didn't have a lot of questions. But she said she might have to call back if she came up with more." Even the idea made him miserable. The last thing he wanted was some stranger poking around in his personal business, digging up bad decisions he thought he'd laid to rest.

Nevin squatted in front of him. "If she does call, you don't need to say a word. Get her number, and I'll give her a ring." He was using a calm, reassuring tone, probably the same one he used when he spoke to the victims in the Vulnerable Adults Unit.

"Okay."

Jeremy still leaned against the sink, but now he was poking at his phone. "I've got a pal who's a great lawyer. I'm going to send her name and number to Rhoda."

"I need a lawyer?" Parker wailed. He didn't question why Jeremy knew a lawyer; the guy had connections all over the city.

"Unlikely. But just in case. How complicated were your personal affairs?"

"Huh?"

"You and the ex. Do you have a lease you need to deal with? Joint property?"

Parker shook his head. "I only knew him a few months."

Nodding as if this were a good thing, Jeremy came closer. Nevin moved out of the way, letting Jeremy take his place. "Parker, I'm really sorry this happened to you. Just remember that whatever decisions Logan made were his and none of this is your fault, okay?"

Coming from someone else, these words might have been trite. But Jeremy's ex-boyfriend had been murdered a couple of years earlier in some kind of gangs-and-drugs mess. The investigation somehow ended up involving Jeremy, even though he and his ex had broken up long before. Jeremy was kidnapped and tortured, for God's sake. So he knew what he was talking about, and Parker needed to remember that the world didn't revolve around Parker Levin.

Parker sniffed. "Thanks. Logan was…. He could be really sweet. He was funny too."

"He must've had something special going to end up with you."

Shit. Parker's cheeks flamed, and he hid his face, hoping Jeremy would assume it was out of grief rather than embarrassment. Maybe a guy never completely recovered from his first crush—maybe it stayed mostly dormant, like the chicken pox virus. Anyway, embarrassment was preferable to nausea, and somehow it made Parker feel a little less miserable.

Nevin and Jeremy asked a few more questions, but Parker didn't have much to share. He finally smiled, although weakly. "Thanks, guys. I really appreciate it. You probably have to get back to work, though."

"Not until we deal with the wanker," Nevin said.

"Who?"

"Don't worry about it."

But this sounded interesting—and also nicely distracting. So when Jeremy and Nevin marched out into the main room with Rhoda right behind them, Parker tagged along too.

They paraded to a table in the far corner, where a single customer looked up at them apprehensively. Parker recognized him as the handsome ponytailed man who'd nodded at him outside the café. Now he sat with a coffee mug, a plate full of crumbs, and an expression suggesting that his innards might not be in much better shape than Parker's.

Nevin opened his mouth to say something—probably something profane—but Jeremy spoke first. "You should just go, Wes."

"I will. But I need to say something first. It's why I came here, and I really need...." He swallowed audibly and bit his lip.

"You really need to get your ass out of here." Nevin crossed his arms and looked fierce. And Jeremy, for once, looked scary too, his brow creased in a scowl and his jaw clenched.

Now, if Parker had been in Wes's place, he would have picked up and run like a rabbit. Jeremy and Nevin made wonderful friends but, he suspected, terrifying opponents. But Parker wasn't in Wes's place; he was standing behind the others, noting Wes's desperate expression and acknowledging that he wasn't the only one having problems today.

"Let him talk."

Rhoda, Jeremy, and Nevin turned to stare at Parker, while Wes gave him a look of naked gratitude. That look encouraged Parker to continue. "I don't know what the problem is here, but it's not gonna hurt anyone to let him have his say."

"Thank you," Wes said quietly. And while Jeremy and Nevin looked unhappy, they relaxed their postures. Rhoda cocked her head and gazed at Parker inquisitively, but he'd deal with that later.

Now that he'd been given the chance to speak, Wes couldn't seem to find any words. He picked up his coffee cup and put it down again. He poked at a raisin on his plate. He scratched behind one ear. Finally, when it seemed as if Nevin was going to start swearing again, Wes spoke.

"I... I guess I mostly came to apologize. I screwed up. Big-time. And I've.... God, I've been reliving that day for ten years. I have nightmares about it. I'm going to have to live with what I did for the rest of my life. But I needed to tell you I'm sorry."

Parker was dying to know what Wes had done that was so awful, but interrupting to ask would be rude, so he held his tongue. He could interrogate Jeremy later. Right now he empathized with Wes. Parker knew how awful it felt when you fucked up and had to face the people you'd impacted with your mistake. Not that he'd be facing Logan again, because.... Yeah, that thought could wait until later. When Parker was closer to a bathroom.

Jeremy peered at Wes. "Is this part of a twelve-step program?"

"No. I'm not a drunk or an addict. I'm just stupid."

"Then why are you telling us this?"

"Because…." Wes sighed. "I don't know. It's not like you're going to hate me any less. I just thought it was important for you to know that I'm sorry. That I didn't go tripping off into a sunshiny future, okay? I ruined myself. I have so much regret, I'm fucking drowning in it."

"You expect us to forgive you?" Nevin sounded hostile, but at least he wasn't openly threatening Wes.

"No. I don't forgive myself, even. I'm only hoping that you'll feel a little better if you know that none of what I did rested easy on my shoulders. I've been trying to find the courage to face you for a long time. So I could tell you all this. And now I have." Wes stared down at the table, his shoulders hunched.

After a long pause, it was, surprisingly, Nevin who spoke. And he didn't sound angry anymore. "It's been ten fucking years, Wanker. You wouldn't believe the shit that's gone down since then. It's not like I'm losing any goddamn sleep over *you*." Which should have been insulting but seemed to ease a bit of Wes's misery.

Not looking up, Wes nodded. "I wanted to ask too…. I don't have a lot of money, but if there's some kind of fund… something for the kids?"

Jeremy and Nevin exchanged looks, and then Jeremy answered. "I think there is. Give me your phone number, and I'll see if I can get the details to you."

Wes nodded eagerly and patted the pockets of his denim jacket, eventually producing a somewhat crumpled business card, which he set on the table. Nobody took it, but Jeremy nodded.

Then Wes stood. "Thanks for letting me…. Thanks." He aimed a weak smile at Parker.

Parker's heart broke for the guy. He didn't know why. He knew nothing about him, other than he did something a long time ago that royally pissed off even implacable Jeremy. And he'd been feeling torn up about it ever since, or at least so he claimed. But God, he looked so defeated. And he was brave too, wasn't he? Facing your demons took balls.

With his hands stuffed in the pockets of his jeans, Wes walked slowly past Jeremy and Nevin. Past Rhoda. Past Parker too. And nobody said anything to him. When he reached the door, he looked back briefly, scanning his gaze over the entire interior of P-Town as if he were searching for something. No. As if he were saying goodbye. It was the same way Parker had looked around the doggie day care after being fired or around some of the nicer apartments he'd been forced to move out of. Wes caught Parker's eyes and gave him a tiny wave. Then he walked out the door.

Five seconds later, Parker went chasing after him.

Chapter Four

He hadn't died. He hadn't keeled over from a stroke or exploded in a ball of shame-filled fire, and Nevin hadn't shot him or beaten him to a pulp. This was a good result, Wes reminded himself as he walked out of the coffeehouse door. And he'd actually been courageous enough to do something he'd been dreading for years, which meant he never had to do it again, and that was good too. It was *great*.

But Wes didn't feel great. He felt better than he had before going into P-Town, but that was only because the ordeal was over. The guilt remained. The heavy knowledge of the harm he'd caused others and could never undo.

As he walked toward his van, he reached a sudden decision. He wasn't going to return to his home in Rogue Valley and make a coffee table—at least not now, not right away. He needed distance between himself and the world. He needed flat expanses of highway, bad gas-station coffee, and radio filled with nothing but static. He needed—

"Wes! Hey, Wes!"

He turned to see the kid from P-Town running toward him. Parker, right? And his first and most ridiculous thought was that Jeremy and Nevin had sent Parker after him, maybe because it would be less messy to clean up Wes's corpse on the sidewalk than in the coffeehouse.

But Parker didn't exactly look homicidal. In fact, when he caught up to Wes, panting slightly, he grinned. "Hi."

Wes blinked. "Um, hi."

"Where are you going now?"

"Wyoming." The answer came out of nowhere. Wes hadn't given any thought to a particular destination; he'd just planned to hit a freeway and keep going. Let Morrison lead the way. But now that he'd said it, he liked the idea. Wyoming, he remembered, was the least populated state. There were only two sets of escalators in Wyoming. It was the first state to grant women the vote, *and* it was home to Devil's Tower, site of the alien landing in *Close Encounters of the Third Kind*. All of these seemed reasonable motives for going to Wyoming.

If Parker was surprised by Wes's answer, he didn't show it. Instead he gave a small nod. "Take me with you?"

"What?"

"Take me with you. To Wyoming."

"Why?"

Parker shrugged. "Why not?"

There were ten thousand reasons for Wes to refuse—perhaps twenty thousand, including the reality that he was never going to make it out of Oregon. But he continued walking toward the van. "C'mon, then."

WES DID not get on the Banfield, which would have eventually taken them to Wyoming. Instead he drove around the east side as if getting his thoughts in order. Parker surely must have noticed they were going nowhere, but he didn't comment. He stared silently through the windshield, sometimes turning his head to steal a quick glance at Wes.

After nearly forty-five minutes of aimlessness, as Wes was passing Laurelhurst Park for the third time, Parker finally spoke. "Do you think next time you circle past that McDonald's, we could stop for a minute? I never had lunch."

"Do you really want fast food? Or something better?"

"You're driving. You decide."

Weird that Parker seemed to trust him, especially after the confession at P-Town.

Wes wasn't a big fan of Mickey D's, so he steered Morrison to a food cart pod instead. He got some yakisoba noodles, Parker bought himself a gyro, and they sat at a picnic table under a tent. They had the space to themselves, either because it was cold or because it was late for lunch, but plenty of cars whooshed nearby.

"Are you planning to take me to an isolated spot and perform Satanic rituals?" Parker asked this cheerfully, as if he looked forward to such a thing. "Or just take ten years to get to Wyoming?"

"Neither."

"Okay. Um, my name's Parker Levin, by the way. My mom owns P-Town."

Wes nodded. "I'm Westley Anker. Wes." He waited a beat for the inevitable.

Parker's eyes sparkled when he got it. "Wanker. Nevin kept calling you Wanker."

"Yeah. He's not the first to do it, but he was the most insistent. And that was before he hated me."

That gave Parker an obvious opportunity to ask *why* Nevin hated Wes and what all the drama was about. But Parker didn't take the bait. "Yeah. He calls Jeremy Germy, and ever since the time I dyed my hair blue, I'm Smurf. I'm also pretty sure he's the only person on the planet who calls my mom Rho."

"He's always had a colorful vocabulary."

Parker laughed. "Yeah." He drank some of the Mexican Coke he'd bought to wash down his gyro. "Last year we were doing a little volunteer work and running an errand at a hardware store, and this jerk called me a fag. I think I was wearing something especially, um, colorful that day. I was just gonna ignore him, 'cause who cares anyway. But Nevin ripped into him. Didn't lay a finger on him or anything, it was all just words, but by the time Nevin was done, the guy honest to God had tears in his eyes. Then Nevin topped it all by giving me a big smoochy kiss on the cheek—it's okay, Nevin's husband was right there watching and thought it was funny—and the jerk ran away."

Wes stared at him. "Nevin Ng is *married*?"

"Yep."

"Jesus. He used to sleep with anyone who was willing. I never, ever pictured him settling down."

Looking a little sad, Parker drained his Coke. "I guess almost anyone can settle down if they meet the right person."

Wes grunted doubtfully. Not everyone *had* a right person. Some people were destined to run through life solo.

And then it occurred to him that this was a good opportunity to satisfy his curiosity. "What's with Jeremy Cox in a green uniform?"

"He's a city park ranger. Chief, actually."

"Oh." That didn't entirely surprise Wes. Jeremy had been a good cop, solid and dependable, but always more interested in helping people than arresting them. And he'd also been kind of a nature freak.

"Did you used to work with them in the bureau?" The question was gentle. Parker no doubt had realized this might be a sore spot.

"Yeah." Wes braced himself for more questions, but they didn't come. Instead Parker gathered up their trash and deposited it in nearby cans, and they both got back into Morrison.

"Wyoming?" Parker asked. He was smiling.

"Maybe not. You, um…. Back at the coffeehouse. You were upset about something. Are you sure you don't want to, I don't know, chill somewhere?"

"I *am* chilling somewhere." Parker patted the dash. "I'm chilling in your van."

"Morrison."

"What?"

"The van's name is Morrison."

Parker actually guffawed. "I love that! My last car was a crappy old Ford Focus. I called her Helen Wheels, and this guy I knew painted flames on her fenders. Like, shitty flames, you know? Maybe Morrison needs some decoration. White is boring. What would you paint on it?"

Wes opened his mouth to say he'd never given it any thought. Maybe a piece of furniture would be appropriate. But then he realized Parker had successfully steered the conversation off its intended track. "Maybe you shouldn't ride to Wyoming with a stranger when you're still upset."

Parker answered with only a dismissive *pfft*. He sat there, staring at rain beading on the windshield, apparently willing to remain like that until the end of time.

Jesus. How had Wes gotten into this? He was supposed to spend the day delivering furniture and flaying himself alive, then head back to his quiet home. Stubborn, rainbow-hued boys suffering a personal crisis were not part of the agenda. Not even if they were beautiful.

"Won't your mother be angry you've run away?"

Parker gave him a quick glare. "I'm twenty-six. I can run away all I want to."

That was older than Wes had guessed. But now that he looked closely at Parker's eyes, he saw a depth that would be unusual in a college kid. Parker might be impulsive, but he'd lived through some shit. Wes was sure of that.

"What about Nevin and Jeremy? I really don't want them to come after me for kidnapping." He was serious.

Parker rolled his eyes. But he also pulled out his phone and, thumbs flying, texted a message. "There," he said as he tucked the phone into his pocket. "I've informed them that I'm not kidnapped and they need to leave me alone for a while. They're probably happy to be rid of me."

"I doubt that. They seemed pretty worried about you."

"Hmm." Parker folded his arms and turned to stare at Wes. "I'm not telling you my tale of woe while we're parked here. If you want me to talk, onward. Wyoming, or wherever." He punctuated this with a vague *get rolling* gesture.

Maybe Wes could scare him off. "How about we go somewhere and fuck instead?"

"Okay."

Shit. That wasn't the response Wes had expected. "That's it? Just okay?"

"You're gorgeous, and I'm… single." A flash of deep sorrow, replaced quickly by determination. "I'm not exactly easy, you know, but I'm also not exactly hard to get."

"You're… medium? Just right?"

Parker grinned. "Now you're making me sound like someone Little Red Riding Hood would sleep with."

In truth, Wes was more than a little tempted to do exactly what he'd suggested. To find somewhere secluded, take Parker into the back of the van—conveniently full of blankets to cushion the furniture—and screw until neither of them could walk right. But his conscience said no. Parker was dealing with some kind of disaster, and Wes didn't want to take advantage. He had enough regrets on his tally sheet; he didn't need more. Still, his conscience wasn't assertive enough to force him to drop Parker off at P-Town.

Traffic sped by, the rain grew harder, and Wes tried to steer the right course. "Tell you what," he said. "How about if we opt for Plan C?"

"Which is?"

"No Wyoming. But no quick boinking either. How about if we head down to my place?"

"Where's that?" Parker was interested, not wary at all.

"South. Rogue Valley."

"Okay. Cool."

South it was. As if there had ever been any real doubt where Wes would end up.

Morrison was much more cooperative than on the journey into Portland. Maybe the van was like a horse, eager to get home after a long day. Or maybe having a passenger gave the vehicle a renewed sense of purpose.

Parker remained quiet until they passed a familiar landmark south of Salem. "Enchanted Forest," he said, pointing at the sign. "My parents used to take me when I was little. It's nice that it's still there."

"It hasn't been that long since you were little."

"God, it's been eons."

"Nah. You're still young."

"You say that like you're a hundred. You're not that much older than me."

Some days Wes felt as if he *were* a hundred. "A decade. I'm a decade older."

"Ancient."

Then Parker was silent again. When they reached Eugene, Wes announced that Morrison needed gas. He pulled into a station and, while the tank filled, trotted through the rain to the bathroom. He returned half expecting to find Parker gone—or at least demanding a ride back to Portland. But Parker, still buckled into his seat, smiled. "I can chip in for gas."

"Nope. I was going to have to head home anyway. It's not as if you're costing me anything."

Wes pulled out of the gas station and, soon afterward, back onto the freeway. This situation was so weird—he never picked up strangers, never brought anyone home with him—but it felt oddly comfortable. Maybe because Parker seemed content to simply sit there and watch the scenery roll by. Companionship had been rare throughout Wes's life. Usually he didn't feel it was necessary. But today, well, maybe he could use a bit. For a little while.

"You're not a cop anymore?"

There it was. The best reason to avoid other people: they asked awkward questions.

"No."

"What do you do for a living, then?"

The tightness in Wes's chest eased when he realized Parker wasn't poking into the ugly depths of Wes's past. "I'm a cabinetmaker. I build furniture." That certainly sounded boring, didn't it?

But Parker didn't act as though it was. "Really? How cool! Tell me what you make." And he listened with what seemed to be genuine interest while Wes talked about his work. Parker even asked questions about carpentry techniques and Wes's stylistic influences while claiming that his own experiences were limited to disasters involving IKEA. "I should not be trusted with an Allen wrench."

Wes came to feel as if furniture making really *was* cool and that he might be clever indeed for having mastered it. He rarely felt accomplished or admired—except when Miri handed him a check—so this was nice. But then, as they were approaching Roseburg, Wes made the mistake of asking Parker a question. "How about you? What do you do?"

First Parker moaned, and then he was quiet for a few miles. Finally he sighed. "Unemployed. Except of course Mom will always give me a spot at P-Town."

"So you're a barista."

"On and off. I've also…. Let's see. Doggie day care wrangler. That was my last job, and sort of a dumb choice since I'm allergic, but it was fun. I took antihistamines. Before that I worked retail a bunch of times. Fast food. Receptionist. Messenger. Customer service rep. Inventory auditor—that's a fancy name for counting stuff in stores. I sold cell phone covers at one of those little booths in a mall. I mopped floors. Checked tickets at a movie theater. And I've poured oceans of coffee."

"That's a lot of jobs for a twenty-six-year-old."

"None of them lasted long." Parker turned toward his window as if to end the discussion.

Wes didn't pry, although he still wanted to know what had upset Parker so thoroughly today. He turned on his music, and Eddie Vedder began to wail about a homeless man. To Wes's surprise, Parker sat back in his seat and moved his knees to the beat, humming along now and then. He wouldn't have pegged Parker as a grunge fan. But then, the only thing Wes really knew about the man at his side was that he was… unexpected.

In Grants Pass, Wes finally left I-5 and turned onto a state highway. There weren't many people down this way, mainly farms, orchards, vineyards, and pastures with horses. And a whole lot of weed, although that wasn't visible from the road.

"Almost there," Wes commented after a bit. "Twenty more minutes."

"All right. Hey. Do you mind that I glommed on to you? I didn't ask."

"It's fine."

"Good."

They passed through the tiny town where Wes went for groceries. It contained little more than the general store, a post office, a bar, a gas station with an auto mechanic, and a mediocre pizza joint. There was an elementary school—high school kids had to travel farther—and a Grange Hall that hosted occasional events, which Wes never attended.

He slowed at an intersection and turned onto a county road. Parker shifted in his seat and took a deep breath. "I broke up with my boyfriend yesterday. Logan. It was kinda ugly. And today he died by suicide."

"Holy shit." Wes pulled onto the shoulder, a precaution not entirely necessary since there was no other traffic. But he felt as if he'd been slapped. He twisted to face Parker. "I am so sorry, man."

"Thanks. That was… that was what you saw in P-Town. Seattle police called to tell me—Logan and I lived there—and I freaked out."

Deeply grateful that they hadn't fucked when Parker was clearly so emotionally vulnerable, Wes sought appropriate words to console him. He was no good at that kind of thing. "That's terrible. I'm sorry this happened to you."

"It didn't, though. I mean, yeah, I have to sort of deal with it, but I'm here. I'm alive. Logan's the one who's gone." He played with the hem of his hoodie, rolling it between his fingers and tugging at a loose thread.

"But to lose someone you loved…."

Parker shook his head slightly. "I didn't…. I *liked* Logan. But we weren't in love. We'd only been together a few months, and it wasn't exactly the kind of relationship you'd read about in a romance novel. It was just…." A noisy sigh that was almost a sob. "We worked together and got along okay. We fooled around a couple of times. And his apartment was closer than mine to Barkin' Lot—that's where we worked. Plus one of my roommates used to have sex on the living room couch, which was gross, and another one—or maybe the same one, I dunno—sometimes crapped in the hallway, which was way gross, and everyone was always eating my food and nobody ever did the dishes. So I moved in with Logan."

Unsure whether the word avalanche was over, Wes reached into the pocket of the door and pulled out a couple of the peppermints he always kept there. He handed one to Parker and unwrapped the other for himself. Peppermints weren't going to solve the world's problems, but his grandfather had always given them out when Wes was upset, and they certainly didn't make things worse. At least you ended up with good breath while you were miserable.

Parker crunched his instead of sucking on it. "Anyway, Logan was a good roommate. I thought so, anyway. Turns out he wasn't actually paying the rent. Maybe I would have fallen in love with him eventually? But I found out we were about to get evicted, I yelled at him at Barkin' Lot, we both got fired, and I called my mom to come get me. Again. I guess Logan decided to escape a different way."

"I'm sorry."

"Thanks." Parker leaned his head back and closed his eyes tightly. "Episode 5,892 of the *Parker Makes Bad Decisions Show*, only this time my bad decisions affected somebody besides me."

Wes knew very well how one person's poor choices could lead to someone else's grief. He wasn't sure, though, that this was one of those situations. He spoke quietly. "It sounds to me as if Logan was responsible for what happened to him."

Parker dry-rubbed his face and then turned to Wes with a weak smile. "Sorry. I bet you didn't wake up this morning hoping to get involved in a stranger's soap opera."

"I don't mind." It was kind of nice, actually, to be reminded that he wasn't the only person who had problems—although he didn't wish troubles on Parker, who seemed like a sweet person. "Why'd you come with me today?"

After a long pause, Parker scrunched up his face. "I needed to get away. Mom's great. She loves me and she's always there for me. Nevin and Jeremy are superheroes. But I need to not be with them right now. And you looked like a nice guy when you were going into P-Town, even though I'd guess you were nervous about seeing Jeremy and Nevin. Plus you faced the two of them—that was really brave."

It had been a long time since Wes felt brave. And he had no idea why, but for some reason Parker's presence made him feel calmer. More solid within himself. Maybe that was simply due to Parker's pretty face. But he didn't think so.

"Do you still want to go to my place?" Wes asked.

"I really do."

Chapter Five

PARKER HAD always found it easy to make new acquaintances, although he struggled with finding deep friendship. So hopping into Wes's van wasn't exactly out of character for him. Heck, he'd had sex with guys whose names he didn't know. Watching Wes straining to apologize to Nevin and Jeremy had struck a deep chord of sympathy. And of course, Wes had given Parker a handy opportunity to get away from Portland when staying might have crushed him.

All of that explained why Parker had climbed into Wes's van. However, it didn't explain why he felt so comfortable with this man, a relative stranger. Usually emotions—good or bad—swirled inside Parker like a tornado. Now, though, they felt more like a stiff breeze. Still noticeable, still enough to make him shiver, but not enough to carry him away.

And the farther they drove from Portland, the more relaxed Parker became. As far as he was concerned, they could continue forever. But as they neared Wes's home, he recognized that he had to fess up—had to admit what he'd done and what happened—because it wouldn't be fair to Wes otherwise. When he'd spilled his story, Wes hadn't freaked out. He also didn't overwhelm Parker with meaningless condolences or thick pity. He just said a few good words and stared at Parker with his blue-gray eyes full of understanding.

Joining Wes was as impulsive as many of Parker's other decisions. But maybe it wasn't entirely stupid.

Wes turned Morrison onto a gravel road that was full of dips and bumps. A farmhouse stood in the middling distance, its white clapboards visible even in the waning daylight. Parker assumed that was their destination, but Wes rolled right past it, curved around a hill, passed a thick grove of trees, and finally pulled to a stop. "Hope you weren't expecting the Taj Mahal." He turned off the engine and got out of the van.

No palace was visible. In fact, there didn't even seem to be a house. But there was a school bus, most of the yellow paint covered by wild abstract shapes in every imaginable color. Concrete blocks chocked its tires. The area, edged by trees, also contained a couple of small wooden sheds, a tidy collection of boxes and furniture under a large green canopy, and a little pond with a few mallards swimming placidly.

"I thought ducks were supposed to migrate south or something," Wes said when Parker joined him. "But these guys showed up two years ago and evidently decided to hang around."

"You live here?"

Wes looked away from the ducks to give Parker a quick glance. "Yeah."

"That's cool. I never met anyone who lived in a bus before. Can I have a tour?"

After a brief pause and another quick look, Wes nodded. With Parker at his heels, he led the way to the canopied spot, where a green tarp created a weather-protected space. "This is my workshop and kitchen. The bus doesn't have plumbing, but I've got running water here." He pointed out a few features: the sink, propane grill, and oven where he prepared his food; the shed containing the compost toilet; the little wooden enclosure with a cement floor where he showered. He had a propane-powered tank to heat water for washing and bathing.

"Rustic," he said with a half shrug. "I'm used to it."

But Parker was noticing the details, the little touches such as a wooden dish rack with stylized flower shapes adorning its sides. Shed doors that sported fanciful animals carved into their surfaces. Doorknobs and cabinet knobs of glass, painted ceramic, and faceted metal. A half wine barrel heaped with colorfully painted stones. A tabletop mosaic of broken dishes.

"It's homey," he announced. He liked this space. He could imagine lounging in one of the chairs with a mug of coffee in hand, watching Wes create furniture out of pieces of wood. Yes, it was a little chilly now, in the depths of November, but Wes had a space heater out here, and there was a firepit nearby. And an observer could always cover himself in blankets.

Wes had been watching closely, gauging Parker's reaction, and now he gave a slow smile. "Thanks." He led the way up a few stairs into the bus.

Parker wasn't sure what he'd been expecting. Maybe a cot and a few odds and ends, along with the faded smell of school lunches and crayons. Instead he discovered a home. The steering wheel and original controls remained, but the driver's seat had been replaced with a leather recliner that faced the back. Polished wood covered the floors, accented by a couple of long patterned rugs. A platform bed took up the entire rear of the bus, and the middle held a couch and some upholstered chairs, an armoire and a dresser, some cabinets, a bookshelf, a table for two, and a woodstove. There was even a fridge/freezer. Curtains hung at every window.

"Wow," Parker breathed.

"Yeah?"

"Definitely wow. It's so cozy." And it was. Not many knickknacks, but every item looked carefully crafted or chosen with care.

"No plumbing in here, but I have electricity and Wi-Fi."

It was a lot like a trailer home or one of those tiny houses people on TV were always pining for. It smelled of freshly cut wood with a hint of lavender.

"It's amazing. Did you do all this yourself?"

"Mostly."

"How long have you lived here?"

"Ten years."

Parker ran his fingertips down the side of a cabinet. The wood was as smooth as glass, but warmer. He imagined Wes patiently sanding and finishing that same expanse. The brief vision made Parker's heart beat faster, and he felt his cheeks flush. He had a thousand more questions, but asking them seemed intrusive. Wes clearly had unpleasantness in his past that didn't want resurrecting. So Parker settled for a statement instead. "You love your home."

Wes's response came out low and raspy. "Yeah. My grandpa lived in that house we passed. I used to spend a lot of time with him when I was a kid. I helped him dig that pond." He gestured at a window, and Parker viewed the scenery in the waning light. The pond was about the size of Rhoda's urban backyard and ringed with grass and late-autumn remains of wildflowers. It was an intimate and peaceful place, much like the interior of the bus.

Wes traced a finger down the window glass. "Grandpa was still alive when I moved here—the bus was his idea. But he died before I got things really set up." He gave a small smile. "He left me these five acres."

Darkness had fallen, and several lights gave the bus interior a warm and cozy glow. Parker remained near the door, watching as Wes plugged in his phone and then spent a moment poking at it until low-volume music drifted from speakers near the ceiling. The Rolling Stones.

"Do you want some dinner?" Wes asked.

"Not yet. Still full from lunch."

"Okay. I can grill us some burgers or salmon later. If you still want to stay, that is."

Parker wanted that very badly. He strode over to Wes, planning to ask about the beautiful chair nearby. Had Wes built it? What kind of wood was it? What made him decide to carve that particular design into the back? But instead of interrogating him, Parker somehow found himself embracing him.

They were nearly the same height, although Wes was more heavily built, and their bodies seemed to fit together as neatly as two pieces of joined cabinetry. They didn't kiss, didn't grope. But Parker held Wes tight, and Wes returned the embrace—he was solid and smelled of soy sauce and peppermint.

Parker felt that if only they could stand like that for a long time—a week, a month—he might leave the embrace with a permanent sense of who he was and where he wanted to go. He might never make a bad decision again.

Wes snuffled into the crook of Parker's neck. "God, this is.... We need to not do this." He didn't loosen his grip, however.

"Why not?"

"I don't want to take advantage of you."

That made Parker laugh. "Do you think I'm some kind of blushing maiden? Or a child?"

"No, I think you're a man who's gone through a lot in the past two days."

That was true enough. Still, Parker ordinarily wouldn't have hesitated to jump Wes's bones. But the sensible little voice inside his head—the one that rarely spoke up—told him if he and Wes fucked now, that would be the end of it. The next day Parker would find his way back to Portland somehow, and he'd never see Wes again. He didn't want that.

It was physically painful to unwind himself from Wes, but Parker did. Still, he felt fortified by the hug. Well, fortified and half-hard. He sat on the couch and smiled up at Wes. "Tell me about your grandfather."

WES'S STORIES came slowly at first, little dribbles of sentences without much detail or emotion. But then the words came faster, the memories grew lusher, and he talked almost nonstop as he prepared dinner and then while they ate outside under the canopy, as if they were camping. Parker enjoyed having opened the verbal spigot and loved hearing about Wes's grandfather, who'd taught him carpentry.

"If we *had* gone to Wyoming," Wes said, a bottle of beer in hand, "we could have visited the Reliance tipple."

Parker, with his full belly, felt more relaxed and comfortable than he had in ages, even though the night air was cold. "I have no idea what that is."

"It's this place where they used to sort and load coal. They haven't used it in… I dunno. Decades. But the structure is cool. Big and sort of postapocalyptic industrial, out in the middle of nowhere. I've, uh, seen some photos."

"I would like to visit a tipple."

Wes flashed him a grin. "Or there's the desert. Or maybe the ocean."

And then Wes was off again, describing the history of transpacific sailing. Parker listened, realizing Wes probably didn't get much chance to talk to other people, at least not at length. Parker was usually surrounded by people—coworkers, acquaintances, customers, roommates—and it was nice to have just one conversation going, to have somebody focused only on him.

He continued to listen while he washed up the dinner dishes, and then he and Wes went into the bus. Just as Wes was asking Parker what music he'd like to hear, Parker's phone buzzed. He glanced at the screen and sighed. "My mom. I'm gonna take this outside, okay?"

Wes nodded, and Parker stepped out of the bus.

"Hi, Mom."

"You doing okay, Gonzo?"

He looked up at the sky, where a few stars peeked through tattered clouds. "I'm fine. Not kidnapped or anything."

"You're still with Wes?"

"Yeah. I'm an adult, and—"

"I'm not calling to tell you what to do."

That made him blink. Rhoda was generally pretty free with advice—not just to him, but to everyone who ventured within her sphere. "Oh?" he said carefully.

"I just wanted to tell you I love you."

"I love you too." He waited for what felt like a long time, but she didn't say anything else. Didn't hang up either, though. Eventually he puffed out a lungful of air. "You're sure you don't want to tell me that running off like this was irresponsible? Or that Wes is a complete stranger who Jeremy and Nevin hate?"

She laughed. "You already know those things, kiddo. I don't have to tell you. If you need some space to sort out your head and your heart, then I respect that."

He wandered over to the covered area and plopped into the chair where he'd sat for a good chunk of the evening. Something rustled in the trees nearby. Maybe just a bit of breeze. Or maybe… raccoons? Possums? He'd spent his life in cities and suburbs and didn't know what might be lurking here. Still, it wasn't scary to sit out here, even alone. Wes had hung some lights here and there, and they cast a cheery little glow.

"I have no idea what I need," he admitted. "Or what I want."

"Like I said—maybe you can sort yourself out a little now, wherever you are."

"Maybe. But Wes…."

"I don't know what Nevin and Jeremy have against him. I'm sure they have a good reason to be angry. But I thought he seemed very nice. And brave, for standing up to those two to apologize."

Parker nodded to himself. "I like him."

"Good."

Perhaps Rhoda's tacit approval shouldn't have been important, but it was. For one thing, her instincts about people were rarely off.

Wes hadn't closed the curtains in the bus, and Parker caught glimpses of him through the windows, moving around as if he were arranging something inside.

"Mom, I don't know when I'll be back." Or how he'd get there, but that was a problem for another day. "Am I leaving you shorthanded at P-Town?"

"A little, yes, but don't worry. I have backup plans."

Of course she did. Rhoda was prepared for everything and never jumped into stupid decisions. "Okay," Parker said.

"If you hear from the police again, let us know, all right? And do you want to talk to that lawyer Jeremy recommended?"

"Not really. Can you do it?" Because that was totally what an adult did—ask his mom to take care of his legal issues.

Maybe Rhoda expected this, however, because she didn't hesitate before responding. "If you want. I'll let you know if she needs information from you, though."

"Thanks. I appreciate you, Mom."

"You should." She chuckled. "And I appreciate you too, Gonzo. Good night."

After the call ended, he stayed outside for several more minutes until he realized he was shivering. When he returned to the bus, Wes had settled into a chair with a book on his lap.

"Everything okay?" he asked.

"Yep."

Creedence Clearwater now played through the speakers, John Fogerty singing about the Midnight Special. Parker hummed along as he made himself comfortable on the couch. "You're probably thinking I'm too old to be checking in with Mommy."

"Nah, I get it. You're close."

There was a hint of longing or sadness there, and Parker scrutinized him. Wes had spoken a lot about his grandfather but hadn't mentioned the rest of his family. "You're not close with your parents?"

Wes shrugged. If he was trying for nonchalant, he didn't quite pull it off. "They divorced when I was little. They both remarried and started new families. I was kind of a leftover. A reminder of failure. They shuttled me back and forth, you know, but I didn't fit in with any of them."

That sucked. No matter what disasters Parker brought on himself, he was always rock-solid in his knowledge that he belonged to his mother, and she to him. "Are your folks around here?"

"Nah. My mother ended up in Nevada. My dad and his kids inherited the rest of Grandpa's property but sold it right away. Somebody rents the land, the house is empty, and my dad's in California somewhere." Wes lifted his chin. "But I have my five acres and my bus and my furniture business. This is *mine*."

The song ended and another began: "Fortunate Son," in fact, which was rather ironic timing. Wes stared at Parker. "Do you want a ride back to Portland now?" His voice was quiet.

Parker's throat tightened and he lurched to his feet. "I'm imposing. I'm sorry. I'll—"

But Wes was out of his chair and resting a hand—hard calluses and hot skin—on Parker's forearm. "You're not imposing. I just…." He took a step back, letting his hand drop. "I'm not good for you."

If Wes's expression weren't so somber, if Parker weren't feeling choked, he would have laughed. "Good for me? Like health food or something? 'Cause I'm not a big fan."

"I'm not…." Wes bit his lip, clearly struggling to get the words out. Then he shook his head. "My life here is really boring."

Breathing became easier when Parker saw the doubt in Wes's eyes. Wes didn't want to get rid of him. "I like it here," Parker said.

"Why?"

A reasonable question, but Parker had a hard time answering. It was difficult to express. "I like the quiet," he said, but there was more to it than that. And if Wes was willing to put up with him, the guy at least deserved a more complete response.

After a brief hesitation, Parker took two steps, which brought him to the opposite side of the bus. He ran his fingertips down the side of a bookshelf made of a red-hued wood, polished to a warm glow. A swath of blonder wood was inset in a random serpentine pattern that looked as if a lazy river or wandering country road flowed down the bookcase to the floor. "You made this, huh?"

"Yeah."

Stroking the wood seemed to help organize Parker's thoughts. "My parents opened P-Town when I was in high school. It was a ton of work—getting the shop physically set up, collecting all the right permits and stuff, hiring and training people, deciding on menus and suppliers…. Even now, all these years later, Mom probably puts in eighty hours a week. She doesn't have to. But she *wants* to. Her dream. Maybe it's a dumb little coffeehouse to everyone else—"

"It's a really nice coffeehouse."

Parker smiled. "It is. But in the end, it's really not much more than a place to get sugar and caffeine, and Portland is full of those. Still, P-Town's almost always busy, and regular customers come from all over the city even though parking can be a pain in the ass. And I think the reason why is that people can tell it's not just some corporate outpost or a way for someone to make a few bucks. P-Town is my mom's happy place, and that gives off vibes that make other people happy too."

Funny. Parker had never really thought about this before, but the words rang true as he said them, and Wes was nodding as if they made sense to him as well. That was pretty cool. If Parker had made this speech to any of his exes, most of them would have laughed and asked what he'd been smoking. But since Wes wasn't laughing, Parker continued while caressing the bookshelf.

"This place—your bus, your workshop outside—it's like that. You've put your heart into it, just like Mom has into P-Town, and that makes your home a good place to be. It's a warm energy, you know?"

Wes regarded him, wide-eyed. "Yeah."

That made Parker so pleased that he hugged himself, as if holding his body together.

They settled back down again, Wes in his chair and Parker on the couch, Credence still twanging away. Usually Parker would have played on his phone, but after eyeing Wes for a few minutes, he instead stood and examined the books on the shelf. "Can I borrow one?"

"Sure."

Parker had always considered reading a chore rather than entertainment, but after he snuggled back into the couch with *Hitchhiker's Guide to the Galaxy*, he was absolutely content to dip lazily in and out of the story as he listened to the music and to Wes turning the pages of his own book. Even better was when Wes disappeared outside the bus for a few minutes and returned with steaming mugs of minty tea. He set one atop a coaster on the little table beside Parker, then rooted in a cabinet before producing a bag of chips. He poured the chips into a couple of bowls, handed one to Parker, and sat back in his chair with his own.

Yeah. Pretty close to perfection.

An indefinable time later, Parker looked up when Wes began to yawn. "Long day, huh?" Parker asked.

"For both of us."

The memory of what had happened to Logan resurfaced from where Parker had attempted to bury it, and he grimaced. "Yeah."

"Okay. Your choice. We can make up the couch into a serviceable bed. I've slept on it before, and it's pretty comfortable. Or...." He gestured toward his own bed.

Ordinarily Parker wouldn't have hesitated to jump onto that nice wide mattress—naked, with lube and a rubber in hand. He'd thought Wes was hot the minute he laid eyes on him outside P-Town, and the longer they'd spent together, the sexier Wes had become. Tonight, though, a rare hesitancy poked at him. If he and Wes fucked tonight, it would probably be fun. And they might fuck again in the morning, maybe again tomorrow night. But then what if that was that? It would be sort of like sitting down to dinner and eating dessert before you got to the main course. After a big slice of chocolate peanut butter cake, that plate of grilled zucchini wasn't going to be as appealing. And that would be too bad because grilled zucchini tasted damned good—and was long-term healthy to boot.

Parker had the feeling that getting to know Wes more deeply would make for a very satisfying main course.

On the other hand, Parker wasn't in the mood to be alone on the couch, even if Wes was only a few yards away.

Wes waited patiently, eyebrows raised and head slightly cocked. He wasn't rushing Parker into a decision, which was nice.

Compromise. "Your bed, please. But, um, no sex. If that's okay."

"That's fine." If Wes felt disappointed, he didn't show it.

Half an hour later Parker was glad for his decision. Wes's bed was cozy, enclosed on three sides by the walls of the bus and with a painted starscape on the ceiling above them. Wes had shut down the stove, and the room temperature was cooling, but they had flannel sheets and a heavy down comforter that smelled pleasantly of Wes: wood shavings, Dr. Bronner's soap, and mint tea. Wes snored softly beside Parker. They weren't touching, but Parker *could* touch him if he moved his hand a little to the side. Maybe tomorrow.

Chapter Six

Wes couldn't remember the last time he'd awakened with another man in his bed. It was a little strange, especially since he'd just met this particular man the previous afternoon and then enjoyed an oddly domestic evening together—and they hadn't fucked. Hadn't even kissed. Parker was also a decade younger and looked especially youthful in his sleep: orange hair spread over the white pillowcase, long lashes fanned above cheekbones, wide mouth hanging open a bit. Wes hadn't closed all the curtains before they went to bed, and now the morning light bathed Parker's beautiful face and one hand, lightly curled, sticking out from the blankets.

Wes wanted to run his fingers through Parker's hair and across his cheeks. He wanted to taste Parker's lips. He wanted to press their bodies together and bury his nose in the crook of Parker's neck so he could inhale the early-morning scent of him. Instead Wes simply looked, several miles of inches between them.

Then Parker opened his eyes—varied tones of warm brown, like bits of polished rosewood—and smiled. "Morning."

Wes cleared his throat to get rid of the hoarseness. "Breakfast?"

"Wouldn't say no to that." Parker stretched luxuriously. "But let me help, okay?"

Wes was well aware his home setup was unconventional; you had to brave the morning's outdoor chill to simply use the bathroom and wash up. He was used to it, of course, but he expected some grousing from Parker. He didn't get it. Parker seemed cheerful about everything, in fact, and cooked eggs and toast while Wes showered. Wes repeatedly glanced at him over the top of the wooden shower enclosure, and Parker shot him occasional quick grins.

They took their breakfast into the bus to eat. "The eggs are good," Wes commented after a couple of bites. "You put stuff in them."

"Just threw in a few herbs and spices."

"Coffee's good too."

Parker chuckled. "If there's one thing I can do really well, it's brew coffee."

"It's a handy skill." Wes lifted his mug in a toast. "I appreciate it." He took another sip.

"In the grand scheme of things, it's not a big deal. Not like making fancy furniture."

Wes laughed. "And how many people get to use my fancy furniture? A handful. Rich ones with money to burn. Coffee making, however, delights the masses."

Parker rolled his eyes, apparently unconvinced, but let the matter drop. "Did you plan to work today?"

"Yeah. But if that sounds boring, we can—"

"It doesn't. I'd like to watch, if it's okay with you."

"Sure." Wes had never had an audience before. He suspected the show would grow tedious pretty fast.

After Parker helped with the breakfast cleanup, he settled into a chair under the tarp with a blanket on his lap and fresh coffee in hand—and stayed there most of the morning. He asked a few questions about what Wes was doing and listened carefully to the explanations. Wes showed Parker the planks of weathered white oak salvaged from an old barn and talked about his hopes for the current project, explaining that the numerous nail holes would simply add to the coffee table's character. If he cut and joined everything correctly, the tabletop would evoke the keel of a sailing ship. An appropriate piece of driftwood, currently waiting in one of the sheds, would curl around it: a sea monster pulling the ship to its doom.

When alone, Wes had a tendency to mutter to himself as he labored. It was a nice change to talk to another human being. Especially one who was easy on the eyes and willing to fetch him hot drinks. Parker tried to bring him tools as well, but it soon became clear he didn't recognize much beyond a hammer.

"Your mom never taught you handyman skills, huh?" Wes glanced over and smiled.

"No," Parker answered with an amused snort. "I don't think she has any of those skills."

Wes hesitated a moment before posing the next question. "What about your dad?" Parker had mentioned his parents, plural, a couple of times, but although he talked about Rhoda in some detail, he'd said very little about his father.

Parker laughed softly. "He was even worse at projects than her. He used to call himself Captain Klutz, which was an accurate description."

"Um… *was*?"

Parker nodded. "Yeah. He died in a car crash a bunch of years ago."

"Jesus. I'm sorry."

"Thanks. I was in my first semester at Oregon State. I'd seen him the weekend before—he and Mom came down to Corvallis to take me out for my birthday dinner. They dropped me off at my dorm, I said good night, and that was it. He just suddenly disappeared from the world."

Wes nodded, remembering the grief that had torn at him when his grandfather passed away. At least Wes had some warning: his grandfather was in his late eighties and had battled cancer for a couple of years. But still Wes's world shifted in a terrifying and disorienting way. For months afterward he caught himself almost heading down the road to his grandfather's house, almost buying a package of those awful menthol candies the old man loved to suck on when he wasn't in the mood for peppermint.

"I'm sorry," Wes repeated.

Parker looked pensive. "Mom was— It wrecked her, and seeing that was almost as bad as losing him 'cause she's always so strong. She got through it okay in the long run, though."

"Did you get through it okay, in the long run?" Wes didn't look at Parker as he spoke.

"Sure. I mean, I guess." A pause punctuated by a sigh. "I dropped out of school. In theory it was a temporary thing so I could help Mom out for a while, but I hadn't been doing all that great in my classes anyway. I probably would have flunked out. I'd only gone to college because that's what everyone expected. Anyway, I never went back."

"Do you wish you had?"

This time Wes glanced at Parker, who scrunched up his face in thought. "No. I'm not the academic type. How about you? Did you go to college?"

"Associate's degree. Criminal justice."

Parker's eyes widened. "That's right! You used to be a cop."

Parker hadn't pressed him about yesterday's run-in with Jeremy and Nevin, and Wes was perfectly okay with avoiding that topic for, oh, the next century or so.

Frowning, he unhooked the tape measure from his tool belt. "Want to see how a miter saw works?"

PARKER SEEMED to grow a little restless as the morning continued. He wandered over to the pond and watched the ducks for a while. Then he announced he needed a walk and disappeared around the curve in the gravel road. Wes half expected he'd never see Parker again, figured he'd make his way to the county road and hitch a ride. But Parker returned an hour later, his shoulders hunched against the light rainfall.

"That hoodie's not going to keep you dry," Wes said, trying to hide his pleasure at Parker's return. "I think I have a spare raincoat."

"Now you sound like my mom." But Parker made sure to stand under the tarp's shelter. "Want me to make us some lunch?"

"Sure."

"I should be doing something to earn my keep."

Wes was in the middle of sanding, and it was wonderful to look up from his work now and then and see Parker close by, rattling pans and humming to himself. Parker managed well with Wes's somewhat makeshift kitchen. Maybe his varied job experience helped him find his way around, even under rough circumstances.

After they ate, Wes returned to his project. He didn't often put in so many hours in a row, but it was a lot of fun to have someone to talk to, and the time flew by. He didn't know whether Parker was genuinely fascinated by the details of woodworking or just appreciated a distraction from his personal problems. Either way, Wes was happy to be of service.

By dinnertime his back ached and his hands felt stiff. This was one of those few occasions when he wished he had a nice, deep bathtub. Maybe he ought to look into the costs and logistics of building a hot tub. It would be nice to soak under the stars now and then.

Parker insisted on starting dinner—linguini, chicken, and squash—while Wes washed the dust and grime off his hands and face. They ate outside, listening to raindrops patter onto the tarp, enjoying a mostly silent camaraderie. Five meals, Wes realized with a start. This meant he'd shared five meals in a row with Parker. He rarely had company, almost never while he ate, and the last time he'd eaten five consecutive meals with anyone was... while Parker was still in high school.

Parker stared at him as if there was something absolutely fascinating about the way Wes ate pasta. That scrutiny was unusual too, because people didn't often pay Wes much attention. Even his rare hookups seemed satisfied with a cursory inspection of Wes's face and physique before getting down to business. Wes knew he was sort of good-looking, in a bland and forgettable way. Forced to give a flattering description of his own face, Wes would have said his features were regular and symmetrical.

But Parker gazed as if Wes were remarkable. Maybe Parker was so used to colorful, striking people like himself that an everyday model proved momentarily exotic.

"Sorry there's no club nearby," Wes finally blurted.

Parker's eyes widened. "Club?"

"Dance club. There's nothing for miles. You'd have to go to Medford for that."

"Do you want to go dancing?"

Wes chuckled uncomfortably. "I can't dance. I just figured that was more your speed than... you know...." He shrugged and waved his hands vaguely at their surroundings.

"Is that who you think I am? A club kid?" Parker's expression, which had been relaxed most of the day, went tight and angular.

"No. I mean, if you are, that's fine, nothing wrong with it. It's only that you're such a vibrant person. I can picture you out on the dance floor with your gorgeous, cool friends, having a good time. Better than I can picture you on a farm listening to some guy go on about wood glues and joining screws."

Parker's face lightened. His lips even twitched a bit at the corners. "Joining screws? Is this the point when I can make a lot of bad double entendres about wood?" He snorted lightly, then stood and began gathering their dishes. "I like dancing," he said as he carried the plates to the sink. "And sometimes I'm in the mood to go out. Right now, though, I'd rather be here. With you."

Wes was immediately doubtful. But then he remembered Parker was dealing with a number of fresh shocks—a breakup, a job loss, a move, and the death of his ex. Maybe he *did* need some quiet and isolation right now. Retreating to a safe, secluded location made a lot of sense after trauma. The problem with that strategy, however, was that if you weren't careful, a refuge could become a self-imposed prison, and you might never find the key to let yourself out.

That night Parker texted his mother, probably to report that Wes hadn't murdered him yet. Afterward Parker and Wes sat in the bus with their books as the speakers wafted dinosaur rock. They ate popcorn and drank beer. And sometimes Wes would glance over to discover Parker looking at him pensively.

When the hour grew late, they washed up, stripped to their underwear—gray boxer briefs for Wes and tangerine-colored briefs for Parker—and got into bed. Side by side. Not touching.

Having Parker right there, almost naked yet out of bounds? It was a terrible torture, and Wes wanted to groan.

"Question for you." Parker's voice was barely above a whisper, amplified by the darkness and intimacy. "It's personal. So don't answer if you don't want to."

That was intriguing and slightly disquieting. "Okay."

"You can think of it as a game of Truth or Dare. Which means if you answer with a truth, you get to ask me something, and I have to answer too, or else I'll lose. I hate losing."

Wes wasn't usually in favor of spilling secrets, but tonight he was amenable. "What do you want to know?"

"You don't seem to have a whole lot of interactions with other people. Is that because you're a world-class introvert and prefer to be alone? 'Cause if so, that's cool. Or do you wish you were more... social?"

Wes didn't respond right away, in part because he wasn't sure of the answer. He'd always been kind of a loner, or at least most comfortable with just one or two people close by. Crowds made him nervous. Social occasions exhausted him. On the other hand, there was a big difference between needing some alone time and spending a decade barely interacting with the outside world. Sometimes a week or more went by without him seeing or talking to another human being. And sometimes he felt so isolated and forsaken that he wanted to cry.

"Some of each, maybe," he answered at last. "Mostly I feel protected here. Secure."

"Okay." Parker's response seemed to come without judgment or condemnation. He didn't even ask why Wes needed to feel secure. Parker just accepted it. Then he shifted under the blankets. "Your turn."

Although there were about a thousand things Wes wanted to know, he didn't *need* to know them. Not now, when Parker was still emotionally raw.

"What other colors have you dyed your hair?"

Parker barked a laugh. "All of them. Every color of the rainbow, man."

A comfortable silence fell between them, and after a short time, Wes began to slip into a drowse. He wasn't sure if he was dreaming when Parker reached over and touched his hand for a second and whispered, "Night, Wes."

Chapter Seven

As Parker cradled his second coffee of the morning, he acknowledged that he needed to *do* something. Well, something more, because he'd fixed breakfast again, and brewed coffee, and now he was watching Wes turn boring hunks of wood into something amazing.

Parker found Wes more fascinating than any movie or video. Part of that was Wes's magic—the way he could make something valuable from what looked like a pile of kindling. And part of it was Wes's handsome face and the way he bit his lip when he concentrated. Wes's smooth voice contributed too. He talked about foreign places or explained how a tool worked, and Parker hung on every word. And Wes's hands! Parker kept finding himself staring at them, admiring their dexterity and strength, wondering how they'd feel moving across his skin. What were the chances he'd imagine those hands during the next zillion jerk-off sessions? Oh, somewhere in the ballpark of a hundred and ten percent.

But he couldn't just sit there for the rest of his life, rousing himself only to make food and clean up. He was wearing Wes's clothes, which didn't fit him very well, and he'd used Wes's phone charging cord, his razor and brush, his soap and shampoo and toothpaste. He only had his own toothbrush because Wes gave him one from his stash. As accommodating as Wes was being, a man couldn't survive forever in borrowed underwear.

But Parker didn't want to face the real world.

This was like a grown-up version of summer camp, where he got to spend his days being entertained in the great outdoors and his nights tucked away somewhere cozy with a friend. All he needed was s'mores and a poison oak rash. But eventually summer camp ended and school began. His time with Wes had to end too, and Parker needed to go back to Portland, to his mother's house and her coffeehouse, to the ashes of his latest and greatest disaster.

Suddenly Parker was crying.

He hadn't meant to. He wasn't the type to dissolve into tears, and on those few occasions when emotions overwhelmed him, he locked himself in a bedroom or bathroom and bawled in private.

But now Parker was crying so hard, in full view of poor Wes, that he had to put down the coffee cup and bury his face in his hands. He would have run away if he'd trusted his legs to hold him.

Wes put aside his sander, hurried to Parker's side, and knelt on the soft ground. "Parker?" He gave his shoulder an awkward pat.

Parker abandoned his last specks of dignity and threw himself at Wes. He landed on his knees and clung to him like a drowning man trying to save himself. Instead of pushing Parker away—as a reasonable person might want to do—Wes held him, petting Parker's back and letting him get tears and snot on Wes's soft flannel shirt.

When Parker's knees began to ache, he let go of Wes and got to his feet. "Sorry." He swiped his arms across his face. His hoodie sleeve made a crappy Kleenex, but it would have to do.

Wes stood too, his expression concerned rather than grossed-out. "It hit you, huh?"

"Logan was…." Parker sniffled. "He was unreliable. Even by my standards. But he was also funny. And at work he was so good with the dogs. If one was a little fearful or overwhelmed, Logan would just hang and sweet-talk it. Cuddle it, maybe. And pretty soon the dog would be totally chill. All the dogs loved Logan best."

Logan had other appealing qualities too. He'd buy plain white tennis shoes, cheap ones, and doodle all over them with Sharpies. For dinner he liked to eat cereal, the sugary kids' kind with cartoon characters on the box. He knew the theme songs from a zillion old sitcoms. He was mortally terrified of spiders and shrieked anytime he saw one.

God, Parker was going to start crying again.

"He's dead because of me," he said in a tiny voice. He'd made a lot of mistakes in his life, but until now he'd never killed anyone.

Wes shook his head. "C'mon. You're not responsible for whatever bad shit was going on in his head."

"But if I hadn't broken up with him and gotten him fired—"

"What were you supposed to do? Thank him for stealing from you and getting you evicted?"

"I… dunno." More pathetic sniffles. "I could have handled it better, maybe."

"Let's... let's go inside. It's kind of cold out here."

They washed up, and Parker made more coffee. This time when he sat on the couch, Wes took the spot beside him instead of his usual chair. Parker stared into his cup. "Can you drive me to Grants Pass tomorrow? Or if that's a pain in the ass, I can—"

"Why do you want to go to Grants Pass?"

"So I can catch a bus to Portland." Parker hadn't checked the Greyhound schedule, but he figured there'd be a stop there.

Wes stiffened beside him, and when he answered, his voice was strained. "I'll drive you."

"You're not too busy?"

"No."

Silence hung heavy between them, and Parker wasn't sure what to say. He didn't know what he wanted, didn't know what he was going to do. Hell, half the time he didn't even know how he felt. And as for Wes, he clearly wasn't used to much personal interaction.

Which raised an interesting question, one that provided an excellent opportunity for a needed change of subject.

"Why did you become a cop?"

Wes stared at him, brow furrowed, and didn't answer. But that didn't stop Parker from blundering onward. "I know sort of a lot of cops. Nevin. Jeremy—well, he's not one anymore, but he's still kinda coppish. A lot of their buddies hang out at P-Town, so I know them too. And don't take this the wrong way, okay, 'cause I don't mean it as an insult, but I'm sorta having trouble picturing you in a blue uniform. You just don't seem the type."

Parker winced at the words. So what if Wes didn't fit the typical law enforcement persona? Parker didn't care. Preferred it, even. In his current mental state, he was probably better off with Wes's quiet, unpushy manner, with the way Wes could be solid and strong in an unobtrusive way. But telling someone he didn't seem to fit his former career was probably a shitty thing to do.

To Parker's surprise, Wes quirked his mouth into a small smile. "I'm not the type. I was a shitty cop, and I hated doing it."

"But—"

"My dad was a sheriff's deputy. He wore khaki and green instead of blue, but there was no question he was a cop." His lip curled. "The kind who feels like a tough guy because he wears a badge and carries a gun."

Nevin and Jeremy were nothing like that, but Parker knew what Wes meant. "Okay."

"I figured if I followed his footsteps, he might finally…. I don't know. Pay attention to me. Like me. Respect me."

Parker understood completely. He'd never questioned his parents' feelings toward him, and if anything they tended to smother him with attention instead of ignoring him. But still, he'd never been able to shake a niggling sense that he was letting them down. That as their only child, he ought to be achieving something remarkable. Or… achieving *anything*. Maybe that sense hadn't been so overwhelming when his father was alive, since Parker was still young then, still on a somewhat meaningful trajectory. But after his father's death, Parker couldn't help feeling as if he was constantly disappointing his mother. That feeling grew worse every year, with every personal disaster.

"You wanted him to love you."

"I was a dumbass."

"I don't think so."

Wes shot him an unreadable look before shrugging and leaning back against the couch cushion. "Anyway, he didn't give a shit. I invited him to the ceremony when I graduated from the academy, but he didn't show. Never heard a fucking peep from him until I… until I left the bureau. And let's just say he wasn't feeling very respectful then."

Parker was dying to know what had transpired to end Wes's career and make Nevin and Jeremy so angry. Surely it couldn't have been something really bad, like corruption or abuse of force; Wes didn't seem capable of that. Not that Parker knew him all that well. If only he had his mother's magical ability to read the quality of people's souls.

Wes didn't offer more information, and he looked so angry and forlorn that Parker chose not to push it. So he smiled gently instead. "Was there anything you liked about being a cop?"

That brought a small chuckle. "Driving fast. I really liked driving fast."

THEY DIDN'T discuss anything personal for the rest of the day. Parker watched Wes work, and Wes explained what tools he was using and why, and that was good. When Wes got wrapped up in making furniture, he almost became a different person. More confident. Less gruff. A light would shine in his eyes as he spoke about the qualities of different materials and his plans for the pieces of wood that awaited his craftsmanship. It was the same light Rhoda displayed when talking about P-Town or that Jeremy got when describing a hike. Passion, Parker supposed. He doubted his own eyes had ever held that light.

They ate a simple dinner of burgers and baked potatoes—Wes cooked; Parker cleaned up—before holing up with music and books. Tonight felt jagged somehow, though, and Parker had trouble settling. He turned pages without registering what they said. Wes kept changing the playlist or getting up to fiddle with curtains and lights. He hummed something Parker couldn't quite catch. Maybe things would have been easier between them if they'd had more space, but the rain had intensified, the night was cold, and the bus felt really small.

Parker's nerves, already frayed from recent events, buzzed uncomfortably. Fidgeting didn't help, and neither did a mug of mint tea. When he couldn't stand it a minute longer, he lurched across the bus and ran out the door. Despite the darkness and rain, and even though his hoodie offered little protection from the elements and he could barely see the gravel road in front of his feet, he sprinted past the white house that once belonged to Wes's grandfather. He continued to the county road, chose a direction at random, and pounded down the blacktop.

The exertion warmed him despite his soaked clothes and the squishing inside his sneakers. Wet hair hung in his face. Between that and the poor visibility, he fell once. Swore, stood up, wiped the debris from his stinging hands. Continued running. Listened to his lungs laboring and the splashes as his soles slapped the blacktop. Thought about nothing at all.

The headlights hit him before he heard the car approaching from behind. He veered to the shoulder—and fell again as he stumbled into a shallow ditch. This time his hands landed on something stiff and thorny, perhaps the late-autumn remains of a thistle. He was still standing in the ditch and swearing when the car came to a stop beside him.

Not a car—Morrison.

"You're going to get yourself killed." Wes hopped out of the driver's seat.

Before Parker could protest, Wes draped a raincoat over Parker's shoulders, hauled him to the passenger seat, and buckled him in. He tossed a blanket onto Parker's lap before returning to the wheel. After executing a quick three-point turn, he zoomed back toward his property.

"You forgot your phone," he said as he drove. He pulled it out and tossed it onto Parker's lap.

Parker, shivering violently, didn't touch it. He faced the window instead. It was steamed opaque from their breaths.

When they reached the bus, Wes turned off the engine and stared through the windshield. "Go change into dry clothes and I'll drive you to Grants Pass. Probably no bus until tomorrow. I'll get you a hotel room."

Parker finally spoke, but his voice was barely more than a whisper. "You want me to go tonight?"

"No!" Wes shouted, slamming the steering wheel with both hands. "I want you to stay inside where it's warm and dry and some asshole driving too fast in the rain isn't going to run you over. But you seem to have different plans."

"I wasn't...." Parker traced patterns in the moisture on the glass. "I'd rather leave tomorrow."

With a frustrated grunt, Wes shoved his door open and hopped out. He slammed the door hard enough to shake the van.

Parker remained in the vehicle for several minutes, hair dripping onto his face and shoulders. He felt small and stupid, and he was cold. Finally he got out and draped the sawdust-scented blanket over his head, tucking his phone into a fold of the fabric to keep it dry. The stairs leading to the bus door loomed steeply, but he managed them.

As soon as he was inside, Wes reached around him to close the door. "Put these on." He nudged Parker's chest with a stack of folded clothing.

Still shivering, Parker stripped out of his sodden clothes and into the dry ones. Clean boxers, a pair of soft gray sweatpants, and a pinkish sweatshirt that was probably once red. Threads trailed from its raveled hem, but the inside was nice and fleecy, and it felt comforting against his clammy skin.

"Did you hurt yourself when you fell?" Wes had spirited away the wet clothing and now hovered nearby, frowning.

Parker wordlessly held out his hands. They were raw-looking, with bits of gravel and broken thorns embedded in the skin.

Wes sighed, but he sounded more weary than annoyed. "Sit down." Parker perched on the edge of the couch, and Wes left the bus without putting on a jacket.

He swiftly returned with a plastic bucket of steaming water in one hand and a sizable first-aid kit in the other. The kit's plastic case was scuffed and battered; it had clearly seen frequent use.

Neither of them spoke as Wes swabbed Parker's hands with warm water and then antiseptic, although Parker couldn't stop a hiss at the sting. He was a wimp about pain. He remained still, though, even when Wes prodded and then pulled the thorns loose with tweezers.

Finally Wes gave Parker's hands a critical inspection, nodded, and closed the first-aid kit. "Bandages would be more of a pain than they're worth. But keep your hands clean."

"You're good at doctoring. Something they taught you at the police academy?"

Wes barked a laugh. "No. If you work with your hands, they get chewed up sometimes. And you learn how to take care of them."

That Wes had nobody to patch him up when he was injured made Parker a little sad. But he didn't mention it.

Wes went back outside to put away the supplies, and he returned with an oversize mug, which he shoved at Parker. "Drink."

It was hot chocolate, the instant kind, and although it burned Parker's tongue, it also chased away the last of his chills. He was left feeling feeble and weak-limbed. "Maybe I should go to sleep." He had no idea what time it was but suspected the hour was still early.

"Fine."

"I'm sorry I...." Parker let the words fade away. He was so goddamn tired of being sorry. He made his slow way to the bed and, keeping all his clothes on, collapsed onto the mattress. He stared up at the curved ceiling, listening to Wes move around the bus, damping down the wood stove and closing the curtains. Tidying up a few things. Tucking away food because, he'd told Parker the previous day, otherwise mice inevitably found their way into the bus.

Parker must have drifted into a doze, because he was slightly startled to find Wes standing at the foot of the bed and frowning down at him.

Parker sat up. "Do you want me to sleep on the couch?"

"You're young. And... bright. Vibrant."

That didn't seem to answer the question. Parker cocked his head. "Okay?"

"I'm not any of those things. And I'm a miserable son of a bitch most of the time."

"I don't think—"

"I am. You haven't been around me long enough to see, but you would, in time. You've had enough trouble without having to deal with my shit. Go back to Portland tomorrow. You'll find what you need there."

Parker had no idea what prompted this conversation or why Wes would say these things, and he didn't have the emotional energy to argue. "Let's just get some sleep, okay?"

After a moment Wes doused the last of the lights, leaving the bus in almost complete darkness, and joined Parker in bed. They lay beside each other, breathing in tandem.

"I'm not always a huge mess," Parker said after a long time. It sounded pathetic.

"I know."

"Really. Usually I'm kinda happy and easygoing. Too easygoing, maybe. It's like running down that road in the dark—I don't see where I'm heading and end up falling. Drama city."

"But you get back up again."

Parker considered this. "I guess so. I'm just sorry I dragged you into the current mess. Usually it's just Mom who has to deal. This time it's you too." A thought struck him. "And Logan. Christ, Logan."

"We've been through this. His suicide was not your fault."

"Maybe not. But I didn't help either, did I? I mean, we were living together, and I didn't even realize he was that into me. Or that he was depressed. I kinda know some of the symptoms of depression 'cause Qay's talked to me about it before."

"Who?"

"Jeremy's husband. He's a really cool dude, but he has struggled. I think no two people experience depression the same way, but I sure wouldn't have guessed it about Logan."

Wes was quiet for a bit. "But he was having money problems, right? Maybe the stress got to him."

"Especially after I got him fired."

"Parker—"

"I know, I know."

More silence. But then the weirdest thing happened: Parker became suddenly aware of how close Wes was. And that he was probably wearing only underwear. He was handsome, and he'd been patient and generous with Parker even though Parker hadn't earned it. He'd gone out on the road in the rain to rescue him. He'd so carefully dealt with Parker's hands—even though he had nobody to tend to him when he was hurt.

He was right *there*.

And tomorrow Parker would be gone.

Parker rolled toward Wes. Rolled *onto* Wes, actually. Cradled his head between sore palms and leaned in to press their lips together.

For a second or two, Wes remained utterly still. But then he wrapped his arms around Parker and kissed him back with such fervor that their teeth clacked together. Which probably hurt, but Parker didn't care about that any more than he cared about the sting of his hands. What was important was the contact between his skin and Wes's, the way Wes opened his mouth to Parker's tongue and how Wes held his waist with his strong fingers.

Parker liked kissing. It was a hobby he'd engaged in often over the years. Sometimes he liked it almost as much as sex because it felt equally personal without being so... fussy. No messy lube or fumbling over a condom. No awkward getting dressed afterward. No positions where someone ended up with a cramp.

So yeah, kissing in general was good. But *this* one.... Maybe it had something to do with how Parker had lately been on an emotional trampoline, leaving his body oversaturated with hormones and neurotransmitters. Maybe it was just that Wes's nearly naked body felt so good against Parker's clothed one. In any case, this kiss sent him straight into overdrive. Every one of his senses became superhero acute while the cognitive centers of his brain blue-screened into nothingness. He dimly realized that he was moaning and undulating his hips and that Wes strained his own hips upward to meet him, but all of that was less important than the taste of chocolate and the scents of rain and wood shavings.

He almost cried when Wes gently but firmly pushed him away.

"Got enough regrets already." Wes's voice came ragged. "Don't need another."

Hurt cooled Parker's ardor as thoroughly as cold rainwater. "I thought you wanted—"

"I do. Badly. But what about you? This whole situation you're in…. Let yourself breathe a little first, okay?"

The hurt faded, only to be replaced by sorrow. Parker wanted Wes desperately right then, but he didn't know whether that was honest attraction or just a sinking ship heading for the nearest port. Wes didn't deserve to be used. And Parker, well, he could discern his own motives even less well than usual.

He reached over and gave Wes's shoulder a quick squeeze, then turned away. Parker didn't know whether this was an admirably good decision or a phenomenally bad one, but it was his choice for tonight.

Chapter Eight

"I can drive you to Portland." It was the third or fourth time Wes had offered, and as they sat in the van outside the Greyhound station in Medford, Parker shook his head again.

"I've been too much trouble already."

Wes twitched a shoulder. Aside from the mad dash to nowhere in the dark and rain, Parker hadn't been any trouble at all. The opposite, in fact. Wes had enjoyed the companionship. But if he argued the point too strongly, it might lead to Parker being in bed with him again, and this time Wes wouldn't have the strength to push him away.

"If you're sure," he said. He thought about trying to give Parker some money, but his attempts had so far been unsuccessful. Parker claimed he had adequate cash for his fare to Portland, which was enough for now.

They ended up in Medford after learning that Grants Pass didn't have an actual station, just a stop in the middle of an industrial park. Even though this station was small, at least Parker could buy a ticket. There were benches inside, or outside under an awning so he could stay out of the rain while he waited. Now he sat in Morrison's passenger seat and stared at the plastic grocery bag in his lap, containing the clothes he'd worn the day he ran away with Wes. Today he wore the sweats Wes had given him the previous night. Parker said he'd mail them when he was back in Portland, but Wes didn't care about that.

Parker made no move to get out of the van, and Wes didn't urge him to go.

An elderly woman in a puffy down parka exited the station, looked around for a moment, and shuffled to the nearest bench. She had an enormous purse slung over her shoulder and carried two bulging cloth shopping bags from Trader Joe's. A green knitted hat with an absurdly oversize pompom perched on her head. Maybe she'd end up sitting near Parker for the ride north. If so, Wes hoped she was good company.

With a noisy sigh, Parker turned to face him. "Thank you. For putting up with me."

"It was fine." More than fine.

"Next time you're in Portland, come by P-Town. I don't know how long I'll be there, but…."

Wes nodded, although he had no intention of stepping foot in P-Town again. He'd faced Jeremy and Nevin once, he'd had his say, and that was enough. Besides, Parker would find new prospects soon enough and move on. He was a bright kid, willing to work hard, and he picked up new things quickly. He'd land a new job somewhere. A new boyfriend.

"I left my number in your bus," Parker said. "On that notepad near the bed? You could call sometime."

Another lie of a head nod.

Silence followed. And then Wes blurted out the truth that had been eating him like acid for a decade. "I killed a woman."

Parker blinked at him. "What?"

"That's why…. Nevin and Jeremy. That's why they hate me. They *should* hate me."

"You don't come across as a cold-blooded murderer." Parker said it lightly, as if the confession were a joke, but his eyes looked troubled.

"I'm not. I…. Shit. Never mind."

"No. If you want to say this, I want to listen."

Where had Parker learned to give such gentle words of support? Nothing demanding or judgmental; just a promise of a willing ear. Wes couldn't resist such a rare gift. "I was hardly more than a rookie, and I'd already given up on impressing my dad, but I guess I was still trying to impress *someone*. Anyone. Trying to be a big shot and a hero."

He'd never told this story to anyone, at least not like this. Although he'd had plenty of discussions about it with his captain and the detectives in Homicide, with Internal Affairs, with a bunch of lawyers, this was different. Parker was just watching him, not interrogating him.

"I was on patrol in my car, not all that far from P-Town, actually. The Brooklyn neighborhood. And it was a really quiet Tuesday morning." He remembered the details with exquisite clarity, like a movie he'd watched a thousand times. Weak sunlight filtered through wispy clouds and evaporated the moisture on the pavement, an early spring chill hung in the air, and there were very few people in sight because most were at work or school. The trees were just beginning to leaf out; daffodils bloomed in front yards. He drove slowly up and down the streets of the modest neighborhood, bored out of his mind. He was considering how soon he could stop for lunch, and where.

"This guy came running out from the front porch of a triplex, waving his arms at me and shouting. I knew the guy—Ralph Denton—because he had some mental health issues. Nothing dangerous, but once in a while he'd go off his meds and play his music loud enough to piss off the neighbors. He'd turn it down when we asked. Anyway, that morning he was obviously upset. When I stopped the cruiser and rolled down the window, he told me that the man in the unit next door had been screaming and the lady who lived there was crying."

It hadn't been a particularly coherent account. Mr. Denton was upset and tripping over his words, and he offered several wild and contradictory theories about what was going on. Drug dealers. The FBI. Terrorists.

"What I should have done was call it in. I knew that. Standard procedure. But instead I just parked and got out of the car."

"Why?" Parker sounded genuinely curious, not accusatory.

"Because I was a fucking idiot. I figured Denton was hallucinating the entire thing. Or maybe he'd had an argument with the neighbors over his music and wasn't being rational about them anymore. I figured I'd knock on the door, check things out just enough to mollify Denton, and then head off to lunch. Quick and easy."

He couldn't go on with the story.

Parker set a hand on his knee and whispered, "It wasn't, though." A simple statement, not a question.

"I didn't hear anything when I approached the door. Maybe there was nothing to hear, or maybe I wasn't paying enough attention. I don't know. I knocked. Cop knock, you know? When nobody answered, I did it again. I did the cop voice too: 'Portland Police Bureau.' Nothing."

He'd been annoyed with Mr. Denton—hovering nervously nearby—for making him get out of the cruiser, for making him waste his time. This wasn't what he wanted to be doing with his day, dealing with Mr. Denton and the possibly nonexistent neighbors, driving around in a squad car and waiting for somebody to run a red light, wearing a uniform and a badge and a gun and hoping someone might notice he existed.

"I was going to give up. But then I heard a sound. A woman's voice from inside the apartment. I couldn't make out what she said, but it was... distressed. And again, instead of calling it in, getting help from more experienced officers, doing anything a decent cop would have done, I knocked again. 'Police. Open up!'"

Had he been panicking? Afterward he was never sure. The flawless memory of that day became muddled from the point he heard the woman cry out. Lindy Shaw; that was her name. Wes would never forget *that*. But everything else immediately after became jumbled in his mind. Perhaps he was clearheaded at the time and it was only the shock afterward that obliterated the details. He'd never know.

"She screamed. It was a terrible scream—really loud. Then came the gunshots. Four of them." That's what the detectives concluded later. Three bullets in Ms. Shaw and one in her husband. At the time, though, Wes wasn't able to count them.

"Oh no," Parker moaned. His palm still lay on Wes's knee, warm and comforting. "Someone shot her?"

"Her husband. Then he shot himself. I finally called for backup, but it was too late for her. Too late."

"You didn't kill her, Wes. He did."

"If I had handled the situation properly, there's a very good chance she'd be alive today. She had two children, Parker. They'd possibly still have parents." The only good thing was that the kids had been in school that morning, so they hadn't been physically endangered. Emotionally, though… the damage must have been unimaginable.

"You don't know that. The entire bureau could've showed up and things could've turned out the same."

Wes shook his head. "Don't take my side on this, Parker. I don't deserve it. Facts: I was careless and arrogant, I failed to follow procedures or give appropriate credence to the witness's story, and a person died. Two people. Maybe the son of a bitch who pulled the trigger could have been salvageable as a human being, given the proper intervention."

Frowning, Parker gnawed a fingernail. "So… you screwed up. But there was nothing evil about it—just a dumb mistake. I make those all the time. God, look what happened to Logan because of me."

"Not because of you. Because of *him*. And everyone screws up now and then. That's human. But people who choose to enter certain professions have to be held to a higher standard because the consequences of errors are so awful. Surgeons. Soldiers. Police officers. None of them are allowed the luxury of making dumb mistakes."

When Parker looked as if he might argue, Wes held up a hand to stop him. "I mess things up now and then as a carpenter. I've wasted nice pieces of wood by cutting them wrong. I've spilled paint and drilled in the wrong spot. A couple years ago I miscalculated measurements on a fancy bar cabinet and had to tear the whole thing up and start from scratch. Lost a couple days of work. But nobody died."

Parker regarded him gravely. "That's a lot of guilt to be carrying."

"I've earned it."

"What… what happened to you afterward?"

"I resigned. They would have fired me anyway. I was lucky I hadn't fucked up badly enough to face criminal charges. I didn't have many friends, not even then, but the ones I did have were cops, and they all turned away from me."

Parker nodded. "Like Jeremy and Nevin."

"I'd have done the same in their shoes. Anyway, after all the legal things were settled, I moved down here. My dad sent a letter telling me what an embarrassment I was—first time I'd heard from him in I don't know how long. Grandpa let me stay with him, though. Let me work with him in his workshop." The old man had never said a word about what had transpired in Portland, but he wasn't the chatty type anyway. Most of his conversation consisted of curt advice on how to build furniture.

"Why did you tell me this now, Wes?"

"Because you need to know the truth of who I am."

"The truth of you is bigger than that one day." Parker said it with conviction. But he was young, and he didn't know Wes well. His rosy outlook could be forgiven.

Parker looked out the passenger window, maybe watching the lady on the bench, who was eating something out of a paper bag on her lap. Then he faced Wes again. "Will you tell me one more thing?"

Wes shrugged. Why not? He was open and bleeding anyway.

"Why did you go to P-Town the other day?"

Oh. That. Was there a way to explain this that didn't sound ridiculous? Nope.

"I was watching TV a few weeks ago. I hardly ever do, but… I don't know. I was just surfing from one channel to another without really focusing on anything."

Parker nodded. "I do that sometimes, with YouTube videos and stuff on Netflix. A couple minutes here, a couple minutes there. I kind of space out over it."

"Right. So I happened on a religious show. I don't do religion, never have, but the preacher man had on such weird clothing, I thought it was a parody of some kind. Red-and-blue plaid suit and an oversized bolo tie." He chuckled. "Turned out he was for real. I only watched him for a few minutes, I guess, but something he said caught my attention: everyone should try to die without regrets. He said that makes salvation easier. Salvation doesn't matter to me, but the no-regrets part stuck. I lost sleep over it. And I realized I was really sorry I'd never apologized to Jeremy and Nevin for letting them down. They'd been really nice to me when I was new in the bureau."

He'd been right. His explanation sounded even more laughable than he'd feared. And his jaw hurt. He'd yammered more this morning than he had in years, as if a word spigot had opened in his brain. It was time to close it now, though.

"Are you glad you did it? Apologized, I mean?"

As Wes considered the question, a tiny grin flickered at the corners of his mouth. "Yeah. I met you."

"I'm really glad of that." Parker squeezed Wes's knee.

The bus lumbered up the street and parked in front of the station, dwarfing the little building and obscuring their view of the woman on the bench.

Parker leaned over and planted a quick kiss on Wes's cheek. This was nothing like the previous night's heated exchange; it was entirely chaste. But it still made Wes's heart race and his skin flush.

"Good luck, Parker. You deserve it."

Clutching his plastic bag, Parker got out and turned to flash a brief smile. "You too."

WITH PARKER gone, Morrison felt empty. Which was bad enough, but Wes suspected that his bus would feel empty too. His entire property would likely have a forlorn air—ducks and all. So although he returned to the freeway after filling the gas tank, he didn't head north toward home. He went south instead, through Ashland, into the mountains, and over the border into California. On the other side of the range, he dropped through forest and into the Central Valley with its dry farmland, through Redding, all the way to Williams, where he had to stop to refill the tank and buy some bottled water. By then his body felt cramped from sitting too long. The sun shone, though, and that was nice.

Instead of turning north on I-5 to head home, he decided to go west. More farmland, then rolling hills scarred by fires. There was a big lake ringed by tiny communities, most of which appeared hardscrabble at best. Then steeper mountains, a devilishly twisty road beneath towering redwoods, and… the ocean. Somehow Wes had made it to the Pacific, where fog hung in the brine-scented air and seagulls perched on rooftops. His own home wasn't a very long drive from the coast, yet he couldn't recall the last time he'd driven that way. A shame. He liked the ocean.

He seriously considered parking Morrison somewhere near a beach and spending the night in the back. But running water and a hot meal held too much appeal, so he checked in to a budget motel a few blocks from the water in Fort Bragg. He grabbed the spare clothes and basic toiletries he always kept in the van.

The sun was setting when he arrived at the cliff overlooking Glass Beach. The fog hung too heavily to allow the sunset its visual spectacle, and Wes shivered in his old denim jacket. But he remained standing there anyway because he liked listening to the waves crash and tasting sea salt on his lips. He speculated on what secrets lay hidden beneath the water's surface and what adventures might lie over the horizon. Maybe such close exposure to things aquatic would give him inspiration as he completed the sea-monster coffee table. And maybe in the morning he'd find some shells or interesting little stones he could work into the table somehow. Very quietly he sang "Sloop John B." Twice.

It was long after dark when he headed inland. He strolled around the small downtown before settling on Thai. Lemongrass-and-coconut-scented soup warmed him up, pad see ew filled his belly, and a couple of bottles of locally brewed stout mellowed him out.

He didn't think about Parker—not more than every two minutes, anyway. And he tried to rein in those thoughts. Their time together had been a momentary blip. A fascinating little detour in his otherwise quiet, predictable life. He hoped he'd done a good deed by giving Parker respite and a peaceful haven when he needed them. Now Parker could put his own life back together, and Wes would return to making pretty furniture and enjoying his serene existence. An existence in which he had nobody to hurt or disappoint. And one where he was free of regrets, now that he'd apologized as best as he was able.

Except he realized, as he nursed his third beer, that he'd acquired a new regret: the kiss. Not the one at the bus station, but the one last night. The one where Parker was draped—warm and solid and oh so sweet—over Wes's nearly naked body. Where they thrust against each other despite the layers of clothing, and where Wes almost came. That kiss.

He didn't regret the kiss itself. It hadn't been his idea to begin with, and it had been far too wonderful to be sorry about. Besides, he had the impression that the kiss had helped settle Parker's mood—or at least had directed that mood in a more positive direction.

But he'd pushed Parker away, and *that* he regretted.

It was the right thing to do.

Yeah, it was, from an ethical point of view. Even from a practical one since it had been clear that their short time together was nearly over. But from an emotional perspective, pushing Parker away was wrong, wrong, wrong. Now Wes would spend the rest of his life thinking about that night and wondering what it would have been like if he'd allowed matters to proceed. As wonderful as he imagined, based on the evidence of the kiss? Who the hell knew.

"Dammit!"

The waitress took a hasty step back. "Sorry! I didn't—"

"No, no. I'm sorry. I was stuck in my own head. Was swearing at myself, not you."

She relaxed, flashing a broad smile. "Oh, I get you. I talk to myself all the time. Sometimes I get in arguments with myself."

"Probably not in public, though."

She just laughed. "Can I get you another bottle?"

"If I have another I might start doing worse than thinking out loud. I think I'll just take the bill, please."

He slowly strolled back to the motel, arms wrapped around himself as if to keep in the warmth. Nobody else was out except for a homeless man watching him from the doorway of a vacant business. Wes walked a half block past the guy, stopped, and turned back. "Here," he said, holding out a crisp hundred. "Maybe this will keep you warm and fed for a night or two."

The man had a thick beard and multiple layers of clothing, including a long yellow skirt and a pair of tattered ski pants. His shoes were mismatched—one a battered red-and-white Nike, the other a tan hiking boot. He stared at the bill. "That's a lotta money."

"I've had some good luck lately. Feeling a little flush. Don't mind sharing."

Looking doubtful, the man took the money. "You sure, buddy?"

"Yeah. Maybe if you get a chance someday, you can pay it forward."

"Yeah, okay. Thanks. Have a good night."

"You too."

Wes continued on his way. At least he wouldn't wake up in the middle of the night mentally kicking himself for ignoring someone who needed a hand.

Soon after returning to his motel room, Wes took a shower. A nice long one, using way too much hot water. It was a treat not to have to deal with the somewhat makeshift setup he had at home. Plus he stepped out into a steamy, warm little bathroom instead of the great outdoors—which was neither steamy nor warm at this time of year. Although he had the spare clothes in the van, he washed his underwear and socks in the sink and gave them a few passes with the blow dryer before draping them over a chair near the heating vent. Maybe they'd be dry by morning.

He crawled between the sheets—which smelled of bleach instead of Parker—switched off the light, and tried to clear his mind and fall asleep. It wasn't particularly late, but the drive, emotional upheaval, and three bottles of stout had tired him. Nonetheless, despite varied sleeping positions and rearrangements of pillows and blankets, he remained awake. He considered jerking off for the lulling effect of postorgasmic hormones, but he wasn't in the mood. Besides, he'd inevitably end up thinking about Parker, and that felt wrong.

"Argh!" He threw himself out of bed and, wrapped in a makeshift blanket toga, shuffled to the window. He couldn't see the ocean, just the parking lot with its scattered yellowish lights, but staring at that was better than glaring at the dark ceiling. Or turning on the light and confronting the poorly rendered lighthouse painting that hung opposite the bed.

No waitresses nearby to overhear and freak out, so he asked out loud, "How did I get here?" And by *here*, he didn't mean Fort Bragg, because he could have recited that route completely. This was an existential *here*, as in pretty much alone in the world, living in a school bus, surviving more or less hand-to-mouth. Pining over a kid he hardly knew.

"I should get out more often. Meet more people." Next time he made a furniture delivery to Miri, he'd go to a bar or a club. Spend a night or two in town. At the very least he'd use an app and find someone to hook up with. Right. As if that would magically improve his life. "Big deal, Wanker. Big fucking deal."

As a kid he pictured a very different future. He was bounced around like a pinball between his parents and his grandfather, so he imagined that when he grew up, he'd fall in love and marry a girl, have kids, and stay put in a nice little town or suburb, going to Little League games and taxiing children to orthodontist appointments. He'd have a date night with his wife every couple of weeks, putter around the house on weekends, teach woodworking to his sons and daughters in a garage workshop, and go on vacations to Disneyland.

By his late teens he realized girls didn't get his wheels turning. Ethan Hawke made far too many starring appearances in Wes's crankshanking fantasies for him to believe otherwise. But he'd stubbornly refused to admit that his future self should change to reflect that reality. No, somehow, magically, Future Wes was straight as an arrow and living in a four/two ranch with a wife who taught high-school science classes and dragged him to line-dancing lessons every Thursday evening.

In community college Wes fucked around with a couple of guys but wasn't out to his small circle of friends. He remained closeted when he joined the bureau—and felt awful about it every time Jeremy casually mentioned a boyfriend or Nevin boasted about some stud he'd screwed the night before.

Wes never officially came out of the closet, in fact. After the leaving the bureau, he had nobody to come out to—except his grandfather, who never asked about Wes's perpetual lack of girlfriends. And Wes never told.

That childhood version of Future Wes deserved to be scrapped long ago. And since Wes was comfortable with his orientation, shouldn't he have replaced that guy with a different Future Wes? One who loved and was loved by a remarkable man, one who created his own family in his own way?

Wes stared through the window at the parking lot until his eyelids drooped, and then he dragged himself to bed.

HE WOKE up with an idea.

This wasn't uncommon for him. At least once a month, he opened his eyes in the morning to a fantastic plan for that gorgeous slab of olive wood with the cracked heartwood or that vintage cast-iron latch he'd picked up at an antique store. He liked to believe a cabinetry muse occasionally visited him in the night, gifting him with enough clever notions to pay the bills.

But this morning's idea had nothing to do with furniture.

Wes woke up with the deep conviction there was something off about Logan's suicide. He tried to push the idea away since it was really none of his business, and besides, what could he possibly know about the fate of Parker's deceased ex-boyfriend?

Still, the idea niggled at him while he brushed his teeth and hair; put on his dry underwear, slightly damp socks, and other clothing; and gathered his few things before checking out of the motel. With no better options around, he grabbed a quick coffee and breakfast at McDonald's and filled Morrison's tank, then headed north on Highway 101. It was a gorgeous drive, especially the parts that hugged the coastline, but he couldn't concentrate on the scenery or on the music Morrison blasted obligingly.

After leaving Crescent City, where he stopped to gas up, Wes toyed with the problem some more. Thinking out loud seemed to help a little. "The thing with Logan just doesn't add up. First off, why would Logan kill himself? Parker said he hadn't shown signs of depression, and their relationship didn't sound like it was the love affair of the century. Logan was stealing from Parker—is that how you treat the guy you can't live without?"

Morrison chugged along as if in agreement.

"Maybe the breakup isn't why Logan committed suicide. He'd lost his job and his roommate and was obviously having some kind of money issues. But even assuming that was enough to make him want to end it all, why would he address his suicide note to Parker, who'd already moved out? If he really wanted to say something final, wouldn't it have made more sense for him to text instead?"

He took the turnoff for Highway 199, a snakelike route through the mountains of Klamath National Forest. Pines, firs, and cedars seemed to stretch infinitely in every direction, and Wes rolled down the window a little because he liked the way the air smelled. Unfortunately the resulting chill didn't chase away his new obsession with Logan.

"Why would he commit suicide by OD'ing? Assuming Parker was right, Logan didn't use hard drugs, so he wouldn't have had them just lying around. And there are cheaper and easier ways to kill yourself than tracking down a dealer and scoring enough shit to kill you." Wes had taken a couple of psych classes at the community college before training as a cop. Unless patterns had changed drastically in the past few years, which he doubted, men usually shot themselves, hung themselves, jumped off something high, or did something fatal with a car. They were much less likely than women to use poisons or drugs. Which didn't mean a man *couldn't* OD on purpose. But if you put that together with the other odd things about Logan's death, something just felt… off.

Wes made a decision as he crossed into Oregon. He needed to find out what Logan's suicide note had said.

Chapter Nine

Even as Parker collected the assortment of cups and plates from the vacated table, he could feel Rhoda watching him from behind the counter. He twisted his head to shoot her a quick glare, and she didn't even pretend she hadn't been staring. God. It was as if she feared he'd explode if she didn't keep an eagle eye on him.

He carried the dirty dishes back to the kitchen and left them with others near the sink. No two pieces matched, because Rhoda haunted thrift stores and yard sales in search of cheap and interesting china. A few of the most frequent customers had picked out their favorites, which were kept aside especially for them.

Rhoda was waiting for him when he emerged from the kitchen. "Do you want a break, honey?"

"I've been here less than two hours."

"So? It's slow."

He sighed. "Then I'll sweep. And wash the windows." The truth was, he preferred to keep busy. That was always true for him, and especially when he faced emotional turmoil. Scrubbing glass was way better than wallowing—or spinning eternally in his angst vortex. When he'd returned from Wes's place, Rhoda had insisted he take the afternoon off and then made him stay home the next day too. He spent the day cleaning her entire house, which was why she'd relented and brought him in today.

Most grown men did not need to resort to housecleaning as a form of protest.

Now it was late afternoon, and Parker had cleaned the floors and windows and caught up on the dishwashing. P-Town had grown crowded. Lots of students arrived at this time of day, and people who normally worked from home tended to emerge into public, laptops under their arms, for coffee and snacks. The group of older women who did some kind of cat rescue thing met at P-Town most days; each of them had a dedicated feline-themed teacup. Fiona, who lived in an old station wagon, came in to wash up in the bathroom and sip coffee while she read magazines. Parker knew business would stay brisk until closing, slowing down only a little at dinnertime and then picking up again later. Today was Tuesday, which meant live music at seven thirty, and by then every seat would be taken.

Good. The harder he worked, the less he had to think about anything else.

"I like your hair color," said one of the cat ladies when he brought her a refill. "Orange is good for this time of year."

"I thought so too."

"My granddaughter dared me to do something wild with my hair. What do you think?" She patted her steel-gray bob.

"I think you'd look amazing with a crimson streak. Or maybe one of those undercolor things where only your natural color shows until you lift the back of your hair, and then there's a rainbow or something."

Her companions cooed their approval of this idea, and her eyes sparkled. "I'm going to try that! Won't Hailey be surprised!"

"Great! Can't wait to see how it turns out."

He was heading over to bus an empty table when trouble walked in the front door: Jeremy and Nevin. Jeremy looked as buff as ever in his green uniform, as if he'd just stepped out of the newest Marvel movie, while Nevin was resplendent in a custom-made black suit and cerise shirt. Pretending not to notice Parker, they headed to the cash register.

Jeremy lived only a couple of blocks away and visited almost every day, usually in the morning before work, and Nevin rarely stopped by when he was on duty. So the fact that they were both there now, arriving together and sporting work attire, meant this wasn't a casual outing.

As soon as they were seated, Parker marched over and balled his hands on his hips. "I don't need another intervention. Or counseling session or whatever."

Nevin lifted his espresso cup. "We're just drinking our fucking coffee."

"No, you're not. Mom put you up to something."

He should have known. She'd very carefully refrained from asking a single question about Wes or Logan since Parker's return. She must have figured she needed to bring in professionals to give him the third degree.

"She's just worried about you." Jeremy held a hand-thrown mug painted with stylized evergreen trees. Although it was almost comically oversized, it fit his giant paws perfectly.

"I'm fine. I'm functioning perfectly well and not collapsing into a hysterical heap at all. I'm brushing my hair and teeth. Putting on clean clothes. Dotting my i's and crossing my t's. All is well. I don't need babysitting."

Yeah, that little speech had about as much effect as he expected. Jeremy gazed at him blandly, probably the same way he gazed at crank addicts who were climbing park statuary in an effort to escape hordes of invisible bugs. Nevin just made a rude noise. "Be thankful you have a mother who gives a shit about you, Smurf."

"I *am* thankful."

"Uh-huh. That's why you ran off with Wanker, who you don't even fucking know."

"I know him now. And he's a really good guy."

"Pfft. Really good at wanting to get into your pants."

"Wes didn't touch me." Parker chose not to share that he'd thrown himself at Wes on their final night. "He fed me and housed me and drove me to the bus station when I left. And he was nice to me the entire time, even though I was a major imposition."

Nevin rolled his eyes but held his tongue, which was unusual for him. Maybe he wasn't as anti-Wes as he had been before the apology.

Jeremy set down his coffee. "Did he tell you why he was here the other day?"

"To tell you guys he was sorry."

"Did he explain why?"

Parker's stomach clenched when he remembered the raw pain in Wes's eyes as he told his story. He couldn't imagine carrying that kind of guilt for so long. "Yeah. He said he screwed up really badly and someone died because of it. He said he killed her."

To Parker's considerable surprise, Nevin shook his head. "Probably not. That whole situation could very well have gone balls-up even if Wanker went by the book. Domestic disputes like that are unpredictable. They can get fucking ugly, fast."

"Then why do you hate him so much?"

"Don't hate him. But he was a stubborn son of a bitch who never should have joined the bureau—he didn't have the temperament for it—

and shouldn't have acted like a fucking moron. And he should have been fucking honest with people about his own shit."

As Nevin crossed his arms and Jeremy worked his jaw, a revelation hit Parker. They were *disappointed* in Wes. And not just because of what happened to Lindy Shaw. "Did you know Wes was gay?" he asked quietly.

"Not until he left the bureau," Jeremy answered.

Nevin made another of his noises. "We fucking suspected, though. He was, what, twenty-two, twenty-three? But he never even talked about girls, and if you tried to steer the conversation anywhere near there, he just fucking shut down."

Knowing Nevin, the conversation was steered there often and forcefully. Before settling down with Colin, Nevin cut a pretty wide swath through the city's dating pool, male and female. Nowadays he was happily monogamous, but that didn't mean he stopped asking blunt questions about everyone else's sex life.

Parker raised his eyebrows. "Doesn't a person have a right to keep his private life private?"

Jeremy cut in before Nevin could answer. "Of course. And a lot of folks in law enforcement don't necessarily feel comfortable being out. Even more so a decade ago. But he never told *us*, and we were his friends. We would have understood. And we could tell something was eating at him."

"He overcompensated by acting like a macho shithead on the job," added Nevin. "Which is why he fucked up that day."

That made a lot of sense. Back in high school, a jock named Pat Ballard swaggered through the hallways leering at the girls. Whenever he saw Parker, Pat would call him a faggot and laugh as if it were the funniest joke ever. Parker hadn't been particularly surprised when, four years after graduation, he walked into the bathroom of a club and found Pat Ballard on his knees, blowing some dude in faux biker gear. Although Parker couldn't imagine Wes swaggering and calling people names—unlike Ballard, he wasn't an asshole—he certainly might have been an insecure young man who tried to cover up his inclinations with a show of manliness.

Parker set his hands on the table. "That was a long time ago. C'mon. You guys did stupid stuff too, once upon a time. Even you, Jeremy. I do it all the time. It sucks that Wes's mistake had such serious consequences.

But he's…. I like him, okay? He was kind to me. And I think he's been really lonely for a long time." Maybe forever. Parker's eyes stung just thinking about it.

For possibly the first time in his entire life, Nevin appeared abashed. He ducked his head and muttered something under his breath, likely a swear word. Jeremy ran fingers through his buzz cut. And then, mercifully, something in the kitchen broke with a noisy crash.

"I better help clean that up," said Parker.

Jeremy smiled at him. "You were right—you don't need babysitting. But we're still here if you want someone to talk to."

That was comforting to know, although Parker's contentment was tinged with sadness at knowing Wes didn't have anyone. Maybe Parker could do something about that—once he got his own life on track.

PARKER HAD planned to stick around for the music that night but found himself yawning repeatedly. He hunted Rhoda down and found her sitting in her closet-like office, clicking away at the computer. "Do you need me here tonight, Mom, or are you covered?"

She glanced at him. "We're fine. Are you going out?"

"Nope. I'm going to change my hair color. Then a Netflix binge and early bedtime for me."

You'd think a mother would be happy to hear *early bedtime*; she'd spent most of his teen years reminding him to get enough sleep. But she frowned and opened her mouth, probably to ask whether the change in hair color was symbolic of something. He held up a hand to stop her. "I'm *fine*. Just need a change. And the early night is because I told RJ I'd take his early shift tomorrow. He has a dentist appointment."

"Okay." She still looked concerned, but she turned her attention back to the screen.

Parker took a Lyft, which wasn't the best use of his money but was the fastest way to get home. When he arrived, he ate a sandwich and potato chips, changed into his schlumpiest loungewear, and got to work on his hair. He dripped some bleach on his T-shirt and the cobalt blue stained his fingers, but he otherwise deemed the change a success. Climbing into bed with his laptop, he had every intention of spacing out in front of *The Great British Baking Show*, even though he knew it would give him the munchies.

But somehow he ended up googling Wes Anker instead.

He found basically nothing aside from the Black Lightning Interiors website, which included some gallery photos of Wes's furniture. Gorgeous stuff, every piece creative and unique. Expensive too, but worth it, given the amount of time and care Wes put into each. They were essentially works of art. According to the website, they had all sold.

A notion crept into Parker's head, a thought that made his heart race. He reached for his phone and brought up the contacts. There it was: Wes Anker. Parker had found the number on a business card in Wes's bus and added it to his list, although at the time he promised himself never to call. But this was different. He wasn't going to *stalk* Wes. This was business!

Taking a deep breath, Parker tapped the number.

Wes's phone rang several times. Just as Parker decided this was dumb and he ought to hang up, Wes's breathless voice came over the line. "Hello?"

"Uh, hi. This is Parker Levin." He winced. God. It's not as if Wes was likely to receive calls from *other* Parkers.

"Hey. Did you leave something at my place?"

It was really hard to judge Wes's emotions over the phone. He wasn't the most demonstrative person in the first place, and without the cues of facial expression and body posture, his true meaning was unclear. Was he annoyed that Parker had interrupted him?

"No, I didn't leave anything. Are you in the middle of something? I can call back."

Wes chuckled. "I was visiting the ducks and left my phone near the sink. Had to run to catch it. I can talk now."

Okay, but did he want to talk? And if so, about what? Parker blundered on. "I was just kinda wondering…. Hanukkah is in a couple of weeks, and Mom is impossible to shop for. Every time I ask her what she wants, she just says, 'For my son to be happy,' and that's totally not helpful. I don't have tons of money, but I was thinking… maybe you could make her something small? Like that dish rack with the flowers on it. I could afford something like that, and I know she'd love it. Um, if you have time. I know this is short notice."

He mentally kicked himself during the long pause that followed. This was truly a dumb idea. All his ideas were dumb. He ought to know that by now.

But when Wes finally spoke, he sounded happy—or at least Parker thought so. "I'd love to do that."

"Really?"

"Really. Just give me a few days, okay?"

"Of course. I can always take the bus down to pick it up, if you don't mind meeting me in Medford."

Another pause, but shorter this time. "I'll bring it up."

There went Parker's heart, beating a mile a minute. He tried to sound calm. "Thanks. You're saving me again."

"Almost becoming a habit." And then Wes said good night and hung up.

PARKER LIKED Sunday mornings at P-Town. The shop opened a little later than the rest of the week, and customers trickled in slowly, many of them clutching books or the Sunday paper. They dressed casually, moved more languorously, and laughed more often. They even left bigger tips in the jar near the cash register.

Uncharacteristically, Rhoda had elected to sleep in and allow Parker to open up. That meant he got to pick the music, and he opted for 1950s pop-swing. Some Sinatra, Nat King Cole, and Dean Martin. A little Ella Fitzgerald, because Ella was always good. Judging from the customers, he'd chosen well; a lot of toes and fingers were tapping. At a big round table in a corner, several students were ignoring their laptops and piles of paper and lip-syncing instead.

Grinning, Parker laid a pumpkin spice Rice Krispies treat on a plate and set it on the counter. "Here you go. Certified holiday cheer."

The customer, a handsome sixtyish man with a little paunch and gray beard stubble, smiled back. "I have to get in the last of it before we switch to peppermint season. I'm not a big mint fan."

"Peppermint's supposed to be good for digestion." Parker had learned that from Ptolemy, who was a proponent of herbal teas.

"Maybe, but aren't the effects negated if the peppermint's drowned in sugar and fat?"

"Probably."

The guy watched as Parker prepared his caffè macchiato. Parker always used a clear glass demitasse for this drink because the layers of coffee and steamed milk looked pretty.

After Parker put the glass on the counter, the guy hesitated. His face red, he finally ventured, "Um, can I ask something?"

"Sure."

"That lady who works here.... I think she's the owner? The one who wears the bright clothes."

Parker fought to keep his expression neutral. He had a sense where this might be going, and if he was right, he'd be very pleased. "Rhoda. Yeah, she's the owner."

"I just stumbled in here by accident a couple of days ago. It's a great place."

"I agree."

The guy scratched an ear. "And she—Rhoda—she seems really nice. She has a lot of good energy."

"Rhoda's great. Best boss I ever had." No need to disclose right now that she was his mother. That would take all the fun out of it.

"Do you happen to know whether, um, she's single?"

"I do. She is." Parker leaned closer and dropped his voice a little. "Want me to put in a good word for you, maybe?"

Now the guy's eyes twinkled. "I'd be obliged. My name's Bob Martinez. I just moved here from Cleveland two weeks ago. Wanted to escape the Midwest for my retirement years. And I'm single too. Been divorced for nine years."

Although Rhoda sometimes admitted she was lonely, she also claimed her busy work schedule kept her from meeting potential dates. Bob, a good-looking man with an easy smile, could possibly be a solution to that problem. Of course, he *could* be an axe murderer. But Rhoda was an excellent judge of character, and Parker trusted she'd figure out on her own whether Bob was interesting and trustworthy.

"Rhoda will be here in about half an hour. Stick around, and I'll try to steer her your way."

"Thank you, kind sir." Bob winked, took his snack and coffee, and headed for a vacant table.

The adventure of matchmaking put Parker in an excellent mood, especially since his mother had often tried the same for him. A cute guy Parker's age would show up at P-Town, Rhoda's gaydar would go off, and she'd practically throw Parker into the poor boy's lap. None of those attempts had been successful, mostly because Parker stubbornly resisted. Good God, Parker could manage to find his own love interests! Even if they weren't always appropriate or long-lasting. Bob's interest in Rhoda would allow Parker to turn the tables for once.

He hummed along with "Mack the Knife" while he rearranged the contents of the pastry case. It was his third-favorite serial-killer ditty, losing out to "The Ballad of Sweeney Todd" and "Psycho Killer." But it was a close contest.

"Hi."

Parker lifted his head so quickly he almost bashed it into the edge of the glass case. Wes stood there in his denim jacket, hair pulled into a neat ponytail, mouth quirked in a hesitant smile. "Is this the Bobby Darin version?" Wes gestured in the general direction of one of the speakers.

"Yeah. I like the Fitzgerald/Ellington version better, but I already played a bunch of her songs and wanted more variety."

They stared at each other as the sound system recounted MacHeath fashioning cement overshoes for the unfortunate Louie Miller. Wes fidgeted.

"You changed your hair color."

"Yeah. Cobalt Midnight." He was at a loss for words, then suddenly blurted, "You're back in Portland." Parker almost winced. *Brilliant observation, and such witty conversation!*

But Wes gave one of his funny little shrugs that now looked so familiar. "Yeah. I, uh, made something for your mom. Want you to see if it's okay."

"I just asked you a few days ago."

"Doesn't take that long. No big thing." Wes scanned the shop, maybe making sure Jeremy and Nevin weren't lurking somewhere, ready to attack. "Do you have a few minutes soon? Morrison's just around the corner."

Parker's thoughts raced. Did this mean Wes was eager to see him again? Or did Wes feel sorry for him and perhaps want to get this obligation out of the way? Maybe Wes just had other errands in town and had stopped by. Maybe this had very little to do with Parker at all. The world didn't revolve around him, did it?

Hoping he came off as nonchalant, Parker nodded. "I'll take a break when Rhoda gets here. Thirty minutes. Coffee while you wait?"

"Sure." That might have been relief on Wes's face, but Parker wasn't certain.

Parker didn't have to ask what Wes wanted. He chose a large mug—one of his personal favorites, painted with bright whimsical birds—and filled it with freshly brewed organic Kona. He left a little room for sugar but none for milk. "Our pistachio macarons are pretty amazing. Can I get you one?"

"Okay."

Wes held out a ten-dollar bill, but Parker rolled his eyes and didn't take it. "Really?"

Another little shoulder twitch, and Wes tucked the money away. He stopped to add sugar to his coffee, then took his things to a little table in the far back, beneath a painting of a unicorn with a rainbow-hued mane. The same artist had done the one in Parker's bedroom, and the artist's boyfriend often played at the coffeehouse on music nights. Parker glanced at Wes often over the next half hour but didn't approach him—in theory because Parker was too busy, but mostly because he didn't want to say something stupid. Every time he looked at him, Wes was watching him back.

Rhoda swept into P-Town a few minutes early, resplendent in a galaxy-print dress, red cardigan, and shiny red boots. She took off her raincoat as soon as she was inside, but not before she caught sight of Wes. She continued to hold the coat and raised her eyebrows at Parker. He pretended not to notice.

Within less than five minutes, she'd hung up her coat, greeted the other employees and some regulars, and assessed the condition of her coffeehouse. Apparently satisfied that Parker had done a good job of steering the ship, she nudged him away from the cash register. "Cute hair. Go. Lunch."

Normally he might have resisted, due to the obvious way she was indicating Wes, but Parker really did want to see what was in the van. And spend a little time with Wes, even if just in a brief commercial transaction.

"Okay. Hey, see that guy near the window in the green shirt? His name's Bob, and he just moved here from Ohio. He's looking for some good tips on restaurants, shopping… that kind of stuff. You're better at that than me."

Her eyes lit up. If there was one thing Rhoda loved, it was giving advice. And this would be a good test of Bob's temperament and stamina. Could he withstand a full dose of Rhoda's guidance? With her happily occupied, Parker ducked into the kitchen and slipped his hoodie on. Wes was standing when Parker emerged, and they left together, neither of them saying anything until they were outside.

"I'm trying to get my mom a date. That's weird, isn't it?"

Wes snorted. "Yeah. But sweet."

Although it wasn't far to Wes's van, Parker felt chilled by the time they got there. Maybe he should follow Rhoda's advice and acquire appropriate winter outerwear. Ugh. All the affordable raincoats were so boring.

Instead of leading them to Morrison's cab, Wes unlocked the back of the van and gestured inside.

"This is like a scene in a spy movie," said Parker. "Or a kidnapping."

"I promise not to take you anywhere against your will or divulge state secrets to the Russians."

"Fair enough."

There wasn't much room in the back—Parker had to stoop—but at least it was dry. He watched as Wes unwrapped several layers of blankets from something bulky.

"Oh my God," Parker exclaimed when the object was revealed. It was a wooden frame about three feet wide and equally tall, holding three shelves. The wood itself was pale with a dark grain, and other species of wood formed insets shaped like cups and hearts and musical notes. The top and bottom of the frame were fronted with intricately carved pieces that incorporated some of the same shapes. The unit was dazzling without being busy or gaudy. "That's stunning."

"Will she like it?"

Parker blinked at him. "I can't— This is way out of my price range."

"Discount. Most of the wood was leftovers, and I wanted to practice with my new scroll saw."

"Wes—"

"Will your mom like it?"

"She'll love it. God, it's perfect."

"Good." Wes started rewrapping it. "Is there somewhere you want to put it so she won't know?"

"Uh…." He had the better part of an hour before he had to return to work. "Do you mind driving to our place? It's not far. I can hide it in my room."

"No problem."

They climbed into the front seats, and Wes pulled away from the curb. He didn't turn down the radio, which was blasting Lynyrd Skynyrd. Parker had to raise his voice to give directions. He sat on his hands the entire time to stop himself from reaching over and touching Wes. To register the reality of him. Ah, but he could still *smell* him, which only reminded Parker of how sterile his own bed had felt lately. Nice bedding, washed with Rhoda's favorite unscented, gentle-on-sensitive-skin detergent. No odors of sawdust and spices. And no Wes, of course.

Parker had to do yogic breathing to keep himself calm.

Wes backed the van into the driveway at Rhoda's house, Parker unlocked the front door, and Wes carried the blanket-swathed shelf inside, following Parker to his bedroom.

Since Parker didn't have much stuff, there was plenty of space in his walk-in closet. But after they tucked the shelf away, he and Wes stood awkwardly in the bedroom, Wes with the blankets folded under his arm. The situation reminded Parker of the times he'd snuck his high-school boyfriend, Marcus, into the house while his parents were still at work. Parker and Marcus would play video games and fool around, and Marcus would hurry away just in time to not get caught. Although Parker had always been careful to hide any evidence, he suspected Rhoda knew perfectly well what was going on. A suspicion confirmed the day he and Marcus discovered several foil-wrapped condoms oh-so-casually arranged atop Parker's dresser. His ears still burned at the memory.

"Can we talk for a few minutes?" Wes was fidgeting again, staring at the floor and playing with the hem of his jacket.

"Sure. Um...." Parker waved at the bed. Mercifully, the bedding looked rather tidy, and the general condition of the room wasn't bad. The rest of the house remained neat after his cleaning binge the previous week.

Wes sat on the edge of the mattress, and Parker perched next to him with several significant inches between them. As the silence stretched, Wes surveyed the room. And as Parker followed Wes's gaze, he realized very little of the room was *his*. It looked as if he was staying for a while in his mother's guest room, which was in fact the case. But it also meant this space didn't truly feel like his home.

"I live like a fifteen-year-old," Parker moaned.

"I live in a bus."

"Yeah, but it's *your* bus. I mean, it's a totally cool space anyway, but you've also made it your own. Anyone who knows you would instantly recognize it as your home."

Wes responded very quietly. "Nobody knows me."

"I do."

Although they'd met only a short time before and had spent only a few days together, Parker knew that was true. He had watched Wes work, had listened to him reveal hard truths about his history, had seen him face specters from his past and apologize in public. Had been patched up by him after falling in the dark and rain. Yeah, Parker knew him.

Wes picked up a small silver-toned elephant from the nightstand. He turned it over in his hands as if he were fascinated by it, even though it was clearly nothing but a mass-produced knickknack. Rhoda had purchased it as part of her redecorating efforts, and Parker sometimes used it to prop up his phone at night.

"Have you heard anything else from the Seattle police?"

Well, that was unexpected. "No. Why?"

"Do you mind talking about it a little?"

"It's okay."

Rhoda had been carefully dancing around the topic, occasionally coming close to mentioning it but not quite getting there. Parker hadn't taken the bait, mainly because there was nothing he wanted to say.

"I was thinking…. Look, you're a lot closer to this than me. I'm just an outsider. But does something about it feel off to you?"

"Off? You mean like Logan's dead? That's pretty fucking off."

"I know. I'm sorry. But I mean how he died. And why. And the note."

Parker took the elephant and made it hop majestically down his thigh to his knee, where it reared up in a silent trumpet. He'd never named the thing. Should he have? He'd been sleeping next to it off and on for several years. But it didn't even have eyes or a mouth, so maybe a name wasn't necessary. He handed it back to Wes.

"Yeah," Parker admitted. He'd thought it was weird from the beginning, actually, but his reasoning had been clouded by emotions. During the relative calm of the past several days, Logan's death kept popping into his head. Not just the sadness of it and Parker's lingering guilt, but also a general feeling of unease, as if he wasn't quite grasping something.

When he was little, those Magic Eye pictures were popular. His friend Hannah had a whole book full of them, but no matter how hard Parker stared, he could never see the 3-D images she insisted were there. Logan's death was like that. No matter how much Parker turned the suicide over in his head, the story never quite gelled. He just couldn't imagine Logan killing himself, especially over Parker.

He turned to look at Wes, who was regarding him closely. "It feels off."

"Do you want to do something about it? Or let it go?"

Weird. If Wes had insisted on poking at this topic, Parker would have pushed back and refused to discuss it anymore. But Wes hadn't insisted—he'd asked what Parker wanted—and Parker had the impression his preference would be respected. That made him reluctant to walk away.

"Do what?"

Wes's smile looked more grim than happy. "Something that requires some help."

Chapter Ten

Nevin Ng was a dangerous man, and not just because he carried a gun. As far as Wes knew, Nevin had never actually pulled a weapon on anyone, although Parker told him that Nevin's husband, a real estate developer, had shot and killed a serial killer. Nevin's real weapons were his sharp mind and even sharper tongue. Which is why Wes was more frightened of him than he was of Jeremy, even though Jeremy was a foot taller and a whole lot heavier.

Still, as Wes sat at a table in P-Town with Parker beside him and Nevin and Jeremy seated across from them, he addressed his request mostly to Nevin. That was because, of the two of them, Nevin was more likely than Jeremy to bully the Seattle detective into cooperating.

"Why do you give a flying fuck about any of this?" Nevin had his arms crossed and his brow lowered.

"Because it involves Parker."

"So?"

"We're friends."

Nevin gave a dismissive *pfft* and rolled his eyes. "Now that you've crawled out of the closet, you're gonna do favors for all the pretty queer boys?"

"Just Parker."

Interesting. When Wes responded to Nevin's barb without defensiveness, Nevin's posture loosened and his scowl faded. "Parker's not just any pretty queer boy. He's ours."

"Hey!" Parker protested. "I appreciate the support, but I'm a grown man, and I don't need any human attack dogs going after my friends."

"Too bad, Smurf. You're Rhoda's kid, and that means we'll be keeping douchebags away from you when you're a hundred and three."

Wes didn't say anything, mainly because he didn't want to treat Parker like the rope in a game of tug-of-war. Jeremy might have felt the same way; he remained quiet with his huge coffee cup in his hand and his long legs stretched out under the table.

The four of them sat silently.

Wes wondered whether other customers were watching, and if so, what they thought was going on. Four frowning men of various ages and manners of dress, each with a different coffee drink, all of them supervised from afar by Rhoda, who was theoretically running the till. Parker had asked her not to participate, and although she'd agreed, it didn't keep her from watching anxiously.

Parker began to fidget with his paper napkin, folding it, rolling the edges, and tearing it into tiny bits he'd have to clean up later. "Are you going to help us?" he demanded at last.

Nevin lifted his chin. "Jeremy and I will help you. *He* can fuck off back to Podunk and mind his own goddamn business."

"No, he's with me. We're doing this together."

Nevin looked surprised, although not entirely displeased, that Parker was standing up to him. And then everyone was surprised when Jeremy finally spoke up. "No," he said, echoing Parker. "They're together."

That made Nevin swivel his head and raise his eyebrows. "Oh?"

"Yes. Oh. This is Parker's personal business, and he should be the one deciding how he wants to proceed. Besides, as I recall, Wes is a fairly bright guy. He could be helpful."

Nevin muttered something at Jeremy that sounded like "fucking Sasquatch," and Jeremy cheerfully flipped him off, but Wes was dealing with an odd little sensation in his chest. It took him a moment to recognize it as relief. Not only was Jeremy taking his side—well, his and Parker's—but he'd said something nice about Wes. He wasn't treating him like the asshole son of a bitch who'd gotten somebody killed.

Parker let go of the last flecks of dismembered napkin and grabbed one of Wes's hands, causing him to jump a bit. Wes glanced at Rhoda, who was still looking their way but didn't appear upset and hadn't moved from behind the counter.

"Wes is super smart," Parker said. "He can take any old pieces of things and find a way to put them together into something amazing. His home? It's totally unconventional, but he's discovered all these creative ways to make it work. Wes figures things out."

Wes had never thought of himself that way. He wanted to protest but feared he'd come off as falsely modest. Besides, Parker didn't need another person challenging everything he said; Nevin had already done enough of that. And with Parker's soft, long-fingered hand holding his, Wes could almost believe he was something more than a loser who played with tools for a living. So he didn't argue, but he gave the hand a quick squeeze and looked Nevin straight in the eyes. Not challenging, just not afraid.

A tall man with a battered biker jacket, gray backpack, and streaks of silver in his straight black hair entered P-Town, looked around for a moment, and headed their way. He was handsome, although something about his face and posture suggested his journey hadn't always been an easy one. His wide smile seemed genuine, and it broadened even more when Jeremy caught sight of him.

"What happened to your class?" Jeremy asked.

The man, who must have been Qay, Jeremy's husband, rested a hand on Jeremy's shoulder. "Prof let us out early. She has a red-eye flight to Philly for a conference."

Jeremy introduced him to Wes—they nodded at each other—and then had a conversation with Qay about dinner and a hike they were planning for the next day. They didn't speak for long since Qay clearly didn't want to disrupt the rest of them, but even in those couple of minutes, their love for each other was evident in the way their bodies leaned subtly together and they finished each other's sentences. Bitter jealousy stung the back of Wes's throat, not just over their relationship but also over the way jaded, cynical Nevin didn't say a single caustic word to them. He simply waited, absently stroking the wedding band on his finger.

When Qay said goodbye to everyone, waved at Rhoda, and strolled away, Jeremy watched him go.

"When do you want to do this?" asked Nevin, drawing everyone's attention back to the matter at hand.

Parker answered. "Now. Like, tonight. You think you can get hold of her?"

"I can do anything," Nevin replied with a sharp-toothed grin. He pulled out his phone and poked at it for a few seconds, then stood. "Be right back." With a complex hand gesture in Rhoda's direction, and her nod in return, he strode across the room and went to the kitchen, where there would be less ambient noise. Right afterward Parker let go of Wes and hopped up to join his mother behind the counter, where he began to do something complicated with the espresso machine. That left Wes alone with Jeremy.

"Congratulations," Wes said, waving at the door where Qay had exited.

"We fought for what we have. It was really hard for a while, but worth every bit of effort." Jeremy leaned back in his chair, making it creak in protest. "You could have told me you were gay, back when you were in the bureau. I wouldn't have told anyone else."

"I know."

"And now you're comfortable with it?"

Wes nodded. His sexuality was one of the few things about himself he *was* comfortable with. He'd abandoned his childhood dreams of a straight Future Wes, replacing him with queer-but-single Future Wes. Maybe not as rosy an outcome as his imaginary family and ranch home, but a lot more realistic. "Nobody cares if I'm gay." Because nobody cared what the hell he did. Except maybe Parker, but that was brand-new and fragile.

"If I'd known then, maybe.... Well, doesn't matter." Jeremy leaned forward, his handsome face serious. "Do you remember Donny Matthews?"

The name rang a faint bell but was nondescript enough that it didn't carry any associations. But Jeremy thought Wes knew the guy, which meant he was probably connected to the bureau somehow. Somebody they'd arrested? Wait, no. "Was he that jerk from the East Precinct?" Loudmouthed and bossy, always cutting corners in his work. Even as a rookie, Wes realized he shouldn't emulate that officer.

Jeremy groaned softly. "Yeah, that was him. When you were in the bureau, I was dating him."

Wes gaped. "I thought he was a homophobe."

"Not really. He was just messed up. And newly divorced and ready to admit he wasn't as straight as he thought."

Maybe so, but Wes couldn't picture the two of them together. Jeremy had been so honorable and upstanding that some of the guys used to call him Dudley Do-Right behind his back, while Matthews could have been voted most likely to get caught up in graft charges. "You, um, never mentioned that back then."

"We were quiet about it for a long time. Mostly because he wasn't out. After you left we went more public. We stayed together for six years."

"Wow."

"Not sure that's the word I'd use. The whole thing was pretty much a disaster. He drank. And later, toward the end, he was using other stuff too. That's part of the reason I left the bureau—I was caught where I didn't want to be."

Six years. It was hard to imagine Jeremy putting up with that kind of crap for so long, but then love did funny things to a person. Or so Wes had been told. "Sorry."

Jeremy flapped his hand. "Walking away from the bureau turned out fine. I love being a ranger. But Donny, that part didn't turn out fine at all. Five years after we broke up—he'd been fired long before that—he showed up literally on my doorstep, all beat up. And the day after that, he showed up dead."

"Shit!"

"He got caught up with the wrong crowd. I ended up involved too, in some pretty unfortunate ways."

"Jesus, that's—"

"Hang on. I'm not telling this because I want sympathy. The opposite, actually." Jeremy leaned forward, his expression earnest. "I made some bad choices. It's not my fault Donny got murdered—he did that on his own—but there were lots of things I could have handled better. Including how I interacted with Qay when we were first together. I was arrogant, I guess. Figured I could magically fix everyone. I can't."

It was clear this admission was difficult for Jeremy. Strong men often found it difficult to admit weakness. But Wes couldn't grasp the moral of this tale. "So... you learned your lesson?"

"God, I sure hope so," Jeremy said with a bark of laughter. "And I bet you did too."

Ah. "Does this speech constitute my official pardon?"

"I'm in no position to pardon anyone, Wes. You'll have to do that for yourself."

Wes raised his eyebrows and considered a smartass comeback about people who disclaimed their efforts to fix others while simultaneously handing down nuggets of Obi-Wan Kenobi-like wisdom.

But just then Parker returned to the table clutching a tall drink with a frothy top. "Mom is dying to know what we've been talking about," he announced as he sat.

"You didn't tell her?" Jeremy asked.

"Nope. She'd only want to get involved. She'd start bossing everyone around."

"Yes, probably."

"I don't want her to. This is my problem." He took a hefty swallow of his drink, which would have added to his show of firmness if he hadn't ended up with a little foam mustache.

Jeremy and Parker chatted for a while, mostly about a P-Town customer Parker thought Rhoda should consider dating. Jeremy seemed to think it was hilarious that Parker was trying to set her up with someone—apparently because Rhoda had spent years trying to find a perfect partner for Jeremy. Wes watched and listened, quietly pleased by the obvious affection between the two men. Anyone who had Jeremy on his side was lucky. Ditto with Nevin, actually.

And speak of the devil.... Nevin came marching out of the kitchen with phone in hand and his jaw clenched. He threw himself into his chair with enough melodrama to put a teenager to shame. "Fucking *pendejos!*"

"Bilingual insults. Stellar achievement, Nev." Jeremy raised his mug in a mock salute.

"Bureau pays extra if I pick up a second language, *cabrón*." Nevin turned his attention to Parker. "I talked to Detective Saito. She's a stubborn shithead who didn't want to tell me anything, but I finally got her to cave."

"It must have been your tact and charm that did the trick," said Jeremy.

Nevin flipped him off without even glancing his way.

Parker ignored that entire interchange. "What did she say?"

"Blathered all kinds of bullshit first about confidentiality and chain of custody, like I'm some kind of wet-behind-the-ears newbie who doesn't know his Glock from his asshole. But eventually she sent me a photo of the suicide letter." He poked at his phone a few times. "There. It's all yours."

As Nevin spoke, Parker's phone buzzed. He took a quick peek at the message, set the phone facedown on the table, and inhaled and exhaled deeply several times. "Okay," he muttered. He picked up his phone and turned it over.

Everyone at the table sat very still while Parker read the note. Wes wondered whether Nevin had already read it and, if so, what his thoughts were. His face gave nothing away. Jeremy's hands were curled into loose fists on the table. All around them, people talked and laughed and ate and drank as if nothing could possibly be wrong. As if Parker wasn't facing something terrible.

Parker had his lips pressed between his teeth and his brow furrowed. He didn't say anything, and the note didn't occupy him for long. When he was finished, he handed the phone to Wes without looking at him. Then Parker bowed his head.

The note was written with a thin black marker that was drying out or running out of ink, but the writing, blocky print letters that leaned all over the place, was legible.

> *Parker,*
>
> *I can't do this anymore. I thought we had great plans together but now their all busted. That's ok. I want you to go on and live your live like you want to without me to drag you down. Good luck. I guess I'm going to a better place anyway, right? When I was a kid my mom and dad used to tell me how someday I'd go to heaven if I was good. I don't know if I've been good enough, but I hope I'm gonna get that halo and harp now. And no more pain.*
>
> *Goodby.*
> *Love,*
> *Logan*

The signature was bigger than any of the other words, a scrawled and slanted scribble that lacked finesse, as if the writer had never written it before.

"He always was a crappy speller," Parker said, barely above a whisper. "We had to write daily report cards for the dogs at work, and he was always asking me how to spell things." He took his phone from Wes and slipped it into a pocket of his hoodie. For just a moment he looked for all the world like a lost little boy.

Then he firmed his jaw, straightened his back, and raised his chin. "That note's not right."

"Logan didn't write it?" Jeremy asked.

"No, that's his handwriting. It's just…. He never called me my real name. Ever. The day we met, he called me Portland Boy. After that I was always PB."

Parker turned and looked straight at Wes. "I don't think Logan committed suicide at all."

Chapter Eleven

Wes planned to sleep in his van, and Parker thought that was stupid. He could have slept in Parker's bed, which was big enough for two people who didn't mind some closeness. And it wasn't as if they hadn't done it before. Slept side by side on the same mattress, that is. They'd had that one scorching kiss, but they hadn't done "it" at all. Anyway, his bed could have worked, but Parker felt a little weird about that in Rhoda's house. Not that Rhoda was under any delusions her son was a virgin. But still.

Rhoda finally solved the problem by hauling a stack of sheets and blankets out of a closet and dumping them on the couch. "You boys can make this up yourselves. I'm heading to bed." It was early yet, but she'd put in a full day. They all had.

Wes opened his mouth, probably to protest again about not putting anybody out, but she turned and swept up the stairs.

"You can't argue with my mom. You'll never ever win."

"I don't want to cause trouble."

"You're sleeping on our couch. That's not trouble. And you're hardly the first." Rhoda had a habit of taking in temporary strays—people she knew from P-Town who needed a place to crash for a night or two. They usually ended up in Parker's vacant room, but when he was in residence, they stayed on the couch. The last one Parker met was a college student who remained for an entire week because her dorm was closed for spring break and she didn't have any family to go home to. She turned out to be a really good cook who enjoyed having temporary access to a kitchen. Rhoda and Parker were sorry when she and her delicious food went away.

Now Parker unfolded a sheet and began tucking it into the cushions. It was from one of his childhood bedding sets. Cartoon robots rather than Tarzan. He smiled as he remembered lying awake in bed and pretending he was a robot too. He and his mechanical buddies were gathering to plan a coup: no more bedtimes and no limits on the numbers of desserts a person could eat.

Wes pitched in to finish getting the couch ready. Robot sheets, purple fleecy blanket, pouffy duvet with a turquoise cover. Plus three pillows, which was definitely overkill.

"There are towels in the cupboard next to the bathroom," Parker said. "Do you need anything else?"

"No. Thanks."

For a moment they just stood there. And then Parker threw himself at Wes, plastering their bodies together and holding him tight. Wes made a soft sighing noise and returned the embrace.

"I've been wanting to touch you all day." Parker kept his voice low because Rhoda was upstairs. And also just because.

"Yeah."

Did that mean Wes wanted that too, or was he simply acknowledging Parker's desire? Ah well, time to blunder onward regardless. "I've been missing you since I came back to Portland."

"I'm not such great company."

"You totally are."

"I should go." But Wes's voice lacked conviction, and he didn't unwrap his arms from Parker.

"I won't let you."

They remained like that for a long time, leaning into each other. Parker noticed for the first time that Wes was a couple of inches shorter than him. Well, he'd noticed that before, but now he *felt* it, and for a little while, Parker felt big and strong and capable. It was 100 percent bullshit, but it was nice anyway.

They couldn't stand there forever, but Parker didn't want to leave yet. He tugged Wes to the couch instead, and they sat together in the middle, their thighs barely touching. Wes had his hands clasped in his lap, as if he were still trying to be a guest on best behavior, and that triggered a thought for Parker. "When's the last time you had a sleepover?"

"What?"

"I've crashed at friends' places a lot over the years—including yours. I was wondering how often you did it?"

Wes glanced quickly at him, his eyes haunted, then away. "Never."

"Ever?"

"I hook up sometimes. Nobody stays over on those."

"But what about platonic sleepovers? Like maybe you stayed up too late watching movies or partying and you're too tired or too wasted to go home. Or your lease is up on your old apartment and you can't move into the new one yet. Except you own the bus, so no problems there. But you know what I mean. Visiting someone who lives far away, maybe."

With his gaze fixed on the floor, Wes gave a little head shake. "Never."

"Not even—"

"The last time I spent the night at a friend's house was in eighth grade. Craig Stephens. His mom took us to see *The Mask*, and then we had pizza and I slept in a sleeping bag on his bedroom floor. It was great. We made plans to do it again, except a week or so later my dad decided he'd had enough of me and shipped me off to my mother in Roseburg, and that was that."

The realization hit Parker as heavily as a physical blow. Wes had nobody. No family, no friends. Nobody to do him a favor when he needed one—or to send him dorky texts just to make him laugh.

"I'm glad you're here tonight."

Wes slumped a little in his seat, perhaps implying he was more relaxed.

"Hey, Wes? How busy are you with work?"

"You want me to make something different instead?" Wes pointed toward the stairs to clarify his meaning.

"No! God, she's going to love it. I was just hoping maybe you could stick around a little longer to help out some more with the Logan thing."

"I haven't helped at all. That was Nevin, remember?"

"Yeah, Nevin made the phone call. But you're the one who brought up the topic and confirmed my idea that the detective's story didn't feel right. And you sat with me and gave me moral support, which I still really, really need." Parker grabbed one of Wes's heavily callused hands and held it in both of his.

It took a while for Wes to answer, and Parker was sure he was going to refuse. But finally he nodded. "I can stay for a day or two."

Parker squeezed his hand. "Good. Maybe together we can figure out what to do next. 'Cause dude, that note didn't make any sense."

"Because he didn't call you PB." Wes didn't sound skeptical, just curious, as if he truly wanted more details.

So Parker gave them. "It's just… it didn't sound like him. Halos and harps? He always told me he thought religion was bullshit. And we didn't have great plans together. We didn't have *any* plans. I couldn't even get him to decide what to have for dinner most of the time, not even when it was past eight and we were both starving. And we'd just had this huge fight because he stole my rent money and was getting us evicted, remember? I think he'd be a lot more likely to write *Fuck you, PB* than anything about love and good luck."

Since Wes continued to listen intently, Parker warmed to his subject. "Logan was never mushy or sentimental. He could be funny, but he was never really all that nice. He was… well, he was a lot better at dealing with dogs than people, actually. All the dogs loved him. There was this lab mix who used to come once a week, and all she wanted was to snore in a corner. She was, like, ninety in people years. But when she saw Logan, she'd bounce around and fetch toys like a puppy. Shy dogs would climb into his lap. Hyper ones that barked too much would calm down as soon as he started petting them. But human beings? Not so much."

Wes hadn't tried to pull his hand away. Now he stroked his chin with the free one. "But you said you thought he wrote the note."

"Yeah. I know that shitty handwriting and even shittier spelling. But why would he write an inauthentic suicide note?" It was a mystery, and Parker always sucked at those. He didn't have the patience to collect clues and puzzle out who shanked Colonel Mustard in the billiard room.

"Maybe you should talk to Detective Saito," said Wes. "Express your concerns."

Ugh. Parker didn't want to talk to cops—except the ones Rhoda was friends with. But it was probably the smartest course of action. The most adult option. After a moment's consideration, he nodded. "Yeah, okay. But will you go with me?"

"Go where?"

"Seattle, of course."

THEY STAYED up late. First Parker had to convince Wes that meeting with Saito in person was better than calling her. A phone call would feel distant and impersonal, and Parker wanted to converse with her. He wanted to see her facial expressions and posture as she responded to him.

And if this gave him an excuse to spend a little more time with Wes, away from Rhoda's prying eyes and sensitive ears, so much the better.

Once Wes was on board, Parker texted Nevin and asked him to set up the Seattle meeting. That dragged on longer than expected, mostly because Nevin insisted *he* could take care of confronting the douchecanoes in Seattle. But Parker held steady, and eventually Nevin caved. That was a red-letter occasion in itself.

After that Parker had to wait for Nevin to contact Saito, worrying the whole time it was too late at night or she'd blow him off. But apparently Nevin overcame those potential barriers. It was almost eleven when he texted:

3pm tomorrow. Sveglio Cafe on Spring St. I'm going too.

Smiling, Parker replied:

Thanks, and no, you're not. How about if I just call if I need you?

After a long pause, Nevin sent the eggplant emoji. Parker decided to take that as acquiescence.

Parker and Wes could have gone to sleep at that point, but Parker had the munchies. They crept into the kitchen, giggling like a pair of misbehaving schoolboys, and pigged out on crackers, cheese, and Rhoda's not-so-secret stash of Oreos. Parker could replace the cookies after he returned from Seattle. They whispered to each other while they ate. Well, mostly Parker whispered, telling Wes the entire drama of how Jeremy and Qay got together and how Jeremy was kidnapped and tortured by a psychotic but dumb drug dealer. It was an epic story.

"—and they met up again on that same bridge in Bailey Springs and decided to stop being stupid and stay in love instead."

"They seem successful at it."

Did Wes look wistful? Maybe. Parker *felt* wistful. Jeremy and Qay had faced pretty enormous obstacles, yet they made things work. Nevin and Colin too. Parker's parents had been together for over twenty years when his father died. A lot of his friends were married now too. Or in serious relationships—the kind where they shared living arrangements, went grocery shopping together, and named each other as life insurance beneficiaries. Or at least got matching tattoos.

Wes yawned.

"You've had a long day," Parker acknowledged. "Let's get some rest." They tidied up the kitchen, walked into the living room, and paused.

"I'll be right there." Parker pointed in the direction of his bedroom. "Let me know if you need anything."

"Okay."

Parker gave him a kiss on the cheek. It wasn't passionate or sexy, but it was nice. It made Wes smile.

"Night," said Parker and headed to his room.

ALTHOUGH PARKER had meant to set an alarm, he awakened to Wes lightly shaking his shoulder.

"We should go pretty soon." Wes was already dressed, his hair in its neat ponytail and his breath smelling faintly of coffee. Yesterday he'd worn a forest green long-sleeved tee, but today a white one peeked out from under an eggplant-colored fleece that looked deliciously soft. Parker wanted to pet him.

Parker looked at his phone. Shit. He didn't intend to sleep so late. Rhoda would have left for P-Town hours ago. "Crap. I wanted to talk to my mom and tell her what we're doing."

"I told her. She says be careful." Wes looked as if he was trying not to grin.

Parker showered and dressed and considered a late breakfast. But Wes suggested they grab lunch along the way, and that sounded like a good idea. Parker was still yawning as they walked through the drizzle and climbed into Morrison.

"You'll have to give me directions." Wes pulled out of the driveway.

"Sveglio's downtown. I've been there a bunch of times. Do you know downtown Seattle very well?"

"Never been."

Parker blinked. "You've never been to Seattle?"

"Never been anywhere in Washington except Vancouver."

"But that's only a few miles away. I thought you traveled a lot. Did you skip our neighbor to the north for some reason?"

Wes didn't answer. In fact he remained silent all the way up I-5 through North Portland, over the Columbia, and into Vancouver. His music was playing—Heart, Pink Floyd, Van Halen—and he didn't say a single word until they were passing the fireworks stores in Hazel Dell.

"I lied," Wes said, his voice startling Parker as much as the particular words. Wes was staring resolutely through the windshield.

"What?"

"I lied. I haven't been to Wyoming. Just read about it."

"I don't think you ever told me you'd been there. Just that you were heading that way."

A Wes shrug. "Well, I haven't. I've never been anywhere except for Oregon. A little of northern California. And Vancouver."

Parker couldn't remember exactly what Wes had told him about his travels, but Parker had certainly formed an impression of a history of road trips and footloose adventures. It made sense for a guy who had no close personal connections or other obligations and who was self-employed and therefore able to take off at a moment's notice.

"Why?" Parker asked.

"Guess I thought it'd make me sound more interesting."

"No, I mean why haven't you gone anywhere?"

"Don't know."

Parker didn't believe that for a moment. The topic was important enough to Wes that he'd lied about it and then later came clean, which meant he hadn't stayed close to home just because travel never occurred to him. Something else was going on. But Wes was doing him a huge favor right now, so Parker decided to not play amateur psychotherapist. Wes didn't owe him all his secrets.

"I like traveling," Parker said mildly. "We used to do a lot of family trips when I was a kid. Nowhere fancy, usually, but they were fun. I did a school trip to New York and DC in eighth grade. And when I was twenty, me and my friend Denise flew to Spain and spent a couple of weeks in youth hostels. Which was totally irresponsible, because I was broke when I got back and I got fired from my job while I was away, so I ended up having to move in with Mom for a few months."

"But you had an adventure."

"Yeah."

Parker smiled at the memory. Lots of bars where he could drink because he wasn't underage in Europe. Hostels full of new acquaintances from all around the world. Two years of high-school Spanish that proved useless in the face of Barcelona's Catalan. A doe-eyed university student named Lluís, who was eager to practice his English with a native speaker—and eager to put his pretty mouth to other uses too.

Wes and Parker stopped for lunch in Chehalis at a place where Parker and his parents used to eat on their trips north. As a kid, Parker always ordered one of the enormous cinnamon rolls, but today he had a panini and fries. Wes ordered a cheeseburger but mostly picked at it instead of eating. He didn't often meet Parker's eyes either, and he said very little. Hating the awkward silence, Parker blathered on about stupid crap that meant nothing to either of them. He insisted on paying, especially since Wes hadn't even let him pitch in for gas.

"I think Morrison's happy," said Wes when they were on the road again.

"Yeah, why?"

"He's getting to see a little more of the world. More of I-5, anyway."

"So are you." That earned one of Wes's shrugs, which Parker decided to interpret as encouragement to continue. "You know, Seattle's a pretty nice city. I can show you around a little after we're done talking to the detective. We can watch them throw fish at Pike Place Market if you want the full tourist experience. Or we can do the Space Needle."

Wes didn't answer, not even with a shoulder twitch. Parker didn't know what that meant. When a few more attempts at conversation failed, Parker resorted to playing with his phone. Wes hummed.

Traffic grew heavy by the time they reached Tacoma, and Wes grumbled under his breath about the driving skills of the locals. Parker couldn't entirely blame him. On the rare occasions when Parker had possessed a car, or at least had temporary access to one, he hadn't enjoyed his Seattle driving experiences. He generally tried to live close enough to his job to walk or take public transportation.

With Parker navigating, they arrived at an underground parking garage near Sveglio with a little time to spare. Wes had some trouble finding a space big enough for his van, but he proved adept at navigating the narrow areas and then at parking. Lots of practice, Parker guessed, assisted by the driver's training he'd received in the police academy.

After they disembarked from Morrison, Parker grabbed Wes's arm before he'd gone more than a few steps. "What?" Wes asked.

"I don't care that you haven't been anywhere."

"Parker—"

"I don't."

Firm-chinned, Wes shook his head. "Logan stole from you. I lied to you. The last thing you need is another dishonest boyf—" He swallowed audibly. "Dishonest friend."

"It's not even close to the same thing, and yours wasn't a big deal. You stretched the truth to make yourself look better. Big deal. I've dealt with way bigger lies than that just on dating apps. Age, height, weight, marital status, jobs, interests, dick size."

Wes shook his head again and tried to pull away, so Parker tightened his grip and hauled Wes closer. "The travel thing doesn't matter to me, not even with the lies. That mistake you made a decade ago—God, I was still in high school then!—isn't important to me either. Or that you live in a bus, 'cause your bus is actually way cool, and frankly I'd be homeless if not for my mom."

Parker realized both of them were breathing hard, the sound slightly amplified in the garage's concrete confines. Although they needed to get to the café, it was even more important that he tell Wes some things. Right here, right now.

"Here's what I know about you, Wes. Not from what you've told me, but from what I've seen with my own eyes. You are a kind man who took in a stranger in distress at a moment's notice and uncomplainingly let him—let *me*—intrude into your life. You never took advantage of my emotional state, not even when I literally threw myself at you. You take personal responsibility for your choices. You're brave. You aren't remotely greedy. You're an artist who makes magic with ordinary materials. You listen to me and act like what I say is worthwhile, and you don't make me feel like a dumb kid even if I act like one. You drag me out of the rain, give me your clothes, and pick the thistles out of my skin. We hardly know each other, but here you are in Seattle because I asked you to come. You have my back. God, *these* are the things that are important. Not whether you made up a story about going to goddamn Wyoming!"

His voice had risen as he spoke, mainly so he wouldn't burst into tears. Parker wasn't as skilled with words as he would have liked. If he'd been able, he would have described how Wes had a depth to him, an authenticity, that made Parker want to hold on to him like a limpet glued to a rock in a tide pool. Wes also possessed deep sorrow, and that *also* made Parker want to hold him tightly until all the sadness faded away. But Parker didn't hold anything except for Wes's arm—which he let go of now, then sniffled a few times.

Wes remained statue-still, eyes wide and lips parted. "Oh," he said finally, in the tiniest voice imaginable.

Parker was going to suggest they head to the café. But before he could say anything, Wes had him in a crushing embrace. And even though they held each other too tightly to breathe, they somehow managed to kiss. Oh God, that kiss. Whoever was watching the garage security cameras owed Wes and Parker a hefty fee for the honor of seeing the world's most amazing, most satisfying, most soul-ringing kiss. Energy poured into Parker from every spot where Wes touched him, and it poured back out of him too, creating an infinite loop of power and strength and goodness. So many sparks flew that Parker worried they'd ignite whatever gas fumes lurked in the garage.

Parker grew painfully hard and felt Wes against him, just as desperate. But this wasn't just a sexual kiss. It was also a romantic kiss, and a thankful one. A kiss that atoned for past transgressions and promised joyful futures. If Parker could have bottled that kiss and distributed it, there'd be world peace.

"Oh," Parker said when they finally separated. Which was what Wes said at the beginning, so maybe it was now their word, just like this clammy underground space was their parking garage.

"Jesus Christ."

"I'm Jewish," Parker said.

"So was he."

That made Parker laugh, which was a good thing because his body was still threatening to explode. Wes took Parker's hand and they walked to the stairs. Detective Saito was waiting.

Chapter Twelve

ALTHOUGH DETECTIVE Saito was wearing ordinary street clothes, she might as well have had a blinking *COP!* sign over her head. She sat at a table near the window, with her phone in hand and a tall cardboard cup in front of her. She owned her space and emanated self-assurance and control, just like Nevin and Jeremy and most other cops. Wes doubted he'd ever possessed it himself.

She stood up long enough for handshakes and introductions; then, when Wes and Parker were seated across from her, she turned her laser vision on Wes. "What's your interest in this matter, sir?"

"I'm just here to support Parker." He tried not to fidget, but police officers made him uncomfortable. He wished he were back home, feeling confident as he conjured beautiful furniture from pieces of wood. But then he caught the taste of Parker on his lips and was glad to be here.

Saito tilted her head. "And who are you to Mr. Levin?"

Wes didn't have an easy answer to that. He was still trying to find the right word when Parker spoke up. "He's a good friend."

"Was he a friend of Mr. Miller's?"

It took a second for the meaning of that question to register since Parker had never mentioned Logan's last name. But like Wes, Parker must have also caught the slight emphasis Saito put on the word *friend*, and he thumped his fist on the table. "I wasn't cheating on Logan with Wes, and Wes wasn't messing around with Logan, if that's what you're thinking. I didn't even meet Wes until after you called to tell me Logan was dead. So you can put all of those weird ideas away."

"That's a short period of time for two people to become close friends."

"So? Maybe sometimes you find just the right person at just the right time, and the two of you click, and you get attached in just a few hours. Haven't you ever seen that before, Detective?" Parker narrowed his eyes at her.

She frowned, and her voice took on an edge. "I've seen a lot of things."

Her demeanor might have intimidated a lot of people, but Parker had practically grown up with Nevin. Cops with an attitude were old hat to him. Wes almost smiled at the way Parker rolled his eyes at Saito.

"Look, if you want to get yourself sidetracked into a stupid investigation that'll go nowhere, be my guest. But if either Wes or I was trying to hide a skanky affair, do you really think I'd ask you to meet with me *and* bring the 'other man' along?" He made air quotes for the *other man* part.

Saito did an eyebrow thing that might have been her admission of his logic. "Fine. Then why did you want to meet?"

"Because I'm not sure Logan killed himself. And I'm certain he didn't intend that letter as a real suicide note."

She scrunched up her mouth and seemed to consider for a moment. Then, apparently reaching a decision, she pulled a notebook from her jacket pocket and raised a pen expectantly. "Please explain."

Parker did, clearly and calmly, including all the inconsequential details Saito asked for. He remained patient when she asked him to repeat things and when she took an inordinate amount of time to write notes. Wes didn't say a word and might as well not have been there, except that sometimes Parker reached over to give his hand a quick squeeze. Saito probably noticed despite the partial cover of the table, but she didn't say anything.

Finally she snapped her notebook shut and clicked the pen. "Thank you for this information, Mr. Levin."

"Are you going to investigate?"

"I'll do my due diligence to collect all available information and reach appropriate conclusions."

"Right. But will you investigate?"

Saito leaned forward a little and, for the first time, allowed her professional mask to slip and her human face to show. "I'll do what I can. Frankly, our resources are limited, and even when there's physical evidence to analyze, it can take months or longer to hear from the lab. Unless there are some pretty clear indicators of foul play, it's not going to be at the top of our list. I'm sorry. I believe you're telling the truth. I know you cared about Logan. But we can't work magic."

She looked tired and older than Wes had first guessed. She probably wished she could clear all her cases and take a nice vacation somewhere warm and dry.

Parker nodded. "Okay." He sighed loudly. "Logan's, um, body…. Is it…?"

"His family has claimed the remains."

"Good. But I hope they didn't bury him in Oklahoma. He hated that place."

After a few brief words, Saito left, pausing to toss her empty cup in the trash on the way out. Parker seemed lost in thought as he stared out the window at the library across the street. It was an interesting building, all glass and steel and strange angles.

"They're not going to do anything," he said to the window.

"Why is it important to you?"

Parker turned to face him. "Because he *was* my boyfriend. Even if we didn't—God, I feel way more connected to you, and we've never even had sex. But he wasn't even thirty yet and now he's dead, and I don't feel like everyone should just go 'Oh well' and move on."

One of the things Wes lov—*liked* about Parker was his passion. He wasn't ashamed to show his emotions, which so fully animated his face and words. He clearly felt distress over Logan, even if on some level he was coming to accept that Logan's death wasn't his fault. And he felt… something for Wes. That had been obvious enough in the parking garage when he gave that little speech. Wes hadn't necessarily believed everything Parker had said about him. But he saw that Parker believed, and that was a gift.

"Want to give me that tour?"

Parker managed a smile.

SINCE WES didn't feel a particular need to watch dead fish fly, they didn't visit Pike Place Market. They also didn't go to the top of the Space Needle, although they drove past it. Parker said it was illegal to come to Seattle and not at least look at the thing. After stopping to get gas, they switched places inside the van, Parker now behind the wheel so Wes could sightsee without worrying about crashing. They went to Capitol Hill, where Parker pointed out the rainbow crosswalks and the clubs and bars he'd sometimes visited. They drove around the edge of Lake Union. And then as darkness fell, they went to Parker's old neighborhood and stopped in front of the complex where he and Logan had lived.

"Barkin' Lot is just a few blocks that way." Parker pointed north.

Wes snorted. "That's really the name?"

"Yeah. Dumb. It's a pretty good place, though. The guests—that's what we were supposed to call the dogs—are treated well. They have indoor and outdoor exercise areas, with separate parts for different sizes so the Great Danes don't trample the Chihuahuas."

"You liked working there."

"Yeah." Parker spent a minute or two chewing his lip; then he smiled. "Have you ever been on a boat?"

Wes didn't quite understand the non sequitur but decided to go with it. "No."

"Do you need to head back tonight? Or could it wait until tomorrow?"

"Tomorrow's fine." Wes's heart beat a little faster as he tried to imagine why Parker was asking.

"Good. Then I have a plan."

PARKER REFUSED to divulge the evening's agenda. He simply grinned and took them back downtown, where he parked Morrison in front of a high-rise hotel. "My mom stayed here a couple times. It's pretty nice."

"The plan is to sleep here?" Wes hardly ever stayed in hotels. On those rare occasions when he remained in Portland overnight, maybe after a few drinks at a bar, he parked Morrison somewhere quiet and slept in the back. The night in Fort Bragg was the first time in ages he'd opted to check in somewhere.

"Yep. Part of the plan, anyway."

Bemused but intrigued, Wes got a few supplies from the back. Those few changes of clothing and basic toiletries—stored as if he might take off on a spur-of-the-moment adventure, which he never did—had come in handy the previous night at Rhoda's. And now here he was in Seattle with Parker. Who had a mystery plan. Wes felt a small flutter in his gut and tentatively identified it as a sense of adventure.

Parker handed the keys to the valet and led the way inside. He made all of the arrangements at the reception desk while Wes frowned at the mass-produced furniture in the lobby and drank a paper cup of lemon-infused water. Wes tried to pay, but Parker waved him away impatiently. "My plan, my dime. Don't worry. I have enough in my account to cover."

As Wes backed off, a small jab of envy struck him. Parker's only current employment was his mother's coffeehouse, and his only home was a bedroom in his mother's house, but still he felt comfortable throwing away a couple hundred bucks on a hotel room. And that was because he lived with the rock-solid knowledge that whenever he fell, he had somebody to catch him. Wes didn't begrudge that—in fact, because he cared about Parker, he was glad he had such security. But Wes couldn't help but wonder wistfully what it would feel like to know that if you failed, someone would help you back onto your feet.

They went up to their room on the eighth floor, and Wes checked out the view—an alley far below with an old brick building on the other side. They stayed long enough to use the bathroom and drop off Wes's things. He cast a look at the king bed and wondered whether Parker had requested that instead of two beds and, if so, whether that was part of the plan. Then they descended to the lobby, where Parker tapped at his phone to request a Lyft.

"We could take Morrison," Wes pointed out.

"We'd have the hassle of parking. This is easier."

As it turned out, they probably could have walked; the destination was only about a mile away. "There's a hill," Parker explained. "And rain." Neither of which would have killed them. But Parker seemed intent on being lavish tonight, so Wes didn't grumble.

To his surprise, the end of their journey turned out to be a mall, where Parker led him confidently to the fourth floor. On the other side of a big window, men dressed in white were making vast amounts of noodles and dumplings. The restaurant looked crowded, but apparently Parker had made a surreptitious reservation. It had been so many years since Wes had reserved a table at a restaurant that he had no idea how it was done nowadays. Via an app, he presumed. Jesus, he was like a crusty old time-traveler. Or a hermit.

"I hope you're hungry," Parker announced when they were seated. "The key to this place is ordering lots of little plates to share. Everything's great."

"You come here often?" Wes smiled to show he knew how hokey that sounded.

"When I can. They're not open late, which is too bad, but sometimes a group of us would eat here before hitting the clubs. Or we'd come here before seeing a movie—there's a theater in the building. Last year ten or twelve of us pigged out here and then saw the opening day of *Thor: Ragnarok*, which was cool. I'm not a huge, huge Marvel fan, but there are way worse ways to spend two hours than staring at Chris Hemsworth."

Another bittersweet twinge as Wes imagined Parker carefree and happy with a gang of friends—and how he'd never experienced that himself.

Parker was obviously as hungry as Wes, so they ordered a lot. Dumplings, fried green beans with garlic, noodles, steamed buns, rice cakes. It was far too much and, as Parker pointed out, a carb overload, but everything tasted delicious. The company was even better. Wes found himself falling into easy banter about their respective chopstick skills, and then they shared stories about meal-related disasters they'd caused or experienced. Wes had a lot of fun, and if Parker wished he were sitting there with a gaggle of friends instead of just Wes, he never showed it.

Parker paid, of course. Then they waddled out of the mall, both of them rubbing their bellies and moaning about how full they were. "How about if we walk instead of riding?" Parker asked. "The rain's mostly stopped, and we can work off some of that dinner."

Wes didn't bother to ask about their next destination since he knew Parker wouldn't tell him.

He'd worn his raincoat, which was warm enough to ward off the night's chill, but he thought Parker looked cold in his hoodie. It was nice to be walking around a new city at night with him. He kept up a running commentary on everything they passed. They strolled down the hill all the way to the bay, and after they'd walked only a short distance along the waterfront, Wes marched into a souvenir shop. He bypassed the snow globes, shot glasses, and tote bags.

"Why are we here?" asked Parker, hard at his heels.

But it was Wes's turn to be mysterious. "It's a surprise. Go wait outside."

For a moment Parker looked as if he might object. But then he grinned and threaded his way to the door. When Wes was sure he was gone, he quickly perused the racks of clothing, finally settling on a navy jacket with a fleece lining. Perfect. Grinning to himself, he paid for the item and told the bored clerk he didn't need a bag.

Parker waited impatiently just outside the door. "What did—"

"Here." Wes thrust the jacket at him. "Put it on."

Parker took the jacket and turned it around. His eyebrows lifted when he saw the image on the back: a drawing of Bigfoot hanging—King Kong-like—atop the Space Needle. "This is the most touristy thing I've ever seen."

"I could go back inside and get you a Seahawks hat. Now put it on. I'm tired of watching you shiver." To emphasize his command, Wes reached over and tore off the hang tag, which he stuffed into his pocket.

With an odd expression that Wes couldn't read, Parker obeyed.

Their destination wasn't much farther, as it turned out: the ferry terminal. Wes smiled as Parker bought tickets. "Bainbridge Island?" Wes asked when Parker rejoined him.

"Yep. It's not exactly a tropical cruise, but it's fun."

"And I get to ride a boat."

"Indeed you do."

The ferry arrived a few minutes later, and Wes found its size surprising. For some reason he'd expected something smaller, more like a tugboat, maybe. Which was dumb considering how many people commuted daily on this boat—many of them with their cars, which took up the bottom level. Parker and Wes boarded, and although they could have sat inside, Parker took them to the deck at the ship's bow. Wes was especially glad he'd bought Parker the jacket.

"We won't have a great view since it's cloudy," Parker said, leaning forward against the rail. "And sometimes there are orcas, but it's too dark to see them now."

"This is nice."

Parker made a happy noise and stood closer.

And it *was* nice. The ferry chugged across the placid surface, water lapping the sides and distant lights sparkling like fairies. The gentle rocking of the boat felt a bit disconcerting, but it helped to have Parker's arm around him. Parker made a few obligatory *Titanic* jokes, but mostly they stood there side by side, listening to the muffled chug of the engines. They had the deck entirely to themselves, and it was easy to imagine they were alone on a private vessel, leaving together on some great adventure. Maybe the best journey he'd ever have, no matter how long it lasted.

They disembarked on the island, and a few minutes' walk brought them to a small downtown with brick and wooden buildings. The shops had closed already, and Wes and Parker certainly didn't need any more food, so it was pleasant to simply stroll. The air smelled of saltwater, wet pavement, and green growing things, and Wes felt very far from home—in a good way.

"I used to watch *Gilligan's Island* when I was little," Parker said. "My dad had the whole series on DVD. Mom hated it—she wouldn't even stay in the same room—but Dad and I would get pizza and watch a bunch of episodes in a row. I used to make lists of what I'd take with me if I went on a boat trip, just in case a three-hour tour turned into a shipwreck on a deserted isle."

"All you brought today was the jacket I got you."

"And you. I brought you." Parker caught Wes's hand and brought it to his lips, giving the knuckles a kiss before letting go. "If I'm gonna be stranded, I want it to be with you."

It must have been a night for mixed emotions, because Wes's chest felt tight with sorrow yet light with… something else. Affection? Gratitude? Happiness? Could a person be happy and sad at the same time?

They returned to the ferry dock and waited for the boat to arrive. "We should stay longer," Parker said, sounding a little dreamy. "Three or four days. Then I could really show you Seattle."

"I think your mom probably wants you back before then."

Parker gave a single humorless laugh. "No. She probably—"

"It's Thanksgiving in two days."

That was clearly news to Parker, who blinked at him. "It is?" He took out his phone and checked the date. "Shit, it is. I guess I have to get back to Portland, then. Mom always does an event."

"She'd want you there."

Parker grabbed both of Wes's hands. "You're coming too."

"I can't—"

"No, you have to. It's a thing. The house always fills up with people, there's tons of food, we play dumb party games."

A tightness tugged at the corners of Wes's eyes. "Thanksgiving is for family, Parker."

"Rhoda defines family very broadly. Look, when I was growing up, it was just the three of us. And after Dad died, I thought she was gonna give it up altogether. Maybe we'd go out or something. Instead she invited people over. Jeremy came, and a bunch of other people Mom collected at P-Town. It was so fun that we almost forgot to be sad that Dad wasn't there. So it became a tradition." Parker momentarily scrunched up his mouth. "A few years ago we had a little glitch because Jeremy was hospitalized after getting himself kidnapped and tortured. But even then Mom delivered food to Qay while he was waiting in the hospital."

"I'm glad Jeremy recovered okay."

"Me too. But Jeremy's Big Adventure isn't the point of my tale. You joining us on Thursday is. You have to come, Wes."

Wes didn't bother with an excuse about having other plans, because Parker would know better. And he didn't try to describe the anxiety he'd feel among all those strangers—people who, knowing Rhoda, led fascinating lives—because Parker wouldn't understand. Wes didn't even explain that he hadn't had Thanksgiving with anyone since his grandfather died. And even when his grandfather was alive, it was usually just the two of them—and a couple of steaks, because a whole turkey seemed excessive.

"We'll see," he said.

Parker narrowed his eyes as if seeing right through him, but he didn't say anything. Nor did he let go of his hands.

The trip back to Seattle was magical, with the city lights appearing through the low-lying clouds, as if in a fairy tale. Seattle liked to call itself the Emerald City, most likely due to all the trees, but from the ferry deck, it could almost be the fabled capital of Oz. Ah, but much of Oz's magic turned out to be a sham, didn't it? The Wizard was just a con man from Omaha. And tomorrow Wes would drop off Parker in Portland and then return to his bus and his wood scraps and his ducks.

But just for tonight, couldn't he pretend to believe in magic? It wasn't so hard right now, with Parker leaning against him, blue hair ruffling in the wind, soft palm warm in Wes's callused one. For tonight Wes would allow himself the luxury of wanting. Wanting the company of a friend, wanting a handsome, bright lover in a big hotel bed. He already knew what Parker's lips tasted like; now Wes wanted to taste the rest of him. Wanted to know whether Parker was quiet or noisy while making love, what kinds of touch drove him wild. God, wanted to know what it would feel like to give himself up and over to Parker for just a few hours.

The lights of the Emerald City drew closer, and Wes didn't let go of Parker's hand.

THEY WALKED the few blocks from the ferry terminal to their hotel. Parker pointed to a building as they walked past Pioneer Square. "Do you know about the underground tours?"

"No."

"Touristy but fun. The city used to be lower, but they raised the street level 'cause of floods and backed-up toilets. Now you can walk around what used to be the first floor."

"Interesting." But Wes's mind wasn't on Seattle's architectural history. He was thinking about what might happen when they reached their room and how, if Parker kissed him this time, Wes wouldn't push him away. And if Parker didn't initiate things, should Wes? He had been the one to start the most recent kiss, the one in the parking garage, and Parker had enthusiastically participated.

Maybe he should stop overthinking things and just let them happen.

When they were a block from the hotel, Parker grabbed Wes's hand and tugged him along. "Keep up, old man," he said with a laugh.

"Old man?"

Wes pulled his hand free and took off at a sprint. Parker was younger and taller, but Wes was in decent shape, and his old sneakers worked better for running than the combat boots Parker wore. Wes beat him to the front door by a yard or so, and they were both laughing so hard that it was hard to walk. They half stumbled through the lobby to the elevators, then jostled each other playfully for access to the buttons. Wes won that little contest too, but when they reached their floor and raced down the hallway, Parker reached their room first and unlocked the door. They wrestled each other through the opening, and as soon as they were inside, Wes closed the door with a thud that probably annoyed their neighbors. He threw himself at Parker, driving him up against the wall.

He didn't exactly mean to do it; he'd intended to let Parker lead the way. But he didn't regret it either, not when he had Parker in his arms and Parker grabbed Wes's head, mashing their lips together in a sloppy kiss. Salty lips, slippery tongues, heat and moisture and *want*. They'd kissed before, of course, and those were wonderful experiences. This was too. But Wes wanted more, and judging by the needy moans Parker was making, so did he.

Clothes got in the way. Parker's dumb new jacket and hoodie, Wes's trusty old raincoat and favorite henley. Not willing to break contact, they kept their mouths together while scrabbling ineffectively at each other's zippers and buttons. Wes managed to shed his jacket and both of his shoes, but Parker remained entirely clothed, his hoodie and T-shirt rucked up to his neck and his unfastened jeans hanging on his hips.

"Wait!" Parker gasped.

Wes backed off at once, silently cursing himself for presuming. He shouldn't have thrown himself at Parker. He shouldn't have—

"Better," Parker said as he shrugged out of his coat and then pulled his hoodie and shirt over his head. He threw them aside, hitting a lamp and nearly knocking it over. "I've been waiting for this. Let's take our time and not end up in the emergency room, okay?"

Wes's lust hadn't diminished, and now relief made his ardor burn brighter. He tried to undress himself slowly, helped by the fact that his hands were trembling. He kept his gaze averted from Parker in an attempt to remain relatively calm, but he could still *hear* him—the rustle of cotton and creak of leather, the heavy rasps of his breaths. And he could still feel Parker, even though they stood a couple of feet apart. It was as if Parker had an aura that reached out to Wes, enveloping him, bathing him in warmth.

Wes was naked first, mostly because he didn't have bootlaces to undo, but Parker took only a little longer. They stood, simply staring.

They'd caught sight of each other naked before; it was inevitable in the close confines of Wes's bus and with his outdoor open shower. And Wes was honest with himself—he appreciated the glimpses he'd seen. But now they could gaze openly, and that was a major improvement.

Parker was beautiful. His pale skin contrasted with the dark patch of hair at his groin and the tousled cobalt falling over his forehead. Wes suspected his hairless chest and belly were due to waxing or some other form of manscaping. Parker was lean and sharp-hipped, with his abs clearly but not starkly defined, and his half-hard cock perked up a bit more as Wes watched.

"Nice," Parker said, leering broadly. "God, really, really nice."

Wes glanced down at himself. His forearms and lower legs still bore a bit of a tan; southern Oregon got more sun than Portland or Seattle, and he liked to work in a T-shirt and shorts when he could. He had never manscaped in his life, but he'd never been especially furry, and in any case, the dusting of dark blond hair on his torso wasn't too visible. He used to work out, back when he was a kid and then again when he was in the bureau, but for the past several years his exercise regime had consisted mostly of walking a lot and lifting heavy pieces of furniture. Because he was naturally somewhat burly, that was enough to keep him looking solid. And his cock was as eager as Parker's.

He was, Wes realized with surprise, proud of his body and pleased to offer it to Parker. *I've put that spark in his eyes.* It was a heady feeling.

Parker took a step closer. "I want to touch now."

They didn't grab at each other, although the greedy part of Wes's psyche wanted to. Instead they stood inches apart, watching as they traced each other's bodies with their fingers. No skin had ever felt so soft and smooth, so hot. No joints had ever been assembled so cleverly, no muscles felt so firm, no nipples had ever tasted so sweet.

Oh. Tasting. Wes became aware he was licking Parker—nuzzling at the crook of his neck, rasping along his collarbone, sucking delicately on pebbled nubbins of flesh. Parker, meanwhile, had removed Wes's hair tie and was combing fingers through his still-damp hair. Parker shivered.

"You're cold."

"No."

Wes was willing to believe him; he felt a bit quivery himself. When Parker moved his hands to Wes's ass and began a caress, Wes's knees went wobbly. "Bed."

They did not proceed elegantly to the mattress. Parker almost tripped over one of his boots, Wes banged a leg on an ugly little table, and they got slightly tangled in each other's limbs. But they made it to the bed, Parker falling onto his back and dragging Wes down on top of him.

Perfect.

They both seemed to remember there was no hurry. An uncertain future stretched ahead, but at least they had all night. Wes wanted this to be far different from the rapid grope-and-fuck he was accustomed to. This was special.

Parker ran his hands down Wes's back, returned to his shoulders for a quick little massage, and then down again to settle on Wes's ass. "God, you feel amazing," he said. "Solid. And you're really here."

"I'm here." All of him. Because right now the past didn't matter and the rest of the world was a universe away. He had Parker's lips against his and then more of Parker to explore with his mouth. Sternum. Ribs. The divot of his navel. The tender skin inside his thighs. The muskiness of his balls. Wes took a single broad swipe the length of Parker's shaft, but when Parker responded with a hip jerk and garbled curse, Wes decided to be cruel. He repositioned himself and moved back up Parker's body. Slowly. Nibbling here, tongue-tickling there, until they were face-to-face, and then he dug his teeth gently into Parker's lower lip and gave a light tug.

Parker did not passively succumb to this process. He had his hands all over Wes, kneading and smoothing. He brought them back often to Wes's head, where he pulled at Wes's hair. Not hard enough to hurt, not even close, but firmly enough to imply some possessiveness. His touches said *You're mine, at least for now*—and Wes was thrilled to hear it.

They kissed some more, bodies softly undulating against each other. Heat built inside of Wes, and he was glad they hadn't managed to pull the blankets over them. They rubbed their cocks together. Hard. Wet. So, so good. Parker tilted his head back on the pillow, granting Wes better access to his long, vulnerable neck. He splayed his legs, and when Wes's cock slipped lower to press against the tender spot behind Parker's balls, Parker shuddered beneath him. "Rubbers and lube. Please tell me you have rubbers and lube."

Wes froze. He hadn't planned for this. He usually kept supplies in his toiletries bag in case he was in the mood for a hookup during a visit to Portland. But he hadn't been thinking of that this time, when he expected to simply drop off Rhoda's shelf and return home. He couldn't remember when he had last restocked the bag.

"Hang on."

Separating himself from Parker was almost physically painful. He hurried to the bathroom—dick bobbing annoyingly—where he rooted desperately in the small zippered bag. And…. "Got 'em!" He ran back to Parker, waving his prizes triumphantly. Parker clapped as if Wes had just won an Olympic gold medal.

Fortunately the interruption didn't break the mood. In fact, seeing Parker spread out on the bed, eagerly awaiting him, made Wes giddy with want. Parker grabbed his arm as soon as he was within reach. "How fast can you get that rubber on yourself?" he asked with a smile.

The stupid foil packaging was almost impossible to open. Wes dropped it twice before managing to rip the damn thing and get the condom out. Then he had to roll it on, which usually wasn't difficult, although it certainly was tonight. That was because Parker was staring at him, big-eyed, jacking himself slowly and firmly.

Wes muttered a quick entreaty for the gods to help him last more than five seconds.

The next step, of course, was to get Parker nice and slippery. Wes would have enjoyed that task, yet he wasn't the least disappointed when Parker poured some lube on his own fingers and, lips curled in the world's most wicked grin, worked two fingers inside himself.

"Jesus."

"Told you. I'm Jewish."

How could Parker manage to be heart-droppingly sexy and so impish at the same time? It was a superpower, perhaps. All that mortal Wes could manage was to avoid exploding at the brush of Parker's fingertips.

They slid a pillow under Parker's hips. "Come here," he said and then wrapped his legs around Wes's waist, pressing his heels against Wes's butt as Wes gradually pushed into his body. "Perfect. God, so perfect."

The tightness, the friction, the intimate noises of bodies moving together—Wes was accustomed to those. Alone, they wouldn't have overcome him. But Parker pulled him down for another scorching kiss. That kept Wes from thrusting as freely, yet it connected them completely, closing a circuit and sending electrical impulses thrumming through them in a dizzying loop. And *that* was enough to overwhelm Wes entirely. He became aware of every fluttering cell in his body and in Parker's, of every sparkle of life, and he came with such intensity that his vision went gray.

Parker fell right after, arching against Wes's belly and crying out into their kiss.

A measureless time afterward, they lay squashed together with the blankets over them. One of the lights was still on, but neither had gathered the energy yet to do anything about it. The used condom, its empty wrapper, and the bottle of lube lay on the nightstand like a still-life painting. It would be titled *Afterglow*, Wes decided.

"So that was worth waiting for." Parker's head lay against Wes's shoulder, and he was playing with the fingers of Wes's left hand.

"Agreed."

"I love the way your calluses feel when you touch me. It's... really butch." He laughed.

"Good." Wes realized he was being even more taciturn than usual, but his ability to speak hadn't completely returned. Probably a lot of his blood was still way south of his brain. He was content to be tickled by Parker's hair and warmed in the cocoon of blankets.

Suddenly Parker went still. "Do you want to see something totally stupid?"

"Um, okay."

Parker sat up a little and pointed to a spot on his chest, just over his heart. "Look."

Wes didn't see anything. "At what?"

"Look closer."

Obediently Wes narrowed his eyes and leaned in. "A freckle?"

"That's not a freckle. It's the world's tiniest tattoo."

On closer inspection, it did look more black than brown. "Why do you have the world's tiniest tattoo?"

"It wasn't supposed to be. It was supposed to be a really awesome sailing ship. You know, the old-fashioned kind with tall masts and a winged unicorn figurehead. And it was going to be in the middle of a wavy ocean and have a cloud with a face blowing on it from the sky. Rhoda's friend Ery is an amazing artist—one of his paintings is in my bedroom—and he drew it for me. It was going to symbolize my journey to find myself and be like a talisman to help me find my life path."

"It sounds like you gave it a lot of thought."

"I did! Like, for months. I asked around a lot and found a really good tattoo artist who was willing to adapt Ery's drawing for me. I saved up money for this. I'm not usually very good at saving."

Wes nodded and chose to hold his tongue about that issue. "What happened?"

"The big day arrived. I showed up at the studio with this guy I'd sort of dated but we broke up but we were still friends, and his new girlfriend who was really cool, so they could provide moral support. I signed all the forms. And... then the tattoo artist stuck the needle in me."

"It hurt?"

Parker sighed. "Yeah. And I've never been great about needles anyway. I always hated getting shots when I was a kid. But it was more than that." Another sigh, with Parker's expelled breath puffing pleasantly over Wes's bare skin.

"What else?"

"My mom. I was suddenly worried about what she'd say."

That surprised Wes. Rhoda hadn't struck him as judgmental or narrow-minded. Most of her employees sported visible ink, as did a good portion of her clientele. "She disapproves of tattoos?"

"Not exactly. It's just…. We're Jewish, right? Traditionally Jews don't get tattooed. I think there's something about it in Leviticus. But Mom and I are not very observant at all. I mean, we eat ham and that's in Leviticus too, and for that matter, I think there's some antigay stuff in there and Mom certainly never cared about that. But still. I was lying there on the table thinking, what will Mom say? 'Cause maybe she'd think that spending all the money on something like that was dumb *and* that a great big spread of ink was something I'd regret when I'm older. So I chickened out. And that's how I ended up with the world's tiniest tattoo."

"I like it," Wes said. He kissed his fingertip and touched it lightly against the tiny dot.

"You don't think I'm an idiot?"

"Parker, you are many things. An idiot is definitely not one of them."

Smiling with what might have been relief, Parker grabbed Wes's fingertip and pressed his lips briefly to it. Then he let go and slithered completely under the blankets.

Wes took a deep shuddering breath and decided he was capable of a second round.

Chapter Thirteen

Wes was so damned hard to read. But he didn't regret the previous night, Parker was certain of that. Wes had awakened with a smile on his face and an eagerness to participate in Round Three. Morning sex was the best kind. Maybe not as earth-shaking as the First Time—and holy fuck, that had been amazing!—but slower and sweeter. The First Time was like some kind of Asian fusion dish, all succulent meats, delicious veggies, and firecracker spices. The Second Time, right before they fell asleep, was a filling side dish of carbs and complex sauces. But the morning sex was dessert. Rich bread pudding with fruit and caramel sauce, the kind of treat you savored slowly, exclaiming all the time that you were totally full and couldn't possibly eat any more while continuing to spoon it into your mouth.

Parker was hard just thinking back on Round Three. He squirmed a bit in Morrison's passenger seat.

So yeah, Wes had definitely been on board with all three courses. But he wouldn't commit to Thanksgiving dinner, which was weird because a shared feast seemed a smaller commitment than sex. And now as they navigated through traffic south of Seattle, Wes was monosyllabic at best.

On the other hand, Parker babbled. He knew he was running at the mouth—going on about music and movies and the time he worked for three months at a mail store. "You wouldn't believe the things people try to ship and the creative ways they wrap things," he said. Wes laughed in the right places, so he was probably listening.

But even Parker wasn't paying full attention to his own ramblings, because his mind was in turmoil. He had so many whirling emotions that he couldn't begin to deal with them all. Delight at hooking up with Wes. Joy over a perfect date night with dinner and a late-night cruise. Uncertainty about his own future and his future with Wes. Anxiety over informing Rhoda that he and Wes were maybe sort of a thing. Curiosity about what had happened with Rhoda and that Bob Martinez guy. Sadness at Logan's fate. Distress over the knowledge that the real story of what happened to Logan would likely never be resolved.

Those final couple of thoughts finally stopped his chatter. "Thanks for going with me," he said. "Not the fun parts, although thanks for those too. I mean the part with Detective Saito."

"That wasn't fun."

"Not even a little." Parker drummed his fingers on his leg, then on the armrest. He recognized the current song as something Rhoda listened to occasionally, but he didn't know the band's name. Why did Wes have such an old-fashioned taste in music? Parker didn't mind—in fact he liked Wes's music—but most people Wes's age weren't that into groups from the sixties and seventies.

"Seattle PD isn't going to do anything about Logan, are they?"

Wes hesitated before answering. "They might poke around a little more. But no."

"I get it. I do. He's dead already, and all the investigating in the world won't change that. I'm sure they have lots of other things to worry about—people to save and bad guys to send to jail. But Logan…. They look at the case and see a twentysomething queer guy who just got fired from his job babysitting dogs, who owed back rent even though he was spending a lot of money on a bigass tattoo, who liked to smoke weed and play video games. He wasn't going anywhere in life and wasn't especially important to anyone." He sniffed and added the rest in a whisper. "Not even to his boyfriend."

Wes reached over to pat his knee. "You cared about him. Maybe you didn't love him, but you cared."

"Yeah. It would be nice if the cops did too."

WES DROPPED Parker off at P-Town, where he was going to put in a few hours of work. He felt a little guilty for abandoning the place on short notice again, and Rhoda probably needed the afternoon off to get ready for Thanksgiving. "You can come in, you know," he said to Wes as he slid out of Morrison. "Hang out. If Nevin's there, I'll make sure he plays nice."

"Thanks. I have stuff to do."

"Okay. Will you be back tonight? You can spend the night again. On the couch or in my bed." Because Rhoda would just have to deal.

Parker wasn't a kid. And now that he thought of it, the idea of making love in his mother's house, having to stay really quiet in the process… that was kind of hot, in a kinky fantasy kind of way.

"Probably not."

Wes didn't offer an excuse. Not that he owed Parker one; a one-night fling didn't chain them at the hip. But God, it sure would be nice if Wes would be clear about what was going on in his head, because Parker didn't have a clue.

"Okay," Parker said.

"Last night…. Thank you. It's the best time I've had in… well, ever."

"Me too." And that was the truth. Even without the sex, the company had been wonderful. Wes had truly listened to Parker, no matter how much Parker blathered on. As if Parker was really interesting. And when Wes made a little joke, which he didn't do often, it was like receiving a special gift.

Somebody beeped at Wes, who was double-parked.

"I hope you join us tomorrow at least," said Parker. "Food's usually ready around threeish, but people start showing up a couple hours before that, and we keep eating until it's late and we're ready to burst."

"Okay."

"And no need to bring anything. In case you wondered, I mean. Some people bring dishes to share, but we always have way more food than we can possibly eat. Mom makes it her mission to ensure everyone gains five pounds no matter what."

Wes's little smile was enough to break Parker's heart. "Sounds nice. But I can't—"

"Maybe you can. Don't say no. Or even if you do say no, you can come anyway." He was three seconds away from begging, and the only thing that saved his dignity was a longer honk from the car Wes was blocking.

"Take care, Parker."

"You too." Parker shut the door and watched Wes drive away. He had no idea if he'd ever see him again.

IT WAS almost midnight by the time Parker got home. A barista named Clover had stayed to help him close P-Town for the night, and she'd been nice enough to give him a ride to Rhoda's house. Wes hadn't shown up.

Although Parker tried to creep inside so as not to disturb Rhoda, it turned out he didn't have to. She sat at the kitchen table with a mug of what was probably herbal tea. She wore neon green leggings, a Pink Floyd T-shirt that once belonged to Parker's dad, and her frumpiest gray cardigan. "Thanks for closing tonight, Gonzo."

"No problem. But shouldn't you be asleep?"

She waved toward the oven. "One last pie. Salted caramel apple. It'll be out soon." The entire house smelled amazing, like sugar and cinnamon and cookies. Rhoda generally wasn't fond of cooking, but she got into it for Thanksgiving.

"What time should I get up to help tomorrow?"

"Before noon?" She winked. "Things are mostly under control. You can make some cranberry sauce, if you like."

"Sure." That had been his dad's duty, once upon a time, and they still used his recipe.

Parker filled a glass with water from the refrigerator dispenser and sat opposite her. She looked tired, which made sense since she'd probably gotten up at five. But it was a relaxed kind of exhaustion, the kind that meant satisfaction in a job well done.

"How was Seattle?" Rhoda asked.

Parker's cheeks flushed with a quick memory of exploring Wes's naked body. But of course she wasn't referring to that. "Sucky. The detective was polite, but nothing's going to come of it."

"I'm sorry, honey." She reached across to take his hand. "You tried."

"I guess."

"And what about Wes? You enjoyed your time together?"

Dammit. Now he blushed even worse. "Yeah. He's pretty great, actually. I invited him for tomorrow, by the way, but I don't think he'll come."

"Why not?"

He groaned and laid his head on his arms. "Because I suck at relationships." The table muffled his words, but he was pretty sure she understood anyway.

"No, you don't. You're everything I could hope for in a son. You're a good friend too."

"I suck at romantic relationships." And that was the heart of it. Guys had fun with him for a night or maybe even a week or so, but that was it. Then they decided he wasn't boyfriend material and moved on. Wes was a special case, of course—he might never decide *anyone* was boyfriend material—but that was even sadder, because Parker really liked him and hated for him to be lonely.

"Maybe you're thinking too hard about it. You don't need a steady partner to be a complete person, kiddo. You're valuable in your own right."

He groaned again, mostly because he'd heard this speech before. Then he thought of a way to change the subject. He lifted his head and blinked at her with faux innocence. "Any interesting new customers lately, Mom?"

She blushed this time, and that was astounding. He'd never seen her do that before. In fact, he would have sworn she was nearly incapable of embarrassment. One day when he was in seventh grade and she was home with a cold, Parker got sent to the principal's office for throwing an apple at another kid. The office called her, and Rhoda showed up at school wearing flannel rubber-ducky-print pajamas, a fuzzy lavender bathrobe, and a dorky knitted pompom cap, and yelled at the principal for ignoring the fact that the apple victim had been bullying and taunting Parker for months. Parker had wanted to both melt under a desk and give her an enormous, thankful hug.

"You instigated this," she said now, pointing a finger.

Parker fluttered his eyelashes and clapped a hand to his chest. "*Moi?*"

"You didn't even tell Bob you're my son."

"True, but he figured it out, didn't he?" He raised his eyebrows. "He's another cop, isn't he?"

"Prosecutor. Retired."

That made him snort. "Better yet. Anyway, he seemed nice."

"Nice."

"You're valuable in your own right, Mom, but that doesn't mean you have to stay single. You can at least give him a whirl."

She flapped a hand at him. "I'm too busy to date."

"Bull. You can take an hour off and have lunch with him." Then Parker had a thought. "Does he have Thanksgiving plans? He's new in town, you know. Probably spending tomorrow alone. Eating a TV dinner." Did they still have TV dinners? Maybe they should be called internet dinners now.

"I don't have any way to contact him."

"You know his name and that he lives within a few blocks of P-Town. Give Nevin that much info and I'll bet he could track Bob down in less than an hour."

She flapped her hand again and gave him a dismissive *pfft*, but he recognized that glint in her eyes. He'd planted an idea. And once Rhoda got an idea, she rarely let it go.

He swallowed his water in one long chug, stood, and carried the glass to the dishwasher. "Night, Mom."

"Sweet dreams, honey."

Parker curled up in bed and was nearly asleep when his phone buzzed. He almost ignored it, but when it buzzed again, he looked blearily at the screen. His heart sped when he saw it was from Wes, but the message puzzled him:

Where was Logan getting his tattoo?

Chapter Fourteen

After dropping Parker off at P-Town, Wes stopped at a gas station. He leaned against the van as the tank filled and tried to think about his next project. He hadn't quite completed the nautical table because he'd constructed Rhoda's gift instead, but another day or so of work would finish the piece. Since his bank account was getting a little low, he was thinking of making something very expensive next. Something a well-heeled Portlander could use and enjoy. A desk, maybe. Not overly large, but with lots of cubbies and interesting visual details. And incorporating something really unique as drawer pulls. Maybe those vintage cufflinks he found in a thrift shop several months earlier? He'd gleefully picked up an entire box of them for a few dollars.

He climbed into Morrison and headed toward the freeway. But as hard as he tried to steer his thoughts toward that desk, they kept veering in a different direction altogether. To Parker, of course. Who'd somehow managed to pierce a heart Wes long ago judged impregnable.

Wes couldn't even put a finger on what drew him so hard to Parker. Sure, Parker was handsome, but Wes had fucked prettier men and then walked away without a second thought. Parker was also interesting and vibrant, a splash of bright color in Wes's drab life. Even more important, though, he seemed to look at Wes and see someone of value. Someone worth his time.

Snorting at his own ridiculousness, Wes neared the freeway. But when he got there, he impulsively took the northbound on-ramp instead of the south.

The traffic hadn't improved since the previous day's trip to Seattle. Most people were probably heading up to meet with family for Thanksgiving. Wes felt a sharp pang, imagining what it would be like to spend the holiday with Parker, surrounded by good food and laughter and companionship. But that kind of thing was for friends, not outsiders. As an adult he'd never spent his solitary holidays mooning around. In fact, the peace and solitude were big improvements over his childhood, when stepparents and half-siblings squabbled around him, somehow reminding him with every word that he didn't belong in their house.

No, Wes would complete this little errand, and if nothing came of it, he'd return to his bus and his tools. In the unlikely event he *did* discover something, he'd send a text to Parker. And then he'd go home to his bus.

Barkin' Lot was crowded with dogs of all imaginable kinds. Maybe the place was always busy, but he suspected Thanksgiving was also a contributor. Parker had mentioned that his former employer boarded dogs as well as entertaining them during the day. Most likely a lot of people had dropped off their pets and left the city for the long holiday weekend. Wes waited just inside the doorway while a fortyish woman provided information and then said goodbye to a German shepherd named Courtney. When the young woman behind the counter finished getting Courtney checked in and settled with another employee, Wes stepped forward.

"Hi. Do you have a couple of minutes to answer a few questions?"

The woman—her tag read Ophelia—blinked at him. "Are you doing a poll? The election's over, thank God."

"No, nothing like that." Wes took a deep breath and metaphorically donned his best bullshitting shoes. He hadn't worn them in years. "I'm a private investigator. I'm inquiring about a former employee."

A sensible person would have asked to see some form of ID or even his license. But as he'd hoped, Ophelia's eyes widened and her jaw dropped. Clearly she was caught up in the unexpected appearance of something more exciting than dog shit. "Is somebody wanted by the law?" she asked.

"No. It's Logan Miller."

He hadn't known whether she'd even be aware of Logan's death, but sorrow descended on her face. "Oh, poor Logan," she said with a sniff. "He killed himself, right? That's what I heard."

"I'm sorry. I'm not at liberty to share details."

"Oh. Right."

"Did you know him very well?"

She shifted uncomfortably. "Um, sort of. We worked together for about a year, I guess, and we talked. But we didn't hang out or anything."

"I understand. Do you know who he did hang out with?"

"Parker mostly. He used to work here too, and they were dating. Nobody was officially supposed to know, but we all totally did. I don't know what Parker—" She shut her mouth quickly.

Wes cocked his head. "What?"

Ophelia looked around as if she was afraid someone might be listening. Then she spoke in a voice not much above a whisper. "Parker's super sweet, but Logan is—Logan *was* kind of a jerk. I know you're not supposed to say bad things about the dead, but he was. He was fantastic with dogs. But he didn't treat people very well. And he owed me a hundred bucks."

Although Wes was saddened to hear Parker's ex hadn't been worthy of him, that wasn't the point at the moment. "Why did he borrow money from you?"

"He said his little brother was sick and didn't have enough money to buy medicine. That was, like, a month ago. Logan was supposed to pay me back when he got paid next, but he didn't. And now he can't."

"I'm sorry. Did he owe money to other people too?"

"Yeah. A couple people chipped in 'cause everyone thought his brother really needed it."

Interesting. "Okay. So aside from Parker, did he have any particular friends?"

"Not here. Parker only worked here a couple months. Before that, Logan mostly kept to himself."

Wes asked a few other questions, but she didn't seem to know anything else useful. When a father and young son entered the building with something small and yappy in a carrier, Wes thanked Ophelia and left.

His next stop was Parker and Logan's old place, an apartment complex that had seen better days. A helpful sign designated the manager's unit, and Wes rang the bell.

A tiny woman in her fifties answered, peering at him dubiously. "Yes?"

Wes repeated his private investigator story. The manager bought it as easily as Ophelia had, but with no apparent sympathy for Logan. "He owed three months' rent," she said, leaning in the doorway with arms crossed. "They can afford to hire you, but they can't pay what he owes?"

"I'm sorry. I can't do—"

"I know, I know. What do you want from me?"

"I'm trying to learn more about his death. Can you tell me anything?"

She seemed to consider for a moment before giving a quick nod. "All right. Come inside."

It was a small apartment crammed with too much big furniture and a lot of knickknacks, most of them frog themed. Photos of, he assumed, her children and grandchildren crowded the walls. She led Wes into the kitchen, which smelled faintly of fish and onions and where dirty dishes rested in the sink. He sat at the table and accepted a mug of instant coffee. He was surprised anyone still drank the stuff, at least in the Land of Starbucks.

Now that she'd allowed him inside, she seemed inclined to small talk. Her name was Cathy, and Wes sipped his coffee as he politely listened to her complain about tenants who made too much noise, trashed their units, or parked in the visitor parking spots.

"Did Logan do those things?" he finally asked.

"No, he was pretty good until he stopped paying. I thought things would improve when that boy with the colorful hair moved in—nice boy—but they didn't. Now that boy's gone, and Logan's dead." She moved her fingers as if she were used to having something in them. A cigarette, Wes guessed. He wondered how long ago she'd quit.

"I'm sure you already spoke with the police—"

"I'm the one who called 'em! I found him." She made a shuddery motion.

"Can you tell me about that?"

"Well, I went to see about the rent. Again. But the door was open a crack. I knocked, and nobody answered, and I thought maybe he'd just skipped out. It happens. Anyway, I pushed the door a little so I could see inside—I wasn't going to step in without permission; I know the rules—and there he was, right in the middle of the floor. I called 911."

Would someone with suicidal intent OD in the center of the room rather than somewhere more comfortable, like on a couch or the bed? It was possible Logan started out someplace comfy and then staggered away before collapsing. But that didn't explain the door being ajar.

"It must have been traumatic for you," Wes said.

"I've found bodies before. It happens. I was surprised with this one, though."

"Why?"

Now she rubbed her palms together, making a dry, papery sound. "He just didn't seem like the type. He lived here almost two years, and until lately he was a good tenant. Paid on time, never had loud friends over. He smelled like pot sometimes, but they're all doing that nowadays. I didn't think he was a druggie. When I saw him, he'd talk about how he wanted to start his own business someday."

"What kind of business?"

"Dogs. Like the place where he worked. But he hadn't mentioned that in a while. Actually I hadn't seen him. He was probably avoiding me because of the rent."

Wes asked more questions about Logan's past and his habits, but he learned very little. Before Parker moved in, Logan occasionally had a male friend over, sometimes for the night. But not often. And once Parker was there, never. "Except for the one with the tattoos," she said. "He came over a few weeks ago."

Wes had been starting to slump in his chair, but now he sat up straight. "Tattoos?"

"Everywhere." She ran a hand over her arms and neck. "Everywhere I could see except his face."

"Do you know who he is? Or anything else about him?"

"He'd parked his car in one of the resident spots, and I went out to ask him to move. He said he was there to visit Logan. I asked why. He didn't look reputable, and not just because of the tattoos. He said he was there to consult about a tattoo with Logan. That's the word he used: consult. I told him they couldn't do that in the apartment—I don't want blood and ink stains—and he just laughed and walked away."

Cathy described the man's car without much detail. An older gray Ford, she thought. And that was all the information she had about him.

Wes's stomach had begun to grumble. He hadn't eaten anything since a bowl of oatmeal at the hotel restaurant that morning, and it was clear Cathy had told him everything she could. He thanked her for her time and the coffee, then left.

Not too far away, he found a modest little sandwich-and-burger place. He ate slowly, thinking about what he'd learned from Ophelia and Cathy. Not much, but he'd unearthed a few nuggets that might prove valuable. When he tried to puzzle them out, though, his mind strayed to a related matter. Why had Parker become close with Logan in the first place? It didn't sound as if Logan had many endearing qualities. Surely

Parker couldn't have simply been desperate for a place to live. He always had Rhoda to fall back on for that, and even his mother's house would seem a better option that shacking up with an asshole. No, it must have been more than a need for housing.

What about a need for affection? Maybe. But Parker could have found someone better than Logan. Unless Parker thought he didn't deserve better. He seemed to overlook his own value, which was ironic given his gift for seeing the strengths of others.

The burger gone, Wes lingered over mediocre coffee. He wasn't thinking about Logan at all now, but rather about himself—and Parker. Somehow Wes had never pictured himself having an evening like last night. A nice dinner with a fascinating companion, a walk through the city, a small water journey. Those things seemed too special for a guy who made furniture and lived in a bus. But he'd had them, at least for one night, and they'd fit him surprisingly well.

Could he possibly have a future with somebody else? Not just anybody else. Parker Levin. God, he found himself turning toward that concept like a plant leaning toward the sun. But just because he wanted it didn't mean he could have it. He didn't know whether he was capable of a relationship, assuming Parker was willing to give it a try.

Why couldn't people be like furniture? You found the raw material, you cut pieces to fit, and you put everything together. With care, that table or bookshelf could last for decades. Centuries, even. But humans came in all sorts of weird shapes and never seemed to mesh with each other very well, and even if you did your best, they almost inevitably fell apart. They abandoned you or died, and then you were left with great gaping holes where they used to attach to you.

The waiter came by for the third time to see if Wes needed anything else. Taking the hint, Wes paid the bill and wandered out to Morrison. He drove around the city for what might have been two hours but could have been longer. Not really thinking of anything and with no destination in mind. Just going in large random circles.

He finally found a modest, quiet residential neighborhood and parked Morrison at the curb, out of the glare of the streetlights. No hotel for him tonight; he'd sleep in the back. He'd last used some of the old blankets to protect Rhoda's gift, and now as he wrapped himself inside them, he imagined them as his connection to Parker.

Maybe he should give up this stupid thing he was doing in Seattle. Maybe he should drive to Portland in the morning and spend Thanksgiving with Parker and Rhoda and a cast of thousands. Maybe he should drive to Wyoming. Or maybe he should just drive home and start on that desk.

After endless tossing and turning, he reached at least one decision. He pulled out his phone, which was low on charge, and sent a text.

Where was Logan getting his tattoo?

Parker didn't answer for a long time, which could have been because he was angry at Wes or because he was asleep. Finally he sent a single word: *Why?*

Wes didn't want to explain, mostly because he didn't want Parker to get his hopes up when Wes would likely not receive any answers. So after gathering his courage, he made a promise instead. *I'll explain over turkey tomorrow.*

Good. I want you here, Wes. I miss you.

Me too.

Funny how admitting that truth was harder than spending the afternoon lying to people. But it felt good once it was out.

I think the name of the place was Anza something.

Thanks. Good night, Parker.

Parker replied with a heart emoji, which made Wes laugh.

ANZA RISING was located in a two-story triangular-shaped building in a neighborhood that might be on the edge of gentrifying but hadn't gotten there yet. The upper floor was probably an apartment; the windows there were curtained and dark. But those on the ground floor remained brightly lit, even though it was past midnight. Maybe people had sudden urges to get inked in the wee hours before Thanksgiving, perhaps in hopes of impressing or appalling their relatives.

There were no spaces big enough for Morrison in front of the building, so Wes parked on a side street two blocks away. Even though his shoes had rubber soles, his footsteps seemed loud in the empty night.

When he got near, he saw an old Ford parked nearby. It was hard to tell in the darkness, but it could have been gray. He paused in a shadow to look through the building's windows. The studio itself looked more upscale than he expected, with plush furniture and potted palms in the waiting area, tasteful framed drawings of fantasy animals on the wall, and good lighting overhead. A woman with long straight hair the color of champagne sat on a tall stool behind a counter, looking at her phone. Behind her, a heavily tattooed man in his early thirties looked as if he was just finishing some work on a bearded man's arm. While Wes watched, the artist wiped the other man's bicep clean and put a large bandage over it. But the customer, who didn't seem inclined to leave yet, remained in the chair, chatting with the artist.

I'm in this far.

Everyone looked up when Wes entered the shop. "Sorry, we're closing," the woman said. "I can make an appointment for next week."

"I actually just wanted to ask a few questions, if that's okay."

She glanced at the artist, who shrugged, then looked back at Wes. "Okay. Just a sec."

Wes sat in a leather chair to wait. He liked the music playing softly over the speakers—Black Sabbath, he thought, although he wasn't well-versed in heavy metal. A large binder lay on the coffee table in front of him, and he leafed through the photos of tattoos, many of which featured animals. He wasn't an expert by any means, but it looked like quality work. He thought idly about what he'd get if he ever decided he wanted ink, but nothing seemed important enough to be permanently inscribed. He remembered the faded blue marks on his grandfather's arms, relics of his time in the Korean War. His grandfather never spoke about them. Maybe Wes should get a tiny dot like Parker's.

"What can I do for you?"

While Wes was lost in memories, the customer had left, and the artist approached him. The woman was wiping down the chair.

Wes stood and held out his hand. "Wes Anker." He'd considered a pseudonym, but what was the point? This guy had no idea who he was anyway.

The artist gave his hand a brief but firm shake. "Leo Cavelli."

"You do nice work."

"Thanks, man. But it's late. If you want a consult, come back Monday and we can talk."

"I'm not here for a consult." Wes raised his chin a little. "Did you know Logan Miller?"

Was that sudden wariness on Cavelli's face? Maybe. He glanced at the woman, who was still cleaning the area around the chair. "Yeah, I know him. I'm doing some work on his back. Big piece. Why?"

"Did you know he's dead?"

Something flashed very quickly across Cavelli's face before his expression settled on a facsimile of surprise. "Nah. What happened?"

Wes decided to throw the dice. "Murder, maybe. We're not sure."

Another fleeting expression. Alarm, maybe? "Shit! Who'd do that to Miller?"

"We're trying to find out. Maybe you can give me some useful information."

"You ain't no cop."

It was funny. Although Cavelli spoke coarsely and wore battered jeans and an old Judas Priest tee, Wes had the impression it was an act. He suspected Cavelli came from middle-class suburban stock. His nice, straight teeth were clearly the result of orthodontic work, for instance, and his shoes looked expensive. His hands were smooth and uncallused except for the parts in contact with the tattoo gun.

"I'm a friend of the family," Wes said with a small degree of accuracy. "We're just looking for the truth."

Cavelli squinted at him for a long time before apparently reaching a decision. He turned and called to the woman. "I'll get it, Coco. You can go home."

She dropped her cleaning supplies at once. Within moments she'd gathered her phone and jacket, said good night, and left. Cavelli locked the door behind her. "Don't want any more walk-ins tonight," he explained.

"You're working late."

"Gonna take a long weekend, but bills gotta be paid."

"I know how that is."

Cavelli crossed his arms. "So whatta ya wanna know about Miller?"

"How well did you know him?"

"Told you. He was a customer. A big piece like his, that takes a lot of hours. Ya get to talking with a guy, you know?"

That relationship sounded too casual for Cavelli to have paid a visit to Logan's apartment. "What did you talk about?"

"Dunno. Regular shit, I guess. He was really into dogs, so I heard a lot about that." He gave his lips what might have been a nervous lick. "And, uh, he talked about his boyfriend. Sounds like they were having problems."

"What kind?"

"Not exactly sure. I think Logan had an expensive little problem, though, you know? His boyfriend was probably pissed about that."

At this point Wes was certain Cavelli was delving into pure fiction, which probably meant he had something to hide. But Wes needed more if he was going to get Saito to take him seriously. So he pushed further. "What kind of problem? Gambling? Shopping?"

"Drugs."

That fit neatly with the fact that Logan had overdosed, but it contradicted Parker, who believed Logan just used weed. Even a pretty big pot habit wasn't usually enough to cause troubles for someone. Plus it sounded as if Logan had been reliable at his job, which tended to be inconsistent with a bad addiction.

"Do you think his drug problem could have got him killed?"

"I dunno, man. He didn't tell me much about it."

"Do you know who his dealer was?"

"No! Like I said, he didn't talk about it much. Just the damn dogs."

Wes doubted dogs had anything to do with this, but he needed a few moments to consider his next line of inquiry. "What about dogs? Breeding them?"

"Nah. He was gonna open a business, he said. Like a pet supply store—really high end—plus a kennel. He said it was gonna make him rich. All these assholes who work in tech, they make a ton of dough and they don't have time for real kids, so they have dogs and cats instead. And they're willing to spend a fortune to make sure Fifi has fancy collars and leashes and a kennel like the fucking Ritz."

That made some sense, especially because it fit with what others had told Wes. It didn't necessarily sound like the plans of a guy who was zonked out on drugs. And Cavelli seemed to know a lot about Logan's dream, which belied his initial claim of them having only a casual relationship.

While Wes thought about this, Cavelli cocked his head. "What makes you think someone murdered him anyway? I mean, he was pretty down about his boyfriend. And he was a heavy user. Shit happens."

Even more bullshit. "There are some indications," Wes said vaguely. "Things that don't make sense."

"Well, I don't know any more than what I've told you."

"How much was the tattoo costing him?"

"I'd have to look at my books. Prob'ly around a grand. Lotta hours going into it."

Wes nodded. "Sure. Had he paid for it already?"

"Nah. He was doing installments."

"Did he ever mention he was having money problems? Aside from the drugs, I mean?"

"Dunno. Might've." Cavelli shifted his feet. "You wanna take a look at the piece I was doing for him? I got photos."

"Sure." Wes didn't particularly care what the tattoo looked like, but it would give him an excuse to delay a little longer and try to extract something incriminating. By now he strongly suspected Cavelli was somehow involved in Logan's death, but he didn't know how or why.

Cavelli walked to the back of the shop and disappeared through a door. When he returned a minute or two later, he carried a binder similar to the one on the table. "These are my ongoing pieces." He handed over the binder. "I like to take pics for reference."

Wes began to slowly flip pages as Cavelli looked over his shoulder. "There. That's him."

Wes could see only Logan's back, which disappointed him. He'd hoped for a glimpse of Parker's ex-lover's face. Would Wes see any similarities to his own? Did Parker have a type? And if so, was Wes it? What he could see was light brown neck-length hair, a little crooked at the edge, as if it were cut by an unskilled barber or had grown unevenly. Beneath that, an expanse of pale skin. Logan had broad shoulders and a slight suggestion of love handles above the waist of his blue jeans. A substantial man, although Wes couldn't tell how tall.

The tattoo took up almost his entire back, although parts of it had only black outlines and hadn't been shaded or colored yet. A large black lab sat in the center, staring intently forward. It was beautifully detailed, every strand of fur seeming to stand in relief. Even in the photo, it looked almost three-dimensional. Smaller versions of other breeds encircled the lab. They held a variety of poses—running, lying, jumping. A border collie, suspended in midair, was about to catch a ball. A Saint Bernard pulled a cart. A shaggy black dog swam.

Would someone really put this much time and thought into a body decoration and kill himself before it was finished? Seemed unlikely.

"Wow," Wes said, bending to look closer. "That's—"

Something moved fast at the corner of his eye. Wes started to whirl to face it—which meant he caught the blow on the side of his head. He staggered and dropped the binder, but he didn't hear it hit the floor because his world had gone eerily silent.

And then the world went dark as well.

Chapter Fifteen

Parker's nose woke him up. The house was filled with the delicious scents of roasting turkey and melted butter and warm spices. He yawned, stretched, and checked his phone, but there was nothing new from Wes. Parker had been too sleepy last night to give proper thought to Wes's question about Logan's tattoo, but now his curiosity redoubled. What was Wes up to?

Parker grabbed some clothes and shambled to the bathroom, calling out as he passed through the hallway. "I'm up, Mom. Be there soon."

He showered quickly, shaved and brushed, and pulled on sweats and a tee for now. Rhoda encouraged him to dress up a little for the holiday, but he'd do that later, shortly before guests were due to arrive.

In the kitchen, Rhoda was swaying to Billie Holiday and chopping celery. Parker swooped in to give her a kiss on the cheek. "Morning."

"Hey, Gonzo. You're in a good mood."

"Hmm." He poured himself a glass of milk, chugged it, and rinsed out the glass. Then he gobbled a ham-and-cheese croissant left over from the previous day at P-Town. "What can I help with?"

"You can get the tables and everything all set up."

Parker went down to the basement, the repository of boxes full of his kindergarten art projects, clothing from previous decades that Rhoda couldn't bring herself to give away, mysterious piles of gardening implements, curtains his parents had replaced after moving into the house, and an ugly couch that had gotten down the stairs via a miracle and was never coming back up. He found the folding table, festooned in cobwebs, leaning against a wall behind the furnace and used a rag to wipe it down. He hoped he was wiping away any resident spiders as well. Then he wrestled the table upstairs.

Thanksgiving involved far too many guests to seat in one place, so Rhoda served the meal buffet style, and people ate wherever. Parker set up the folding table against one wall in the dining room and moved the regular table against the opposite wall. He draped matching colorful tablecloths—sporting turkeys, leaves, and pumpkins—and set out the huge set of white china Rhoda had acquired cheap through one of her food-service sources. He also got out about a zillion sets of flatware, a couple dozen wineglasses, and a bunch of mugs for spiced cider.

Parker once asked her why she didn't just use paper and plasticware; it would have saved a lot of washing up. But she'd shaken her head firmly. "This is an occasion, kiddo. Occasions call for the real thing." Her one nod to convenience was paper napkins, but she used the fancy heavy kind.

After consulting with Rhoda, Parker put out the nonperishable foods and stepped back to assess his work. It looked good. No, better than good. It looked warm and inviting, a promise of friendship and laughter soon to happen. Because it was the right day for it, he took a few minutes to appreciate his blessings. He had a mother who loved him no matter what and who happily opened her home to him whenever he needed it. He never had to worry about going hungry or not having clothes to wear. He was healthy. He had a job at P-Town whenever he wanted one. He had wonderful friends. And then there was Wes….

Parker pulled out his phone and sent a quick text. *Missing you. Hope you're here soon.* There was still no reply after a few minutes. But maybe he was driving now, on his way from wherever he'd spent the night.

Parker occupied some time helping with food prep. Rhoda had bought a bunch of canapé shells she wanted filled with a mixture of salmon, cream cheese, chives, and capers. Filled *artistically*, she emphasized, so he fussed over them. Then he chopped veggies for a huge green salad he thought wasn't really necessary. In his opinion, this was one day when people could skimp on fresh veggies. Rhoda disagreed. It was a pretty salad, at least, with pomegranate seeds adding dots of color. He made a huge batch of his dad's cranberry sauce, which was laced with bourbon. When Parker was a teen, his dad used to let him sneak a little sip while Rhoda pretended not to notice.

Finally Parker changed into somewhat more formal clothing: maroon skinny jeans, a black-and-white-striped shirt, and a silvery blazer. He toyed with his hair too, arranging it various ways until he was satisfied. He turned on the living room speakers and reminded Rhoda to bring up her Thanksgiving playlist. The Beach Boys started singing about good vibrations.

Still nothing from Wes.

The first guest arrived minutes later: a former barista at P-Town who was now a social worker. She came with her six-year-old son and a pumpkin cheesecake. Parker had barely closed the front door when the bell rang again.

"Bob!" Parker exclaimed.

Bob Martinez stood in the doorway holding a bouquet and a cardboard wine carrier. "Your mother tracked me down. She's a resourceful woman."

"You don't know the half of it. Come on in. Mom's in the kitchen."

Then the guests came in a rush. Ptolemy arrived with their boyfriend, an older man who was a high school teacher. They came to P-Town together sometimes, even though Ptolemy no longer worked there, so Parker knew the boyfriend and liked him. Jeremy and Qay came, and two of the cat ladies, and Jeremy's friend Malcolm, and a guy named Al who was homeless when Rhoda first met him but now lived in transitional housing and seemed to be doing very well. John and Carter were there; they brought books instead of food, which delighted Rhoda. Some people stopped by for a while even though they'd be attending dinners elsewhere, like Drew and Karl, who played music at P-Town once a week, and their partners, Travis and Ery. Nevin and Colin would be going later to Colin's parents' house, but they always made a point to come to Rhoda's too.

The house filled with people. It was loud, a little chaotic, and utterly wonderful. Everyone smiled and laughed and nibbled on appetizers. People kept adding their favorite songs to the playlist. Travis dropped and broke a glass, earning the coveted Butterfingers Trophy: a generic football-trophy guy with a candy wrapper glued to his hands. Parker won it the previous year, and now everyone cheered as he handed it over. Travis bowed deeply before accepting. Rhoda was everywhere, cooking, serving, schmoozing. She seemed to spend extra time with Bob, and she just *glowed*. Parker was pretty certain her version of heaven looked exactly like this gathering.

Although Parker circulated, he also checked his phone. Often. When Rhoda took the turkey out of the oven and announced she'd start carving in twenty minutes, Parker couldn't stand it anymore. He sent another text. *Hey, we're about to eat. We'll have plenty of leftovers whenever you get here, but I hope it's soon.*

It remained unread.

Rhoda had used some kind of maple glaze on the turkey, and there was a mountain of fluffy mashed potatoes. Ery had brought the sweet-potato casserole that was one of Parker's very favorite foods. There was an abundance of wonderful dishes prepared with love by people Parker cared about—and it all tasted like ashes.

Although Parker couldn't manage to choke down much food, he tried to at least appear festive. He wasn't especially successful. He was in the process of feeling grateful that Rhoda was too busy to notice his mood, when Jeremy pulled him to a relatively quiet corner of the living room. "What's up?" Jeremy asked.

"Nothing."

Parker tried to walk away, but Jeremy took his arm and dragged him down the hall, then stood there and blocked his escape. "Why are you miserable, Parker?"

Jeremy was a very big man. Parker couldn't push by him, and tackling him was a no-go. That left giving in or standing sullenly in the hallway until Rhoda noticed their absence. "It's Wes," Parker said with a sigh. "He said he'd be here today."

Wincing, Jeremy rubbed the back of his neck. "Look. I believe that Wes is a good person, but he's also troubled. You probably don't want to get mixed up with him."

"Qay was troubled, and you got mixed up with him."

Jeremy's turn to sigh. "Yes, I did. And I'm really glad I did. But it wasn't easy. We love each other to the depths of our hearts, and yet some days it's *still* not easy."

Parker folded his arms. "You don't think I'm strong enough to handle some adversity. Or man enough."

"That is *not* what I think. I admire you. Things happen to you—sometimes bad things—and you keep picking yourself up and trying again with a kind of optimism I really envy. And you're never ashamed to be who you truly are, which is something a lot of us don't achieve until we're a lot older."

His handsome face was open and sincere, and Parker's anger evaporated. He'd always assumed Jeremy viewed him as Rhoda's dumb kid, not as someone to be respected. "I don't mind a challenge if the guy's worth it. And I think Wes is."

"Maybe. But here's the thing—and it's something I didn't understand until well after Qay and I started dating. Until I almost lost him, actually.

You can't fix someone else's problems. Nobody can. You can support them and love them. You can give them advice if they want it. You can let them know you'll still be there even when they screw up. You can *understand* them. But in the end, each of us has to heal ourself."

Instead of being dismissive, Parker took a few moments to honestly consider what Jeremy had said. It made sense, really. After all, Parker knew that however much Rhoda cared about him, she couldn't make him get his life together. But it sure helped to know she was there—like a security blanket—while he was trying to figure things out. And Parker was willing to be that for Wes, if Wes would have him.

"I understand," he said.

Jeremy gave him a long, thoughtful look and then nodded. "I think you do. But he's not here today."

Parker decided to air a thought that had been creeping around his brain. "I know Wes has faults. But is being unreliable one of them? Or lying?"

"Not that I've seen."

"If he changed his mind about showing up, I think he'd say so. Maybe not very elegantly, 'cause he's not great at expressing himself that way. But I don't think he'd just ignore me."

"Then why isn't he here?"

"I don't know." Parker finally admitted what had been bothering him. "I'm worried about him."

"Why?"

"He sent me this weird text last night."

Parker showed Jeremy their conversation. Jeremy's face settled into a concerned frown, and he asked, "You don't think.... Was he trying to investigate Logan's death on his own?"

That would be stupid. But why else would he ask about the tattoo? Because he wanted one from the same artist as Logan? That made zero sense.

"I don't know." Parker felt miserable.

"Let me talk to Nevin about this."

"No. *We* talk to Nevin."

They returned to the living room, where Drew and Karl strummed "Hey Jude" on their guitars while everyone sang along. The room was so crowded that a lot of people had to sit on the floor or lean up against walls, but the event was still beautiful enough to make Parker's heart ache. He was immensely grateful to be a part of this. And God, he wished Wes could be a part too, even if they were just platonic. Wes deserved to belong to a family, and while Parker's extended family might be weird, he wouldn't trade it for any other.

Nevin and Colin stood with their arms around each other. Colin was clearly audible—he had a great voice and loved to sing—but Nevin appeared to be mouthing the words. Jeremy approached him and gestured at Parker and then the front door. Nevin's cop sense must have kicked in—Parker saw the lines of his face harden—and he whispered in Colin's ear. After Colin nodded, Nevin strode for the door with Jeremy and Parker close behind.

It was cold outside, but at least the small porch gave them protection from the rain. "What's up?" Nevin asked. Parker loved how Nevin and Jeremy were willing to jump in whenever they were needed, even on a holiday.

Parker explained the situation as succinctly as possible. Nevin listened attentively without interrupting and then eyed Parker closely. "You care about Wanker?"

"I think I'm falling in love with him."

"Well, fuck a duck." He sounded only mildly annoyed.

"You're not going to tell me I'm being stupid?"

"Of course you're being stupid. Love is stupid. The heart is the dumbest fucking organ in the body—even the asshole's twice as smart as the heart, and my dick's a genius compared to this." He thumped his chest. "But life requires more than just smarts, Smurf, and the heart's also really fucking strong."

"'An Ode to Ardor,' by Nevin Ng," Jeremy said.

"Shut up, Germy. You're an asshole. And hang on. I'm going to go get reamed out by Saito for calling her on a holiday." He jogged down the sidewalk and to the corner, where his purple GTO was parked in front of a hydrant. It was possible he couldn't find anyplace else to put his car, but Parker suspected Nevin enjoyed flouting parking regulations—especially since it annoyed Colin.

Parker and Jeremy watched the rain while they waited. "What do you think of Bob?" Parker asked, mainly to distract himself a little.

"Seems like a good guy. Did you arrange for him to be here?"

"I… enabled a little."

Jeremy chuckled. "You're a lot like your mother."

"No, she's always in control and on top of things. I'm a mess."

"You're really not."

Parker tried to imagine what Rhoda would do if someone she cared about went missing, possibly while investigating a suspicious death. She'd probably have SWAT teams and the FBI deployed immediately, and she'd be there, hovering overhead in a helicopter and shouting commands through a bullhorn. But not Parker. He'd dithered all through dinner and then still wouldn't have said anything if Jeremy hadn't cornered him. And even then, what did he do? Bleat helplessly and then stand by while Jeremy and Nevin took care of things.

Speaking of Nevin, he was jogging up to the porch, his face set in a deep scowl. "Mother Mary's tits. Detective Head-Up-Her-Ass is pissed," he announced when he arrived. He assumed a screechy falsetto more reminiscent of the Wicked Witch of the West than Detective Saito. "'What was he doing there? Why the fuck was he poking around my case?' I told her nobody would need to be poking around if she actually took care of her case."

Parker shook with anxiety. "What is she—"

"She's sending the goon squad to check the tattoo parlor. She'll call me when she hears from them."

Okay. A few deep yoga breaths. Something was being done.

Nevin continued, "How about if we go inside and pour you a few shots of whatever's strongest? Vodka with a vodka chaser."

"No." Parker wasn't much of a drinker, and he doubted even an entire bottle would make him feel better.

Jeremy put an arm around Parker's shoulders. "At least go inside. It's cold out here."

But Parker didn't feel the chill. He was numb, in fact, except for the shards of glass churning in his stomach. Nevertheless, he allowed himself to be steered indoors.

Rhoda was right there to intercept them. "What's wrong?"

But when Parker shot Nevin a desperate look, Nevin gently moved her out of the way. "Boy shit. We got it." Then he took the lead, Jeremy stepped in behind Parker, and they headed for Parker's room. Parker felt a little as if he were being guarded by the Secret Service, which would have been funny if he wasn't ready to puke with worry.

Inside the bedroom, Nevin motioned him to sit on the bed, then perched next to him while Jeremy stood guard at the closed door. "What do you suppose Mom thinks we're up to?" Parker said.

"Boy shit."

"Yeah, but what *is* boy shit?"

Nevin cocked an eyebrow. "Hard-on. King-Kong, pants-tenting, effects-lasting-more-than-four-hours, save-us-Superman hard-on. You needed to be shielded from innocent people's eyes until the horror abated."

Parker nodded sagely. "Savagely ingrown whiskers."

"An attack of latent heterosexuality. We're stopping you from going to Hooters because you have the sudden urge to eat deep-fried foods and ogle underpaid, underdressed waitresses."

They continued on like that for a few minutes. It was stupid and they all knew it, but better to be inane than to make himself sick wondering what was going on with Wes. Just as Parker was ready to try Nevin's vodka suggestion on the grounds that it couldn't hurt, Nevin's phone rang.

"Yeah?" Nevin listened for a moment, blank-faced, then looked at Parker. "What does Wanker drive?"

"Morrison." Ooh, smooth answer, Levin! Parker shook his head to clear it. "A white van."

"Oregon plates?"

"Um, yeah."

Nevin's mouth thinned to an unhappy line. "Yeah," he said into the phone. He listened again, then looked at Parker. "Try texting him again."

Parker's thumbs flew across the screen. *Are you there? I'm worried. No obligation—just tell me you're okay.*

The text bubble sat there with no response. He sent another. *Kinda freaking out here. Please just answer.* Nothing. Oh God. His heart felt like it might beat right out of his chest, but he tried again. And again. Fuck. Fuck. Fuck. Fine, he'd try calling instead. The call went straight to voicemail.

Parker looked helplessly at Nevin, who said something to Saito that Parker couldn't hear over the rushing in his ears. Nervelessly he dropped the phone onto the mattress as his vision blurred. He might have fainted if Jeremy hadn't lunged over to kneel in front of him.

"Breathe, Parker." Jeremy settled his heavy hands on Parker's shoulders, grounding Parker and making the buzz in his head clear a bit. "Breathe."

Bad air out, good air in. Out. In. Out. In. Nice and simple, and he concentrated on that.

Nevin poked irritably at his phone before tucking it into his jacket pocket. When he gazed at Parker, he radiated calmness and control, and his voice was even. "Shop's closed. No sign of anyone there. There's a residence upstairs, but nobody's answering the door. Saito's going to talk to her sergeant and see if she can get a warrant."

"Warrant?" Parker moaned. "Doesn't that need judges and courtrooms and—"

"No. She can get a phone warrant, and that's quick. But she has to have probable cause, and that's iffy with what we've got. So she's going to talk to her sergeant and see if they can make a persuasive enough case."

"They should just go in! Wes might be—" Parker swallowed, unable to voice any of the things Wes might be.

"Or he might be taking a walk after letting his phone battery go dead. I know being patient sucks balls, Smurf, but give the system the time it needs."

"I can't."

"You *can*," Jeremy said. "We're here with you. Let's just sit tight."

So Parker sat tight.

Chapter Sixteen

Wes was in his grandfather's basement. He recognized the familiar odors of damp concrete and wood and heard the familiar woosh-roar of the furnace, but he couldn't remember why he'd come down here. Was he supposed to bring up a tool? And... he was on the floor. The cold, hard floor. What the hell was he doing there? Groggy, he tried to get up.

He couldn't move. He thrashed in panic as he tried to free his hands and feet, but he couldn't untangle them, and he couldn't see, and he couldn't breathe, and oh God was he buried alive had a tree fallen on him was he dead and—

He quelled the urge to vomit, which ironically cleared his head slightly. He fought not to choke on his bile, since something blocked his mouth. And Jesus Christ, his head hurt.

With all the will he could muster, he made his body go limp, slowed his breathing, and got his bearings. He was... tied. Hogtied, actually, and the bindings dug deeply into his skin. He was gagged with a thick cloth, which he couldn't push out. That made sense when he felt tape—duct tape, probably—across his cheeks and pulling his hair.

Okay. Bound and gagged. Was he blindfolded too? Evidently not. As he turned his head, he could make out a faint light leaking around the edges of what might be a small covered window near the ceiling. So he was in a very dark room. In a basement. But not his grandfather's basement, obviously. His grandfather had been dead for years. Besides, his grandfather's basement was in southern Oregon, and Wes was... in Seattle. At the tattoo parlor.

Fuck.

He had received first-aid training at the academy, and his brain was at least clear enough to recognize its own injury. Concussion. That explained the loss of consciousness, the confusion, the headache, and the goddamn nausea—which he'd continue to fight because vomiting with a gag in his mouth would probably kill him, and that wasn't the way he wanted to go. Hell, he didn't want to go at all.

He ran through the other concussion symptoms—dizziness, blurred vision, slurred speech, noise and light sensitivity—but in his trussed condition, he couldn't assess whether he was experiencing any of them. Not that an accurate diagnosis was necessarily his biggest priority right now.

With more deliberate movements than before, he tried to loosen his bonds, which felt like nylon rope. But they wouldn't budge. He owned a dozen or more tools that could cut that rope easily, but those tools were over four hundred miles away. Hell, even if they were four feet away, they'd be useless without the use of his hands, and fantasizing about them wasn't doing him any good.

Few other options remained. Thanks to the gag, he could make only muffled moans. Even he could barely hear them over the rattle of the furnace. He could sort of squirm a little on his side, but it didn't get him anywhere and made his stomach heave, so he stopped. Fine. He would wait. But for what? For Cavelli to come and finish him off?

It was a small solace to know that Cavelli apparently didn't want him dead, at least for now. After all, if homicide were the primary goal, Cavelli could have slit Wes's throat while he was unconscious. Instead he'd tied him up and, judging from the bruised feeling along Wes's back, dragged him down the stairs. Wes didn't want to speculate on why he was still alive, but as long as he was breathing, there was hope of escape.

And hope of seeing Parker again. Jesus, Parker, whom he'd promised to see for Thanksgiving dinner. Wes found himself yearning for him with an intensity so sharp it made his headache feel like nothing in comparison. If Wes got another chance with Parker, he'd seize it. If there was a Future Wes, he belonged with Parker, wherever and however Parker would allow him into his life. Wes would hang on to him until Parker was ready for him to go—and whether that was in a day, a week, or a month, every minute would be treasured. Just the tickle of Parker's technicolor hair, the dancing joy in his eyes, the ring of his laughter. His scrutiny, so sharp, so *present*, and the way he jumped into things without looking twice, like a kid leaping into a swimming hole in August. The taste of his soft lips....

Okay. This wasn't getting him anywhere, although it was better than panic and *much* better than worrying about what was going to happen next.

Hey, cheer up, he told himself. *At least you've apparently solved the mystery of Logan's death.* Now if only he could get a chance to tell Parker.

HE SLEPT for a while, although he'd heard you were supposed to stay awake with a concussion. But he was so tired, and his skull felt like someone was jackhammering it from the inside, and there was really nothing else for him to do. So he dozed on and off, slipping in and out of fitful dreams about his childhood. And then the lights went on, spearing his eyes with bolts of agony.

Yes to the light sensitivity, then.

Two sets of feet thudded down wooden stairs behind him. Wes couldn't turn to face them, which was especially unnerving, but they obligingly tromped around until they were in his line of vision.

One of them, not surprisingly, was Leo Cavelli. The other, with fewer tattoos, looked older and resembled Leo closely enough that they had to be brothers. Both frowned down at him.

"Motherfucker," said Leo, giving a hefty kick to Wes's unprotected stomach. Wes shouted into the gag and spent another several minutes fighting the urge to barf. By the time he was in control of himself again, the brothers were deep in conversation.

"I don't know who sent him," Leo whined. "He didn't say."

"Well, who the fuck is he, Leo?"

"I dunno. Some dude from Buttfuck, Oregon. He had his license on him, one credit card, and a few hundred bucks. That's it."

"No keys?"

"Nah."

"Then how the fuck did he get here?"

Wes wouldn't have volunteered the information even if he hadn't been gagged, but his keys were tucked in a small metal box hidden under Morrison's chassis. Wes had welded the box there himself a couple of years ago, after an unfortunate incident in which he lost his keys in a Portland club—probably while fucking a guy in a bathroom stall. That had been a major pain in the ass, and ever since, Wes preferred to stow the keys when he was on errands of a dubious nature. Like tracking down killers.

"What about his phone?" the older Cavelli demanded.

"I can't unlock it."

"You're totally worthless, you know that?"

"Shut up, Curtis."

Even if the Cavellis weren't responsible for kidnapping him and, most likely, killing Logan, Wes would have disliked them immensely. They were assholes.

The Cavellis returned to bickering about who Wes was, why Leo had been stupid enough to attack him, and what they should do about him. Although all of this was directly relevant to Wes, his attention wandered. It was weird, but fear wasn't the most prominent emotion roiling through him. Regret had that honor. And not even regret about the stupid-ass things he'd done, such as prancing into the clutches of a murderer. Wes regretted what he *hadn't* done. He hadn't had sex with Parker earlier. He hadn't spent every minute of his life with Parker since they'd met. He hadn't told Parker how amazing he was and how much he meant to him. He hadn't allowed himself to fall in love.

God, he hoped Parker didn't blame himself for Wes's fate the way he felt responsible for Logan's death.

Apparently having reached some decision, the Cavellis turned their attention back to Wes. Curtis kicked him—in exactly the spot where Leo had—and it hurt. But at this point *all* of Wes hurt: bruised stomach and back, bound ankles and wrists, cramped limbs, light-sensitive eyes, stretched mouth, and of course his battered skull. Hell, even his bladder ached; he had to piss pretty desperately. But his heart ached worst of all.

Curtis reached to his lower back and pulled out a handgun, which he pointed at Wes's head. His hand was distressingly steady. "We're gonna take away the gag so we can have a little powwow. If you shout or scream, I pull the trigger. Got it?"

After Wes nodded, Leo bent over him and ripped away the duct tape. It hurt, of course, but it was a relief when Leo pulled the cloth out of his mouth. Wes tried to gather enough saliva to spit away the taste of cotton.

"Why'd you kill Logan?" he croaked. It wasn't the wisest move, but he was curious. Besides, these two weren't likely to untie him and send him on his merry way, no matter what he said.

It was Leo's turn to kick him. Wes grunted but didn't cry out.

"Who sent you here?" Curtis demanded.

"Nobody."

"Don't fucking lie to me."

Wes laughed with the stupidity of it all—or maybe because his head was more addled than he thought. "I'm not. I came here of my own accord."

"I'll blow your fucking brains out."

"Then you'll never know, will you?"

That seemed to stymie the Cavellis. Wes was beginning to suspect they weren't the brightest bulbs in the pack. He didn't know whether idiot criminals were more or less dangerous than genius ones.

The Cavellis had another brief whispered conversation, after which Leo stomped up the stairs. Curtis scowled at Wes and lowered the gun but didn't put it away, and shortly after, Leo returned with Wes's phone in hand.

"How do we unlock it?" asked Curtis.

Wes didn't want that, because then they'd see Parker's texts. Logan's suspect suicide letter suggested the Cavellis already knew who Parker was. Wes didn't want them to track him down.

"You can't. I have to swipe a particular pattern with my finger." A partial untruth because anybody's finger would do. He hoped the Cavellis wouldn't know that.

And apparently they didn't, because after another whispered exchange, Leo approached him again. "I'm gonna free your hands. Don't try anything funny."

Wes rolled his eyes. Did they expect him to bust out some kung fu moves? Leo pulled open a pocketknife and began to cut the rope at his wrists.

Okay, that hurt too. Wes's arms and legs had been in the same position for Christ knew how long, and they protested movement. He had to bite his lip hard enough to draw blood to keep from shouting. After a few moments, though, he slowly straightened his legs and used his arms to raise himself to a sitting position. The room seemed to sway and rock as if he were on a ship at sea, causing him to turn his head and vomit profusely. Leo didn't leap away fast enough, and his shoes got splashed. Good.

"God damn it!" Leo pulled his foot back for another good kick, but Curtis pushed him hard, sending him off-balance.

"Knock it off! Just give him the fucking phone."

Swearing, Leo handed it over. "Unlock it," he snarled.

Wes looked down at the phone in his shaking hands. He took a deep breath. And then he hurled the phone to the floor with all his strength—and stomped on it with his bound feet for good measure. The glass and plastic crunched satisfyingly.

Curtis clomped closer, gun upraised, but didn't pull the trigger. Instead he thumped it against the sore spot on Wes's head.

Wes collapsed.

HE WOKE up shivering. The world was blurry, even after he tried to blink his eyes clear, and for several minutes he couldn't remember anything. Who he was, or where he was, or why he was cold and in pain. He was tempted to close his eyes again and sink into oblivion. The void would be so much easier than struggling. But the image of a man with cobalt blue hair appeared in front of him, urging him to stay in the here and now. To keep on fighting.

"Parker," Wes tried to say. He was gagged again, and all that came out was a low groan. But even thinking the name was enough to bring him back to himself.

He wasn't hogtied any longer, which he supposed was an improvement. Instead someone had sat him against a support post, his hands tied behind the post and his legs straight in front of him and bound at the ankles. His ass and crotch felt clammy, and a moment later the reek of urine registered. Fantastic. Well, at least his bladder wasn't complaining anymore.

As for his skull, he now had a newly enhanced headache, twice as strong as before.

The Cavellis had left the lights on, two bare bulbs hanging from the ceiling. Although Wes could look around, there wasn't much to see except for the usual crap that tended to accumulate in basements. Off in a corner, the furnace rumbled. Wes had no sense of what time it was. The basement's single window was obscured by black fabric, except for one top corner that hung down an inch or so and let in weak light. He thought it was sunlight but couldn't judge its angle.

He leaned his poor head against the post and tried to picture what Parker was doing right now. Had he eaten yet? If so, was he angry Wes had never shown up? Wes hoped his absence hadn't hurt Parker, who seemed so genuinely eager for his company. He hoped Parker would still give Rhoda the shelf Wes had made. He'd put a lot of time and thought into it.

He wondered what would become of his bus—which he realized he loved very much—and his tools and the bits of wood and pieces of hardware he'd collected over the years. And what about his five acres? He hoped whoever ended up owning it didn't drain the pond and displace the ducks.

Oh, and Morrison. The city would certainly tow the van eventually, and it would molder in a yard until they scrapped it or sold it at auction. He felt bad that he hadn't treated Morrison a little better. More frequent oil changes. Car washes. Nice covers for the seats.

Jesus, didn't he have anything left but regrets? That was a hell of a way to leave the world, and he'd been trying to die without them.

But no, he was also proud he'd made beautiful furniture that people might treasure for generations to come. And he'd apologized to Nevin and Jeremy, making amends as best he could. He was glad of that. And he'd had that short, glorious time with Parker. Wes didn't regret that at all, not even if it had led him to this basement.

He couldn't smile with the gag and duct tape, but at least his heart settled more peacefully in his chest. He hummed the Beach Boys.

Heavy footsteps sounded on the floor above him, probably boots and likely more than one person. He assumed he was beneath the tattoo parlor, and since the shop was closed for the holiday, Cavelli feet must be making all that noise. He tried to imagine what they were doing up there but didn't really have the foggiest idea, and anyway, such conjuring did nothing good for his mental health.

He let his mind wander for a while and was surprised when it settled on a childhood memory, a pleasant one involving his parents. He didn't realize he had any of those. He'd been five or six, and their marriage was already irreparably damaged, although they hadn't acknowledged it yet. They spent a lot of time screaming at each other. And screaming at Wes, when they weren't ignoring him entirely.

But on this particular day, nobody yelled, and everyone was smiling. His mom had filled a cooler with sandwiches, potato chips, apples, and cans of pop, and the three of them piled into his dad's Chevy truck. Along the route, his dad told funny stories about things that had happened at work, like the time somebody called the sheriff because they saw a camel wandering past their house. Wes's mom laughed and ruffled Wes's hair.

They'd driven over the Coast Range and parked at a beach, and for once the sun shone warmly and the sky was clear. They ate their lunch while sitting on chunks of driftwood and then poked around in tide pools, marveling at starfish and watching tiny fish dart around. They found hermit crabs and had races with them. And then they'd simply sat together, all in a row, watching the sun sink into the Pacific. Wes told his parents that when he grew up, he'd be a sailor and take his boat all over the ocean. By the time they left, he was so exhausted that his dad had to carry him back to the truck, and Wes fell asleep on the ride home, tucked between the warm, comforting bodies of his mom and dad.

He was grateful now to have rediscovered that memory.

THE CAVELLIS came slowly down the stairs, as if fearful that Wes had gotten loose and might attack them. But he remained tethered to the pole, trying to ignore how dry his gagged mouth felt.

"You're gonna answer our questions now." Curtis brandished a blade bigger than the little pocketknife Leo had used earlier. He gestured at Leo, who again tore the tape off Wes's face with unnecessary force. This time it felt as if he ripped off some skin. Wes coughed once the gag was out of his mouth.

"Okay, now," Curtis said. "Who sent you here?"

"Nobody."

"Wrong answer." Curtis bent down and thrust the tip of the knife into Wes's left thigh.

Wes didn't quite scream—it was more of a grunt—and when he instinctively jerked his body away, the blade only cut more deeply. He grunted again when Curtis yanked the knife free, and immediately hot blood soaked through his jeans and trickled to the underside of his leg.

"Who sent you here?" The blade, now streaked red, shook slightly in Curtis's hand.

Frantic to keep from being stabbed again, Wes blurted, "Logan's parents."

"What?"

"Logan's parents asked me to come check things out." Okay, maybe he was throwing them under the bus, but right now he didn't give a shit. They lived too far away to be in immediate danger.

Leo came closer and crouched near him, narrow-eyed. "Why?"

"Th-the suicide note. They thought it sounded fishy."

"Where do Logan's parents live?"

Shit. Parker had mentioned this, but Wes couldn't remember the detail. Not Wyoming. Somewhere in the middle of the country. "Kansas," he said with as much certainty as he could muster.

"Fucking liar!" Leo stomped on the stab wound, which hurt more than the blade itself had, and as if he didn't want his thunder stolen, Curtis plunged the knife into Wes's other leg. Wes almost dislocated his shoulders trying to twist out of reach, even though he knew it was futile. All the squirming and struggling in the world wouldn't save him.

"Who?" Curtis demanded.

Time began to pass in weird jerky movements, speeding ahead and slowing down like someone playing with a video camera. One moment Curtis was dragging the knife tip down Wes's cheek with agonizing slowness; the next, both brothers were screaming at him so fast he couldn't catch the words. The chill of the basement shifted to a burning heat that enveloped his body, and all the myriad pains melded together into a single agony so huge it wasn't even a sensation anymore but rather an entity of its own.

"Like Godzilla," Wes slurred. His tongue was heavy in his mouth, making it hard to speak. "Like Bigfoot on the Space Needle."

Curtis growled inarticulately and poked his knife very close to, although not quite *into*, Wes's balls.

I haven't told them anything. I'm stupid and useless, but I'm strong when I need to be. Wes smiled at that even as he sagged in his bonds. His eyelids had grown so heavy. But that was all right. He was going to leave this world with self-respect and with the knowledge that he'd done what he could to keep the man he loved safe.

Loved.

He loved Parker. Wasn't that a miracle?

In the shop above, something thudded, then crashed. A lot of footsteps thundered overhead. Loud voices.

Wes gathered the dregs of his strength and took a deep breath. "Careful!" he screamed. "He has a gun!"

This time, Curtis pulled the trigger.

Chapter Seventeen

THEY HAD been waiting a thousand years for Detective Saito to call back—Parker was sure of it. Or it might have been two thousand. He'd tried pacing, but his bedroom wasn't big enough, especially with Jeremy taking up space. He ended up back on the bed again, next to Nevin, who was shooting death glares at his phone.

"You should go," Parker finally blurted.

"Go where?"

"Aren't you supposed to go have Thanksgiving at Colin's parents' house?"

Nevin lifted his eyebrows. "Do you honestly think I'm going to go eat more goddamn pumpkin pie when you're in crisis, Buttercup?"

"But they're your in-laws and—"

"And they can fucking eat without me. I'm not sorry to miss that circus, anyway."

Oh good. Something to think about besides Wes. "I thought you guys got along."

"We do. They're so goddamn perfect it hurts my teeth. But Collie's sister has a new boyfriend, and he's a turdbucket. Nowhere near good enough for her. Plus Collie's niece is mooning over some boy at school. She's sixteen, for fuck's sake. Too young. But she rolls her eyes when I tell her that."

Despite everything, Parker gave a small smile at Nevin's attempt to be an uncle. It was good to know that even the mighty Nevin Ng was no match for a stubborn teenager.

Nevin's phone beeped, and Parker nearly jumped out of his skin.

"They got the warrant," Nevin said. "Serving it now."

This time ten thousand years passed.

Nevin's phone finally buzzed again—several times in quick succession—and he spent so much time reading the texts that Parker almost screamed. When Nevin looked up, his expression was grave. Parker stopped breathing.

Softly, Nevin said, "They found him. He's... on the way to the hospital."

THERE WAS some kind of discussion about who would take Parker to Seattle, but Parker didn't follow it. He could see Rhoda, Jeremy, and Nevin in his bedroom and hear the strident tone of their voices, but none of the meaning got through. All he could hear was the echo of a single word. Hospital. Hospital. Hospital.

Finally Rhoda wrapped him in a suffocating hug. She smelled of coffee and spices and wine—all very fine scents—and she was warm and soft against him. And strong. Always so strong. "Honey?" she said when she let him go.

"I'm okay."

She looked doubtful. "You can wait here until there's more news."

Parker shook his head. What he didn't tell her was he didn't really want to go to Seattle. He wanted, in fact, to run away. Very fast and very far, although he had no destination in mind. Wyoming, maybe.

But Wes was in a hospital in Seattle, and he was.... Well, Parker didn't know how badly he was injured, but Nevin and Jeremy looked somber. And the thing was, Wes had nobody. Nobody but Parker. And Parker couldn't bear the thought of Wes alone, in pain, with no friends there to comfort him. No one to hold his hand and tell him he was loved.

"I need to go, Mom."

"All right."

Nevin stepped forward. "I'll drive you."

"But Colin—"

"Is a big boy who understands priorities."

"I can drive myself." He could borrow someone's car or rent one or—

"No, you fucking can't. In your state you're liable to wrap yourself around a power pole before you've even left the Portland city limits. Then you'll end up in the hospital all right, but not in any shape to help your boy." Nevin looked up at Parker, narrow-eyed. "There's nothing weak or childish about asking for help when you need it, Smurf."

Parker still felt guilty about initially roping Nevin into his problem, and now drawing him in even more, but arguing would only waste time. So he shrugged off the blazer, marched to the closet, and grabbed his jacket. The new one. It was silly and touristy but also warm—and Wes had bought it for him. It would make an appropriate talisman. "Let's go, please."

The good thing about having Nevin as chauffeur was he drove with complete disregard for speed limits. Traffic was heavy with people going home after Thanksgiving meals, but Nevin cut in and out as if he were competing in the Monaco Grand Prix. He did it effortlessly too, with a steady string of obscenities flowing from his mouth.

Somewhere around Longview, red and blue lights flashed behind them. "Son of a bitch," Nevin grumbled as he pulled to the shoulder. When the state trooper came to the window, Nevin showed his badge, then let loose a volley of words that ended with the cop apologizing for pulling him over.

Nevin looked smug as he zoomed back into traffic.

"You can bully your way out of anything," Parker said admiringly.

"It's my talent. Be glad I use it for good instead of evil."

A few more miles sped by before Parker gathered enough courage to ask the question that had tortured him since they left. "What happened?"

"Don't know all the details. That fuckwad tattoo artist had him. When the goons served the warrant, they heard shouting from the basement—and gunfire."

Parker made a small pained sound but gestured for Nevin to continue.

"Turned out fuckwad had a buddy with him. Buddy's dead now, courtesy of Seattle PD. Fuckwad's in custody. And Wanker's banged up pretty badly, plus he caught a bullet or two."

This time Parker made a strangled noise, and Nevin shot him a sympathetic look. "I don't know what kind of shape he's in now, and I'm not gonna give you any false promises. But remember, Colin got shot straight in the chest, and he bounced right back to his usual pain-in-the-ass self."

That reminder did help, at least enough that Parker could breathe. But his heart remained in such a tight ball it was a wonder it could beat. He wrapped his coat more firmly around himself, even though Nevin had the GTO's heater cranked.

He'd never felt like this before, and he hated it. The closest he'd ever come was when his dad died. But that had been a different pain, because by the time he learned of the accident, his father was already gone. Hearing the news had been like having a limb suddenly hacked off—a horrifying numbness followed by excruciating agony and a long recovery. But this thing with Wes today? It was slow torture. Like being split open and watching someone remove his organs bit by bit with a soup spoon.

"Nevin?" He spoke quietly, having decided talking was better than fretting.

"Yeah?"

"When did you know you loved Colin?"

Nevin snorted, called the guy doing seventy-five in the fast lane a crab-sucking whoreson, and then was quiet for so long that Parker thought he wasn't going to answer. When he did speak, he kept his gaze carefully ahead. "I interrupted Collie at work to have a meltdown because my brother was getting married and I was feeling abandoned. And instead of telling me I'm a selfish piece of shit, he took me on a picnic in the Rose Gardens. In the rain. Then he took me to an old house he'd just bought and fucked me silly."

"Um, okay. That's... romantic. So you knew you were in love because the sex was good?"

"The sex was fucking spectacular," Nevin replied with a leer. "But that's not why." There was another long stretch of silence. "I realized that day that he could see the worst of me, and instead of kicking me to the curb, he just held me tighter."

Was that what love was? Knowing someone's biggest flaws and wanting them anyway? Not the kind of sentiment you'd put on a Hallmark card or commemorate in epic poetry. But it felt right.

NEVIN HAD to work his magic again at the hospital, where at first nobody wanted to tell him or Parker anything. Only next of kin, the staff kept insisting. But Wes *had* no next of kin. He had nobody at all. Eventually Nevin wore the staff down, and he and Parker were allowed into a waiting room reserved for family.

It wasn't a happy place. These were people who'd planned on having a nice holiday with loved ones and ended up instead on thinly upholstered chairs, surrounded by ancient issues of *Golf Digest* and *Prevention*, waiting for news about someone they cared about. One young woman frowned as she furiously knitted a long green scarf. An extended family chatted quietly in Spanish. A middle-aged couple peered at their phones. And an exhausted-looking mother attempted to entertain her toddler. Nevin steered Parker to a chair and barked, "Stay put," then went stomping out the door.

Parker remained, staring blankly at some health channel on the overhead TV.

When Nevin returned maybe thirty minutes later, he carried two cardboard cups of coffee and wore a scowl. He handed one of the coffees to Parker. "Tastes like crap compared to Rhoda's," he said and then plopped down into the adjacent chair.

He was right—it was shitty coffee. But at least it masked the bile that scorched the back of Parker's throat.

"You want updates?" Nevin asked.

"God yes."

"Wanker's in surgery. Serious condition."

Parker's throat threatened to close. "What does that mean?"

"Means the docs don't know shit yet. But serious is better than critical." He sipped his coffee and made a face. "He was shot once in the shoulder. Probably not life-threatening. But he also got cut with a knife pretty badly, and he has a lot of bruising to his head." He started to say more but paused, maybe to let Parker process.

And Parker did process. He pictured Wes—handsome, kind, talented Wes—captured by two assholes. The same ones who'd murdered Logan, most likely. And it sounded as if they'd taken their time hurting Wes.

A new emotion surged through Parker: rage.

"Those motherfuckers!" he growled as he dropped his cup into the nearby wastebasket, leapt to his feet, and rushed toward the door. To do what, he didn't know. One of the motherfuckers was dead and the other in jail. But Parker's fists itched to punch something, and he wanted to scream until his throat was raw. He wanted to make those men suffer just as they'd made Wes suffer. He wanted to rip their—

"Whoa!" Nevin caught him in a tight grip likely perfected during his days as a patrol cop. He was small but very strong.

Parker bared his teeth.

"C'mon, Bruce Banner. You've given enough of a show already." Nevin gestured toward the others in the waiting room, who gaped at Parker. Nevin steered him out of the room, down a confusing maze of hallways, and out into a parking lot lit only by a few scattered lights. He kept on dragging until they were at the edge of the lot. Then he released Parker's arm. "Let it out."

A few deep breaths in and out, and then Parker shouted at the top of his lungs—every foul word he'd ever heard Nevin utter and more besides. Possibly enough blasphemies to blister the paint on nearby cars. And when that didn't do the trick, he rounded on a light pole and kicked it hard. Kicked it again and again and then punched it with all his might.

That was a mistake.

Awash with mingled pain, anger, and helplessness, Parker sank to his ass on the blacktop and sobbed his goddamn eyes out.

Nevin waited patiently, possibly a first for him. He didn't try to comfort Parker, which was a good thing because Parker didn't want comforting. And he didn't walk away or look pissed off or act like Parker's explosion was a big deal. He simply waited until Parker pulled himself together.

Sniffling, wishing he had a Kleenex, Parker rose to his feet. He cradled his right hand in his left. "Sorry."

"Don't be. I learned some new words from you just now. Never realized you were so talented."

Parker let out a shaky laugh. "And I didn't realize you knew who Bruce Banner is."

"You live with Collie for three years and you know what everyone in the Marvel universe eats for fucking breakfast." He said it with a combination of fondness and fake disgust that made Parker laugh again.

Then he sobered. "I need to go inside."

"Let's get your hand looked at, numbnuts. Rhoda's gonna have my balls. C'mon."

HE HADN'T broken anything, so that was good. The ER nurse bandaged him up, gave him an ice bag, and told him to stop hitting things. Then Nevin and Parker returned to the waiting room, where everyone watched Parker warily.

The torture of waiting continued. Parker shifted in his seat and gnawed at the fingernails on his left hand. He watched a TV show about how to substitute vegetables for carbs. He leafed through an article about how a solid rhythm would improve his golf swings. Then he turned to Nevin, who was occupied with his phone. "Why'd they do it?"

Nevin looked over at him. "In a practical sense or an existential one?"

"Both, I guess."

"Existential is easy. Some people are evil piles of shit who only care about themselves. Practical? Dunno. Saito's still chatting with the fuckwad."

Parker sat back in his seat and hoped Saito was being a really effective bad cop.

After what felt like three eternities, a woman in purple scrubs came to the door. She glanced at her clipboard. "Mr. Levin?" She looked tired, and Parker was sad she couldn't be with her family on Thanksgiving. She led him and Nevin into a small room down the hall; it contained a round table, a few chairs, and nothing else.

"Is Wes—"

"The surgeon will be here in just a moment."

"Yeah, but Wes—"

"Is in recovery." She left, closing the door behind her.

In recovery. That sounded optimistic, even if it was just the name of a room. Parker played with the cover on his ice pack.

A minute or two later, a brisk knock sounded on the door, and a large white-coated man entered. "I am Dr. Ogochokwu," he said with a slight accent. They introduced themselves, everyone shook hands, and Parker managed to avoid jumping on the guy and demanding information. "You are Mr. Anker's friends?"

"Yes," Parker and Nevin said in unison. Nevin sounded as if he meant it.

"Very good. And he has no family near, correct?"

Parker answered. "He has us. That's it."

"All right. I am very pleased to say that Mr. Anker should make a full recovery."

The doctor said more after that, stuff about scars and infection and healing time, but Parker registered very little of it. Time passed in a weird haze, but Wes would be okay. That was all that mattered. Parker almost cried again, this time from relief.

Some cops came into the room and asked questions, but Nevin did most of the answering. Parker had already told Saito about his suspicions regarding Logan, and other than that, he had little information to contribute. Although Wes hadn't shared very specific intentions, Parker showed the cops the previous night's text conversation. It was slightly embarrassing, but they did a good job pretending not to notice the personal stuff. It probably helped that Nevin had them fixed in his steely gaze, just daring them to say a word.

When Parker was back in the waiting room, dozing, the clipboard lady returned. "You can see him now, but only for a minute."

He could have kissed her.

Nevin opted to remain in the waiting room, and Parker practically skipped through the halls. Until he got to Wes's room, where he had to take a few yoga breaths before going in.

Wes looked weirdly small in his hospital bed. His eyes were closed, one side of his head shaved to the scalp, wires and tubes attached to various parts of him. Two long gashes—one on each cheek—looked red and puffy and had a lot of stitches. The rest of his skin was nearly as white as the hospital sheets. But his chest moved smoothly up and down. God, he was alive. And beautiful.

After a minute or two of uncertainty, Parker reached out and gently touched the back of Wes's hand. His eyelids fluttered open, and when he caught sight of Parker, he tried to smile. "You're here," he rasped, voice barely audible over the beeping machines.

"I'm here. You're safe. Now rest."

Wes's smile widened and his eyes fell closed.

Chapter Eighteen

"That's great, Wes!"

The last time anyone had congratulated him on going to the bathroom, Wes had been two. He smiled thinly at the nurse and shuffled back to his bed. "Does this mean I can leave?" he asked.

"The doctor will check on you this afternoon. Then we'll see."

He sighed and arranged the sheets over himself, careful not to catch the IV line. Drained by his efforts, he lay back and gazed at Parker, curled up in the nest he'd made for himself in a chair. He looked exhausted, with a growth of dark whiskers and his hair in disarray.

As soon as the nurse was gone, Wes said, "I'm fine. You should go find a motel or something and—"

"Are you trying to get rid of me?"

"No, of course not. But you've spent two days here and—"

"And I'm staying longer. Staying with you." Wes remembered Parker mentioning that Rhoda rarely let go of a notion once she had hold of it. Judging by his firm chin and determined expression, it looked as if he'd inherited that trait.

Wes didn't argue. He didn't have the strength for it... or the will. Truthfully, he *liked* having Parker there. His wounds hurt less every time he looked at Parker, who'd rushed to Seattle—leaving a family holiday, no less—and stayed at his bedside every minute. That knowledge healed him better than anything the doctors could do.

But then Wes remembered what he'd seen in the bathroom mirror, and he licked his lips. "Look, you can...." Jesus, this was hard to say. But he had to. "Nobody will blame you for leaving now. Especially me." Without conscious thought, he lightly touched the long line of stitches on one cheek, matched by a similar line on the other.

"I'm staying." Parker rose from his chair and took the two steps to the bed. He touched Wes's face gently, just above the stitches, and then bent to plant a featherlight kiss on Wes's forehead. "Staying."

"I look like Frankenstein's monster."

Parker's eyes flashed angrily. "Did you think a couple of scars were going to chase me away? Do you think I'm that shallow?"

"No. But this… I'm…."

"You're alive. And you're beautiful. So cut this crap out, okay?"

Wes sighed. "Okay." He knew that Parker wasn't shallow and that his dedication to Wes was not dependent on a pretty face.

Parker settled back into the chair. "Anyway, I've always liked Frankenstein's monster. He's sexy."

Wes raised his eyebrows, which pulled on the cuts and made his face ache. "Sexy?"

"Yep. My mom and I have argued over this. She has a thing for vampires, but I think the whole bloodsucking schtick is gross and also the vamps tend to be pretty stalkery, which is creepy. They don't want a relationship—they just want to eat. But Frank's monster, all he wants is to belong and be loved." Parker smiled softly, as if he knew Wes's deepest secrets.

For the next few hours Wes allowed himself to drift in and out of a light doze. He'd never spent so much time doing nothing, although Parker kept reminding him he was doing a lot, busily fixing all the damage the Cavellis had inflicted.

Shortly after Wes's lunch tray had been cleared away, Detective Saito arrived. She didn't look happy, but by now Wes was fairly certain she was incapable of smiling. He wondered whether her profession had done that to her or if she'd been grim to begin with and had chosen a job to match her disposition.

"How are you feeling?"

"A lot better than I would be if you hadn't sent your guys in when you did. Thank you."

Huh. One corner of her mouth twitched upward a micrometer. "You should thank Parker and Detective Ng. They're the ones who were so persistent."

Wes hoped that when he was healthy enough, he'd get a chance to show Parker his gratitude. As for Nevin, who was back in Portland, well, that was going to be a little awkward. But Wes would face that too.

"I'd like to take your statement now," Saito said.

At Wes's nod, she settled herself in the room's other chair, took out a recording device, notebook, and pen, and started asking questions. She had a lot of them, and Wes found the interrogation surprisingly draining. But even though Parker tried a few times to make him stop, Wes refused. He wanted to get this over with. At one point, though, when he was describing some of the Cavellis' gorier activities, Wes glanced at Parker and noticed how pale he was.

"Why don't you take a walk?" Wes suggested.

Parker shook his head, crossed his arms, and hunkered down more firmly into his nest.

All three of them were relieved when Saito finally put away her things and stood. "I don't think this case is going to court—the perp's going to plead it out. The DA's charged him with first-degree murder in Mr. Miller's case, along with a boatload of other charges."

Parker needed his curiosity satisfied. "Has fuckwad—um, has Cavelli said anything about what happened with Logan?"

"He spilled a little before he decided to lawyer up. He mostly blamed his dead brother." She rolled her eyes as if she'd expected that kind of behavior. "Sounds like the two of them and Mr. Miller got screwed in a get-rich-quick con. Cavelli says investing in the con was Miller's idea. When they lost their money, they tried to recoup from Mr. Miller, and when he wouldn't pay up...." She shrugged.

"That's stupid," Parker said, his eyes glittering. "There was no point in killing him."

"There's almost never a point to murder. It's a stupid crime." Saito checked her phone and nodded. "Gotta go." Then she cast a long look at Wes. "I'm glad you're doing well. Next time, though, please leave the investigating to professionals." With another almost smile, she swept out of the room.

THE SURGEON arrived around three, looking jolly. It must feel good to know you'd saved someone's life. He read Wes's chart, checked his wounds, and poked and prodded a bit before announcing him fit for discharge. "But you still need plenty of rest. No returning to work for a week, and no strenuous exercise or lifting anything over fifteen pounds for six weeks. You understand?"

"Yes." Wes had already done a mental calculation of his finances. He'd tucked some money aside, so he'd be all right with not selling anything for a couple of months as long as he lived frugally.

"Good. Contact me if you have any problems. Do you have questions?"

Wes shook his head. The surgeon had already covered everything and handed over a folder full of papers with helpful advice, some of which seemed only tangentially related to Wes's situation. Yes, he believed eating lots of vegetables and exercising regularly were good for him, but they wouldn't have saved him from getting bashed, stabbed, and shot.

After a round of thanks and good wishes, plus promises that the nurse would arrive soon with his discharge papers, the doctor left.

"I have a plan," Parker said. "It involves options."

"Okay?"

"Morrison is parked in the hospital lot. Oh, and Nevin says that's a fucking lame place to keep your keys, by the way. He found them right away. Anyway, now I have them. I'll drive us down south. Your choice is to stay with me at Rhoda's and get waited on hand and foot, or for us to stay in your bus while you get waited on hand and foot."

"Self-sufficiency isn't one of my options?"

"Nope."

"Um…." Wes considered for about three seconds. "I'd prefer to be home."

"Good. I was hoping you'd say that."

"Really? Why?"

"'Cause I like your home. It's… homey." Parker grinned.

Then something occurred to Wes. "Um, I think I'm going to have to make the trip in this." He pinched the thin fabric of his hospital johnny. The clothing he'd worn to Cavelli's was toast, stained by blood and piss and then cut away by EMTs and the staff in the ER.

"I'd appreciate the view, but you're not in good enough health to be appreciated. And it's cold. But I have a solution." Parker hefted one of the plastic bags he'd accumulated next to his chair. "New duds. Um, Nevin bought them, so…." He smiled merrily.

Wes groaned. The black sweatpants were perfectly fine—not his usual style, maybe, but more comfortable at the moment than jeans—and there was no issue with the black sneakers. But Nevin had also bought him boxers printed with hot dogs in buns and socks depicting skateboard-riding T. rexes. The purple T-shirt depicted a unicorn pole dancing. And the jacket? It matched Parker's.

"Where did he find all of this?" Wes asked.

"I have no idea. But he is a detective, after all."

THE RIDE wasn't exactly comfortable; the bumping and jostling irritated every damaged bit of Wes's body. But he was going home, and that was comfort enough. Wes had just stirred awake from a light sleep when Parker spoke.

"Hey, Wes? I don't know how to ask this without maybe being insulting, but are you going to be okay with the medical bills?"

"I have insurance." It had seemed like a good idea for someone who spent his days handling sharp tools and lugging furniture. "Thanks to Obamacare, my premiums are only appalling instead of stroke-inducing."

Parker chuckled. "I'm glad. And thanks, Obama!"

"How about you? Money-wise, I mean. You're missing a lot of work to babysit me."

"I'm fine. I don't need much. And I can rely on the Bank of Mom if necessary. I know I'm saying this from a place of privilege—Ptolemy's lectured me on that point a *lot*—but I don't care much about money. I mean, I want the basics like shelter and food—"

"And hair dye."

"—and hair dye. But stuff isn't important to me. People are." He reached over and gently patted Wes's leg.

"That's a good attitude."

"I've been told I lack ambition."

"Maybe your ambitions don't involve careers and paychecks. Doesn't mean they're unworthy."

Parker's smile lit up the van. "Thanks."

"Are you ever going to tell me what you did to your hand?" Wes touched it gently. The bandages were off now, but the knuckles still looked swollen and bruised.

"Nope."

They stopped at Rhoda's house so Parker could pick up some clothing. Rhoda was at P-Town, but she'd left a bag full of nonperishable groceries and a note ordering them both to eat well and text her often. Parker rolled his eyes, but Wes could tell he was pleased.

"Do you want to go to P-Town and see her?" Wes asked.

"Nah. Let's get you home."

WES'S LITTLE compound looked dark and forlorn as they rolled up. It seemed like a thousand years since he'd been there last. But Parker made him sit in Morrison while he ran ahead to turn on the lights and get the wood stove going, and by the time Wes slowly made his way up the stairs and through the door, everything glowed.

"Straight to bed with you," Parker ordered.

"I have to piss. And wash up."

"I stole the urinal cup thing from the hospital, and I'm going to bring you everything else you need."

"Bossy," Wes said, heart full and warm.

"Yep."

Parker found Wes's favorite flannel sleep pants and softest old T-shirt and insisted on helping him get undressed, even though Wes could have done it himself. Then, as promised, he brought washing-up supplies—and didn't wince at the urinal full of piss. That taken care of, he made and carried in tea and sandwiches and sat on the mattress beside Wes, eating and chatting happily.

"We're getting crumbs in the bed," Wes pointed out.

"You survived being tortured and shot. A few crumbs won't kill you."

"Hmm." Wes decided not to argue, because Parker had finished his food, slipped under the covers, and snuggled close.

"Is this okay? Am I hurting anything?"

"No." Actually Wes didn't care that Parker was jostling him a little. The heat of Parker's body was sinking into him, and his hair was nicely tickling his neck.

"My hair looks stupid," said Wes, remembering. Then he yawned.

"We could pretend it's a new fashion. Like a half Mohawk. I'll dye it purple." Parker chuckled, and Wes enjoyed the puffs of breath on his collarbone. "Or maybe we should just shave it all off and start fresh."

"Okay." Wes didn't really care. Right now Parker was in his bed, and that meant all was right in Wes's world.

Chapter Nineteen

Playing house with Wes was amazingly easy. It helped that the bus already felt like home, and Wes was pretty easygoing. For several days Parker did chores and fussed at Wes if he thought Wes was overdoing it. They had a lot of free time on their hands, but neither went stir-crazy. It was relaxing and comfortable to simply talk to each other, sit on the couch with music and books, take short walks to watch the ducks.

One afternoon when Wes's shoulder was still too sore for him to take the wheel, Parker drove them into Grants Pass. They stopped at a drop-in clinic so Wes could get his stitches out. Then he bought a new phone, which was way more hassle than it should have been. The kid at the store had a hell of a time uploading Wes's contacts and other information to the new device, but he managed it at last. In celebration of their day out, Wes insisted on treating Parker to dinner.

They ordered fancy burgers with sweet-potato fries and sat gazing at each other over the table. Wes kept running a hand over his head, probably because he still wasn't used to his buzz cut. He seemed a little self-conscious when people did a double-take due to his scarred cheeks. Parker found Wes even more handsome than before, especially when a smile played at the corners of his mouth.

"Hanukkah," Wes said suddenly.

"What?"

"Doesn't it begin in two nights?"

Parker, who'd lost track of days, had to consult his phone. "Yeah, I guess so."

"But you're stuck here with me."

"I'm not stuck anywhere, Wes. There's nowhere else in the world I want to be right now."

Wes looked at him gravely. "It's a big world."

"I know." And because a shadow of unhappiness had passed over Wes's features, Parker steered the conversation in a different direction. "Mom's gonna love that shelf so much. I can't wait to give it to her."

"Glad you're happy with it."

Wes seemed to want to say more, but although Parker waited, Wes remained silent. The waitress brought their food, and they exchanged only a few words while they ate. "These are good," Parker finally said out of desperation.

"They're okay."

"You're not impressed?"

Wes shrugged. "You cook better than this." Then he looked down at his plate as though his fries required all his attention.

"Who taught you to cook?" Parker asked.

That made Wes glance up. "Nobody. Grandpa could do a few things, but mostly I taught myself out of sheer necessity."

"God, you're amazing."

"Because I can throw together an edible meal?" Wes looked genuinely puzzled.

"Because you've accomplished so much with zero support."

"I haven't sent explorers to Mars or won a Pulitzer Prize. I make furniture and I live in—"

"A bus. I know." Parker smiled. "But I do not retract my statement. I know you, Wes. I *know* you. And you're top quality, A1. You're the bomb."

Although Wes scoffed and threw a french fry at Parker, his eyes warmed. Maybe if Parker kept repeating these things, Wes would come to believe them.

Back home, Wes spent time playing with his new phone as Parker did some laundry and, while standing outside under the tarp, called Rhoda. She sounded a little distracted. "What's going on, Mom?"

"Nothing. Today was Dina's last day, but Larry and Padma both want some extra hours, so that works out fine."

"And you're okay about me missing the beginning of Hanukkah?"

"That's fine, honey." She hesitated a moment. "Any chance you'll be back for New Year's Eve?"

"Sure." Since that was over a month away, Parker assumed Wes would have had enough of him by then, and Parker would return to Portland and nurse a broken heart. God, that was going to hurt. "You're not planning another shindig, are you?" He didn't think he'd be able to bear much gaiety at that point.

She cleared her throat, an act that was unusual and suspicious. "I was thinking of taking a little vacation, actually."

"Oh?" To the best of Parker's knowledge, she hadn't gone anywhere since P-Town opened—unless you counted her numerous trips to Seattle to bail Parker out of his disaster du jour. On the few days out of the year when the coffeehouse closed, Rhoda was busy with her Thanksgiving extravaganza, or she just stayed at home with her feet up, reading trade magazines. "Where to?"

"Vegas."

"Really? That's unexpected. Really cool, but unexpected."

A long pause, during which Parker tried very hard not to enjoy the nearly unprecedented occasion of Rhoda's embarrassment. "Bob thinks I might enjoy it," she finally admitted.

Parker grinned widely, relieved that his personal drama hadn't scared the guy away. "That's great, Mom. Of course I can take over the shop while you're gone."

"Thanks, Gonzo. Love you lots."

"You too."

Wes smiled up at him when Parker returned to the bus. "Everything's good?"

"Yeah. Mom's planning a trip to Vegas with Bob. That's huge." Parker plopped down on the couch beside him. "Mom's happy on her own, but I think being dragged away for a few days by a man will be good for her."

"You like this guy?"

"I do. I wish you'd been able to meet him. He was over on Thanksgiving." That gave rise to a distressing thought. "You never did get a chance to celebrate."

"Sorry I stood you up."

"Being kidnapped is a legit excuse." And it was. But it meant Wes had missed his first opportunity in years to celebrate. And how many other holidays had he sat out, alone, over the years? Just thinking about it made Parker's chest feel tight—until inspiration struck. "I need a few things. Is it all right if I take Morrison into town tomorrow?"

PARKER WOKE up fairly early, made breakfast for both of them despite Wes's protests that he could do it himself, and afterward grabbed Morrison's keys off the hook near the door. "Need anything while I'm there?"

"I have everything I need."

Parker sang along with the Beatles for the entire drive to Grants Pass. He only had three stops to make—Target, a party supply store, and a supermarket—but he made an unplanned side trip to a bookstore as well.

When he returned, he found Wes standing under the tarp, eyeing a wooden plank he'd set on his work table. Parker came up behind him and tsked. "Really?"

"It only weighs a couple of pounds. And I'm not doing anything with it—just planning. Stupid shoulder's still too sore for me to handle tools properly." He stroked the wood grain lovingly.

"It's really hard on you to not be working, isn't it?"

"I guess. Being a carpenter—it's what I do. Who I am."

Parker had never defined himself by his jobs and found this a little hard to understand. But then, he had other rock-solid identities to fall back on, like being Rhoda Levin's son. Wes had none of that. Parker squeezed Wes's good shoulder. "You'll be back at it really soon. In the meantime, maybe you have some tasks that you can catch up on without violating doctor's orders."

Frowning, Wes rubbed the stubble atop his head. "I've been thinking for a long time about building some kind of roofed structure for my kitchen and workspace. I get cold in the winters."

"Why haven't you done it, then?"

"Money, mostly. I can do most of the construction myself, but I'd have to buy materials, and I'd need help with plumbing and electric." He sighed. "But I guess I can draw up some plans now. That's free."

"Do you need anything?"

"Just some measurements. Want to help?"

Parker spent about fifteen minutes holding a measuring tape in place while Wes scribbled numbers in a small notebook. It wasn't strenuous activity, but Wes was limping more noticeably by the time they were done, and his face appeared drawn.

Parker gently confiscated the tape measure and hung it from its designated hook. "Go rest for a while," he said with a pat to Wes's butt.

"Jesus, I'm useless."

"No, you're healing. Go." Another pat, this one slightly on the gropey side, which made Wes laugh.

As soon as Wes was back in the bus, Parker unpacked Morrison and got to work. After about an hour, he stopped and made Wes some tea but discovered him fast asleep on the couch with a spiral notebook on his stomach and a pencil on the floor. Parker set the tea and notebook aside, picked up the pencil, and managed to drape a fluffy blanket over Wes without waking him up. He resisted the urge to kiss him and went back outside to his tasks.

Thirty minutes later he was finished. He found Wes awake this time, sitting with the blanket on his lap and the tea mug in his hands.

"That tea's cold," Parker said.

"Won't kill me."

"Come out with me and I'll make you some fresh."

Wes stood, stretched, and winced, but he moved smoothly as he put on his boots and the coat that matched Parker's. Carrying the mug, he followed Parker outside and then stopped in his tracks.

"What the...?" He gaped.

"Happy holidays!" Parker said brightly.

"But—"

"Presents first, then food."

"I don't...."

Since Wes remained frozen, Parker took the mug and set it aside. Then he grasped Wes's hand and gave an impromptu tour. "The colored lights on your natural evergreens are for Christmas, of course," he said, pointing. "And in the interest of multidenominationalism, I found a Hanukkah menorah. Which isn't easy in Grants Pass. Those noisemaker things are for New Year's. I got some champagne too; we'll have it with dinner. The paper hearts are for Valentine's Day, and those little US flags are for the Fourth of July. That cake is for your birthday—I don't know when it is, but that's fine; we're celebrating today. It's impossible to find Halloween decorations at the end of November, which is super sad 'cause it's my favorite holiday, so I just got some candy instead. Turkey breast is cooking and will be served on turkey-print paper plates I got on clearance. And there will be latkes too. I love latkes."

Wes blinked several times as if trying to wake himself up, then pointed at a wooden bowl filled with hard-boiled eggs. Parker had used a Sharpie to draw designs on the shells. "What's that?"

"Easter, of course."

"Easter's in the spring."

"Yeah, so's Passover. It's also impossible to find matzah in Grants Pass in November, by the way." He kissed Wes's knuckles. "We're celebrating everything today."

"Why?"

"Making up for a little lost time."

Although Wes still appeared to be in a daze, he allowed Parker to tug him to the workbench, where a pile of gifts waited. Some were bound in Christmas paper, some in birthday wrap, and the rest in blue and silver that had to suffice for Hanukkah purposes. "Open," Parker ordered.

Wes obeyed. Most of the gifts were an assortment of used books Parker hoped Wes would like: some novels, and travel guides to Venice, Tokyo, and Mexico City. But Parker had also bought him a blue knitted beanie to keep his shorn head warm when he worked outside, a bag of good coffee beans, and a vehicle air freshener shaped like Bigfoot.

"That one's for Morrison." Parker paused. "Do you like everything?"

Wes blinked rapidly, then rubbed his eyes with the back of his hand. "Yeah," he rasped. "I do."

It would have been nice to eat outside, lit by the glow of Christmas lights. But Parker was worried about Wes getting a chill, so they ate indoors instead. Astonishingly, Wes had never eaten latkes, but he announced that they were now a favorite food. After they finished eating, he insisted on doing the meal cleanup, directing Parker to one of the lawn chairs under the tarp.

Before they went inside, Parker snagged one final box, unwrapped but hidden in one of Wes's plastic bins of supplies. "How about we do this now?" he said, handing it to Wes.

Wes looked at the box. "A gingerbread house kit?"

"I figured we can handle that much construction tonight."

"We can build a house together."

Something in Wes's tone and expression suggested he meant more than cookie construction. A lot more. Now it was Parker's turn to gape.

Then Wes shrugged and patted Parker's butt, breaking the mood. "Let's go inside."

They set the box on Wes's little table, and while Wes got the Eagles playing on the sound system, Parker removed the gingerbread components from the box. As they began assembly, however, it became clear neither of them had done this before.

"Building real things is easier," Wes grumbled after a wall collapsed for the third time. "Is it cool if I just go get my nail gun instead?"

"I think frosting is easier to digest." To illustrate his point, Parker squeezed a bit of white frosting from the bag onto a fingertip, then smeared it across Wes's lips.

Wes's brows shot up, and he licked the frosting away. Then he snatched the frosting bag and squeezed a dollop onto the tip of Parker's nose.

"You bastard!" Parker laughed, reaching for the bag.

Wes hopped back, Parker tripped over the table leg and fell—still laughing—and Wes collapsed on top of him, frosting and all, pinning Parker flat on his back. For a split second Parker worried that Wes might have been reinjured, but before he could say anything, Wes was spreading frosting over Parker's face. Parker tried to wiggle away, but that only resulted in Wes tickling him.

Between squirming and laughing, he managed to ask, "Is this a technique you learned in the academy?"

"Nope." Wes licked Parker's face and followed up with an interesting wiggle that chased the laughter away immediately.

Parker wrapped his arms around Wes, stilling him. "You're still heal—"

"I'm healed enough for this. I'll prove it." He shrugged himself free, pushed up Parker's shirt, and squeezed a line of frosting from the center of his chest to just above the top of his jeans. When he began to lick the path he'd made, Parker's will to argue wavered. Then Wes unbuttoned and unzipped Parker's jeans, and it evaporated completely.

"Oh my God," he said when Wes adorned his cock with frosting. "That's—"

Wes looked innocently up at him. "Yes?"

"We won't have anything left for the gingerbread."

"You taste better anyway." Then Wes lowered his head and began to suck.

There was something wonderfully naughty about being sprawled on the floor of a school bus, shirt rucked up and pants and underwear shoved down, his dick halfway down someone's throat. Yet it was nothing like any of the quick hookups he'd had, or even like sex with his short-term boyfriends. Wes didn't just turn him on; he also turned him inside out and made Parker want to reach for more. More within himself and more without. Made him want to grow roots and become the kind of tree Wes would fashion into something useful and amazing. God, if only Parker knew how to do that!

He planned to push Wes away and move the party to the bed. He was totally going to do that. In a second. In—

"Gonna come!" he screeched and went off like a rocket.

Wes didn't make any effort to stop, not until Parker lay half-senseless and gaping up at the curved ceiling. Then Wes chuckled, low and dirty. "Much better than building a gingerbread house."

"That was... fast. Sorry."

Another low laugh. "But you're young. We don't have to be finished yet."

As if agreeing, Parker's cock, which hadn't softened in the least, gave an enthusiastic twitch. Wes, still face level with it, laughed. "Told you."

Parker shed clothing as he made his way to the bed, nearly falling twice more as he worked his feet out of his jeans. But he made it there naked and unscathed and threw himself onto the mattress, slowly jacking himself while watching Wes undress. He was gratified to see Wes's nimble fingers turn clumsy.

Although Parker had seen Wes unclothed many times over the past days, Wes still seemed self-conscious about his scars. In contrast, all Parker saw was a beautiful, strong man whose healing wounds simply emphasized his strength. Parker tried hard to let his full appreciation show in his eyes and on his face. And when Wes reached to douse the lights, Parker spoke up. "Don't. Please."

Wes let his hand hover near the switch for a moment before turning away and crawling onto the bed. He didn't touch Parker, opting instead to prop himself on his side and watch, as if Parker were putting on a show for him. Which, to a large extent, Parker was. He even slowed down the movements of his fist and spread his legs a trifle wider. He suspected he looked wanton. Maybe even debauched. Good.

When Wes reached for him, Parker caught his hand. "No. Lie on your back. Touch yourself for me."

Wes's eyes widened, but he obeyed. Initially his movements appeared hesitant, but then he seemed to get off on the avid way Parker watched him, and Wes became more extravagant. He tilted his head back on the pillow and caught his lower lip between his teeth, and the deep-red head of his cock appeared and disappeared in his curled fist.

Watching was good. But touching would be better. Keeping his gaze locked with Wes's, Parker lightly brushed the pad of his thumb over one pale pink nipple, feeling it tighten. Wes shivered, so Parker did it again. He switched to the other one, and this time Wes gasped and arched his back.

That encouraged Parker to explore further. He lightly traced each of Wes's ribs and the indentation of his sternum, carefully avoiding bruises and cuts. He played for a bit with the shallow cup of Wes's navel and the points of his hips. There was a particularly nasty-looking gash on one upper thigh, but it didn't seem to bother Wes just now. He spread his legs wide, allowing Parker access to the inner thigh, to the tender crease where legs met torso, and then to Wes's balls.

Wes made a sound then, deep and guttural, that went right to Parker's core. Never mind that he'd gotten off maybe ten minutes ago; his cock was now so hard it ached. Parker was fairly certain that if he touched himself, he'd shoot really fast, and that wasn't what he was going for. Instead he wrapped his hand around Wes's so they moved together, and after several strokes, he moved Wes's hand away and claimed the prize for himself.

He scooted a little closer so he could whisper in Wes's ear. "I love the feel of you. Soft skin but a hard center. Hot. Slick. I bet you taste salty." He didn't move his mouth to Wes's groin, though, but nibbled delicately at the shell of his ear, the point of his chin, the cushion of his lip. He blew very softly and kissed the corner of Wes's mouth, right at the spot that curled up when he smiled. Kissed the lines radiating from the outer corners of his eyes and the little groove centered above his upper lip. Enjoyed the sound of Wes's breaths and the sensation of Wes's heart beating only inches from his own.

Wes was rubbing Parker's lower back, sometimes venturing down to squeeze his ass, and that was very nice. Even better, though, was the way he gazed so steadily at Parker. Wes's eyes were wide and the pupils so open that almost no blue iris showed. Wes seemed emotionally open too, offering himself freely to Parker without regard for his own vulnerability despite what he'd been through so recently. That trust was the most generous gift Parker had ever received.

Continuing the steady strokes of his fist with an added little twist, Parker scraped his teeth on the cords of Wes's neck, soothing the tiny irritations by sucking on them. Wes's entire face and chest had flushed beautifully, and Parker's grip had grown slick from precome. With a deep moan, Wes started lifting his hips in rhythm with Parker's movements.

"Need... more of you," groaned Wes.

Parker knew that Wes kept rubbers and lube in a little wooden box on a shelf above the bed, but that meant separating their bodies, if only for a moment. But then Wes said, "Please." Parker knelt up, grabbed the box, and fumbled through it so quickly that the box went flying—scattering condoms in its wake—and landed with a crash on the floor.

"It broke!" Parker cried. It had been a beautiful thing, obviously one of Wes's handiworks. "I'm so sor—"

Wes grabbed him in a sort of reverse tackle, bringing Parker back to the mattress with him. "Don't care," he growled. He thrust a wrapped condom into Parker's hand. "More. Now."

Which was better: vulnerable Wes or pushy-bottom Wes? Luckily Parker didn't have to choose; he had them both. He rolled on the condom as quickly as possible. It would have been even faster except Wes had positioned himself on all fours. He had a magnificent ass—not flat and bony like Parker's, but meaty and solid. The kind of ass you couldn't help touching and maybe licking and biting a little. Which was what Parker did once the rubber was in place. Eventually he found the lube in the covers, and he worked some into Wes's tight, grasping heat. His grunts got Parker so worked up that he feared he wouldn't make it to the next act.

"Ready?"

"Have been forever."

Wes's body welcomed Parker eagerly, as if they were made to be joined. Like Legos, Parker thought. Like the dovetail joints Wes used when he made furniture. But this union wasn't intended to be static, so Parker swung his hips long and slow to the beat of "Witchy Woman," which was playing on the speakers. After a few moments Wes made another long, low sound and dropped his chest onto the mattress, raising his ass higher. His head was turned to the side, eyes open but unfocused, his hands clutching the sheet so tightly his knuckles were white. As Parker plunged in and not quite out, he smoothed a palm down the long line of Wes's spine.

"So good. So perfect. I need so much and you give it to me and it's more than— Oh my *God*, so good." Parker was babbling nonsense but couldn't stop, and it didn't matter anyway. Not with Wes under him, around him. And Wes was suddenly rubbing his own cock furiously and Don Henley's voice was howling and everything in Parker's world narrowed, narrowed, narrowed to a few square feet and him and Wes and—

Parker threw back his head and bayed when he came.

Wes collapsed completely, Parker still inside and their skin stuck together with sweat. Parker kissed his nape, so pale after having been covered by hair for so long.

"Jesus Christ," Wes said with a long sigh.

"I told you before. I'm Jew—"

"But wasn't that your second coming?"

A naked, sticky tickle fight was a good follow-up to amazing sex. And then maybe a nap. Cleaning up could wait for later.

Chapter Twenty

"Okay," Wes began. "So a jigsaw is good for a lot of uses, and it's the only decent way to cut curves. But it comes with some challenges."

Parker nodded solemnly. "That thing's not over fifteen pounds, is it?"

Wes tried to suppress a smile. It had been two weeks, and he was already impatient with the doctor's restrictions. He'd tried a few times to sneak in a violation, like relocating a box full of metal scraps he might want to use someday, but Parker was always right there to stop him. Now Wes hefted the saw. "Five, maybe six pounds tops."

"Okay."

"Are you going to babysit or learn?"

"Both," Parker replied with an impish grin.

"Right. The secrets to using a jigsaw are to clamp the wood really firmly so it doesn't shift around while you're cutting, and to keep the saw base level and in contact with the wood."

"Remain in contact with the wood. Got it."

Wes feigned exasperation. "How often are you going to spout lame innuendos about wood and tools?"

"As often as possible. And don't forget nuts and screws! And maybe some nailing." Parker patted Wes's butt—which was, in truth, a little achy from last night's hammering, but in a good way. Parker's ass was probably sore too, since they'd switched off. That had been a lot of fun, very much the best of both worlds. But that wasn't what Wes was supposed to be thinking about right now.

"You also need to choose the right blade. Jigsaws will cut just about any material: stone, metal, tile, wood, plastic. So use the right blade for your job, and make sure it's nice and sharp." He picked up a blade from his work surface. "This is a taper ground blade made of high-carbon steel. It's best for precise cutting of wood." Under Parker's close scrutiny, Wes inserted the blade into the saw.

"It's backwards," Parker said.

"What do you mean?"

"The, um, pointy things—"

"The teeth?"

"Yeah, the teeth are facing the wrong way."

Wes chuckled. "They're fine. A jigsaw cuts on the upstroke." He waited, eyebrows raised, for Parker to snigger over the word *stroke*. "Do you want to see it in—um, at work?" He'd almost said *in action*, which would have produced at least a leer.

"Yeah."

"Okay. Draw a shape on this piece of wood. Nothing too intricate, but don't be afraid to include curves. That what a jigsaw's for."

Parker took a thick pencil, walked several steps away, and laid the wood scrap on a chair seat. He clearly didn't want Wes to see what he was sketching, and that made Wes highly suspicious. But it also gave him a very nice view of Parker's upraised ass, so he wasn't about to complain.

When Parker, smirking, returned the wood a few moments later, Wes wasn't at all surprised by what he saw. "A dick?"

"And balls. Those are nice and curvy."

"You want me to make you a wooden cock and balls?"

"I absolutely do. You can either use it as centerpiece for a really interesting piece of furniture—ooh, it would be cool on a headboard!—or add it to your holiday decorations." He waved at the Christmas lights he'd strung from the tarp supports. Wes was considering keeping them up year-round for their cheery nighttime glow.

Shaking his head in mock dismay, Wes clamped the piece to his workbench and switched on the saw. Parker stood close by and watched Wes trace the blade along the penciled line. He had to reclamp the piece twice in order to get all around it, but when he was finished, Parker's masterpiece was free. Wes tossed it to him. "There you go. You can hand sand the edges, or I can show you how to work the power sander next."

Parker grinned delightedly. "I think maybe I'll figure out how to hang bells from this and make it into a wind chime. The ancient Romans hung dick wind chimes to keep away evil and bring good luck. Which is just about the only thing I learned during my short journey through higher education."

"You could screw some hooks into the bottom. Those would hold bells as long as they're not too heavy."

"Good! Dick chime it is!"

"But are you ready to stop playing with your dick and take a shot at the saw?"

Parker set down his prized bit of wood.

Wes drew something much easier for Parker—a simple straight line. He could manage genitalia when he was more skilled. "Okay. Clamp it."

Parker did, but Wes shook his head right away. "The clamp's going to block the blade. You want to avoid moving the piece if at all possible. Also, make it tighter. You shouldn't be able to shift the wood."

"All right." Parker had a habit of sticking out the tip of his tongue when he concentrated. It was adorable and made Wes want to kiss him.

When after several tries Parker had the wood arranged to Wes's satisfaction, Wes handed him the saw. "The trickiest part is the beginning, when only a little bit of the base plate is in contact with the wood. Once you've moved forward a few inches, it gets easier. Just remember to keep it nice and even and to gently guide it along the line."

"Keep it even. Gently guide. Got it." Parker tilted his head at Wes. "Did you take shop classes in high school?"

"Yep."

"Not me. I did drama, choir, and business classes as electives and earned perfectly mediocre grades in all of them."

Wes smiled. "One good thing about being a grown-up is nobody cares anymore about your old permanent record from school. Which is good for me since I got in a few fights."

That made Parker blink. "You? Got in fights?"

"I had a pretty big chip on my shoulder."

"Huh."

"Are you forgetting my tendency toward being a headstrong asshole?"

Parker reached over and brushed at Wes's shoulder as if knocking away an imaginary chip. "Headstrong, maybe sometimes. Asshole, never." Then he waved the saw. "Okay, now how do I turn this thing on?"

"Put the saw in place first." Wes watched Parker comply. "Even it out a little—you have it tilted. Okay. Now put your left palm across the front, thumb on top. Good. That'll help keep it down and steady. Now just squeeze the trigger with your right hand when you're ready."

Parker took a deep breath and started it up. For a second or two the blade followed the line faithfully. Then Parker must have pulled sideways a little, rocking the saw off its base and sending the blade zigging off at a wild angle.

"Let go, let go!" Wes shouted.

And Parker let go, all right. He dropped the saw. It would have hit his foot if he hadn't hopped back. Instead the saw landed on the cement pad with a distressing clunk-crash.

"Oh my God! I'm so sorry! Did I break it?"

Wes gingerly picked it up. The blade had slightly bent, but the tool itself looked unharmed. When he pulled the trigger, it buzzed like it was supposed to. "It's fine."

"The blade is wack."

"No big deal. They only cost a couple of bucks apiece." Wes removed the damaged blade and dropped it into his metal recycling bin. "Do you want to try again?"

"I'll pass." Parker took a few steps back. "I don't want to amputate a limb."

"It'd be hard to cut off a limb with a jigsaw. A finger or two, sure."

"I'd prefer to keep all my appendages, thanks. I think I'll stick to things I can manage without bloodshed. How about if I make us some coffee?"

"You barely tried. If you give it some practice—"

"I could find a way to kill us both. Coffee?"

Wes sighed. "Yeah, sure."

"Good. That's one thing I know how to do right."

PARKER WAS in a strange mood the rest of that day. His smiles appeared more rarely and looked weaker, not reaching his eyes. He didn't chatter as much, and that evening after dinner, when Wes played Queen's *News of the World*, Parker didn't sing along. Although he sat on the couch beside Wes, each of them with a book—it had become their routine—Parker didn't turn any pages. His faraway expression looked thoughtful.

They didn't have sex that night, although Parker snuggled close, his hair tickling Wes's face. Wes liked the snuggling as much as the sex, really. With Parker in his arms, the world seemed to spin more smoothly and his dreams were sweeter.

Although still somewhat distant in the morning, Parker made them pancakes and sausage and then did some tidying inside the bus while

Wes reviewed finances. Things would be tight for a couple of months, but he'd manage. He'd already texted Mira to explain why he had nothing new to give her. He didn't go into the details, of course; she didn't need to know about the kidnapping. He just said he'd been injured and required surgery. She was entirely sympathetic, assuring him she'd look forward to new pieces whenever he was ready. So once he could work again, which was only a few more weeks away, he'd have income pretty quickly.

Now Wes stood under the tarp, looking down at the notebook on his table. He'd been sketching rough plans for a workshop, and now he was getting to the point where he was almost excited at the concept. He'd be able to keep his things more organized. And more secure, an issue that had worried him a bit in the past, even though it seemed unlikely that thieves would find their way to his hidden little corner of the world. But warmth would be nice, not just when working but also when cooking and showering. He'd still use the bus as his primary living quarters, but a shop would make other parts of his life more comfortable.

Wes gnawed on a pencil as he considered various sizes and placements of the shop. If he worked things right, he could use most of his existing concrete pad, which would save him money in supplies and labor.

Parker, who'd been wandering around near the periphery of Wes's vision, came close and draped himself over Wes's back. His pointy chin dug into Wes's shoulder.

"Hi," Wes said.

"Hi." Parker wrapped his arms around Wes's middle but didn't say anything. His breaths tickled the back of Wes's neck.

"Are you going to tell me what's bothering you?"

When Parker sighed, it tickled even more. "Can we go for a little walk?"

"Sure."

Wes set down his pencil, Parker took his hand, and they strolled slowly up the lane toward the county road. The sky hovered close overhead, steel gray and gloomy. Although Wes smelled moisture, it wasn't quite misting.

His grandfather's old house looked forlorn. No holiday decorations, no lights shining through the windows, no truck parked in front. Wes remembered sitting on that front porch when he was in high school, doing homework and sometimes daydreaming about a mysterious stranger pulling up and whisking him into a life of excitement and adventure. But nobody ever did.

Wes and Parker walked on the weedy shoulder between the paved county road and the neighbors' fence lines. A few birds swooped and tweeted overhead, horses grazed in the distance, and occasionally a dog barked from a front yard, but there were no other humans. Wes looked at dead thistles and remembered the spines he'd pulled from Parker's hand. Like Daniel and the lion, only Parker was no vicious beast, and Wes didn't believe for a moment that he'd tamed him.

They'd walked for about a mile when drizzle started and they agreed to turn back. But when they reached Wes's property, Parker stopped at the pond. He let go of Wes's hand and wrapped his arms around himself, his gaze fixed on the ducks. Wes waited.

Finally, without turning to look at Wes, Parker spoke. "I have to go."

Although Wes had been expecting this, the words hurt worse than anything the Cavellis had done to him. He hoped his face didn't show it, but he couldn't stop a waver in his voice. "Why?"

"What am I doing here?"

"Lots of things. You've been cooking and cleaning and—"

"Yeah. But you can do those things yourself now."

Wes's turn to look away. "I can. I don't want to take advantage of you."

"You're not!" Parker tugged on Wes's shoulder until they faced each other. "I love doing things for you. But you don't need me to do them. You don't need *me*."

I do. But Wes couldn't say that aloud, couldn't chain Parker to him with greedy words. "I like having you here" was the closest he'd allow himself.

"And I like being here. But you belong here. You've created a home, and you make beautiful things. I don't…. I'm not even running a coffeehouse or babysitting dogs. I'm mostly just taking up space."

"You're doing a lot more than that. You're…." Wes closed his eyes and remembered what he'd been thinking when the Cavellis were torturing him and he believed he was going to die. Now he *was* Future Wes, and he wanted Parker as desperately as he wanted life. "I love you."

"Oh God." Parker impatiently dashed tears away.

"I'm sorry."

"Don't apologize for that!" Parker shouted. Then he lowered his voice. "I love you too. I do. You're wrapped around my heart. More. It's like bits of you are in all my cells, and it feels good. But God, it hurts too."

"Why?" Wes was dizzy, as if his soul were zooming around in circles, trapped in a vortex of emotions.

"Because it's not enough. We love each other, and it's not enough. I've spent my whole life going nowhere. Sort of pinging around with no direction, and that's partly because I knew I could rely on Rhoda. If I stay with you, I'll just be relying on you instead."

"I don't mind."

"But I do. I need to be someone—not just this guy who brews coffee. I have to have goals and plans and a sense of where I'm going. I can't just float around and leech off people I love."

Wes grabbed Parker and pulled him into an embrace, hoping to steady them both. "You're not leeching. And you *are* someone."

"I don't believe that."

Wes knew whatever he said, no matter how persuasive his words, he wouldn't be able to change Parker's mind. Even with love in the mix, no human being could force another to see his own worth. That knowledge had to come from within.

"I want you to stay," Wes said, fighting back tears. "But I won't ask it of you. Go find your direction, if that's what you need. I just hope you discover that your direction leads you back to me."

Chapter Twenty-One

Late January always seemed extra busy at P-Town. College students were back from break, swilling coffee as they hit the books, and everyone needed extra caffeine to get through the postholiday rainy gloom. Parker didn't mind. He'd been putting in long hours since the day after he left Wes. Working hard didn't get him any closer to finding his path in life, but at least it kept him from wallowing.

When he wasn't at P-Town, he put in some volunteer time with Bright Hope, a group that Nevin, Jeremy, and their husbands occasionally worked for. Mostly he delivered food to LGBT elders, but he also stayed and visited with them for a while. That didn't give him any career goals either, but it felt good to help others—and he enjoyed their stories.

He wandered city streets aimlessly, scrolled through college websites without finding anything that spoke to him, and hunted job postings. But none of them appealed. None even provided ideas to strive for.

He spoke to his mom and a few other people about moving back to Seattle, but each time he let that notion fade. Seattle was too full of bittersweet memories, and anyway, he knew he'd be just as clueless there as he was everywhere else.

Once every week or so, he found strange solace in poking around hardware stores and architectural salvage shops. Everything there reminded him of Wes, and sometimes Parker found a small item he could afford. An ornate old doorknob. A chunk of pretty wood reclaimed from a house or barn. A ceiling medallion that might have once decorated a mansion or saloon. Parker kept these items in a bin in his closet, hoping to someday give them to Wes.

As for Wes, he seemed to be doing okay. They texted each other daily, and once in a while they FaceTimed instead. Wes had fully recovered and was now back to making furniture. If Parker asked, which he often did, Wes sent photos of whatever he was working on. It wasn't the same as being there. Parker couldn't smell the freshly cut wood or hear the buzz of Wes's tools. And God, he couldn't hold Wes in his arms. But it was better than nothing.

"Gonzo, you're going to rub a hole right through that glass."

Parker stopped wiping the top of the pastry case. "Sorry. Spacing."

"I noticed. You're due for a break anyway. Grab a cup and come sit with me."

Shit. Rhoda had her patented Intervention Expression on, the one that meant she was going to offer forceful advice whether the other person wanted it or not. Even Nevin quailed when he saw that look, but at least he could manufacture a work emergency and manage a quick escape. Parker was stuck.

Since he couldn't fully defend himself, he decided to reinforce instead. He made himself an extra-large cup of coffee and grabbed an oversize chocolate-butterscotch-oatmeal cookie. Then he joined Rhoda at her preferred table, the one closest to the cash register. She had her laptop set up and a thick manila folder nearby, which meant she'd probably been working on something related to taxes. No wonder she'd decided to coach Parker instead.

"You have tomorrow off, don't you, honey?"

"I can come in if you need me. It's no problem."

"I don't. Do you have plans?"

He shrugged. "I was thinking about dyeing my hair." The blue had faded away, leaving it bleached with dark roots. Maybe he'd switch to bright red this time.

"Well, if that's all you have going on, maybe you should go out tonight. Gather some friends and hit a club or two. You haven't been out dancing in…. Well, I can't remember."

"Meh. Don't feel like it."

She gave him a long look over the rim of her teacup. "You haven't been very social lately."

"I spend all day interacting with people here at P-Town. I think it's reasonable to want a little downtime at the end of the day."

"Of course it's reasonable. I just want to make sure it's what you're comfortable with and not because I'm overworking you. Or because you're distressed."

Ugh. He wasn't distressed. He was more… numb. Like when the dentist shot you up with novocaine and your lips felt all big and rubbery and in the way. His entire body felt like that now. Hell, his mind did too.

"I'm fine, Mom. But if you want me out of your house tonight, I can go see a movie or something."

She clucked. "Why would I want you out of the house?"

"I dunno. So you and Bob can have some alone time."

"We can have that at his place," she replied. "The house is your *home*, Parker. Always."

"I know." And that knowledge both comforted and confined him.

Rhoda picked at the chipped magenta polish on one fingernail. "Speaking of Bob…."

That perked him up. "Yes?"

"His son Gabriel is coming to Portland next month. Would you be willing to join us for dinner?"

"Is that the gay one?" Parker asked, narrow-eyed. Bob had four sons, three of whom were straight.

"Yes."

He crossed his arms. "Tell me you're not trying to set me up with your boyfriend's kid."

Rhoda thinned her lips and furrowed her brow. Shit. She didn't often get angry, but when she did, the earth shook. "No," she snapped. "How about we assume that just for once, it isn't all about you, Parker Herschel Levin. Maybe this is about me meeting a boyfriend's family for the first time since the last millennium, and maybe I'm a little nervous about it."

Oh. "Sorry, Mom." He hung his head.

"And Gabriel has been going through a tough time lately and could use a little distraction and support, *not* a date with a boy who's already in love with someone else."

Parker snapped his head up so fast his neck cracked. "I never said I was—"

"I'm not stupid. And I know you, kiddo. I changed your diapers, went through four rounds of pinkeye and one bout of fifth disease with you. I survived the seven months when you wouldn't eat anything that wasn't beige. I can tell when my son is in love." Miraculously her anger had melted away, replaced by the fond concern that always made him want to sniffle.

"Augh." He buried his face in his hands and waited for her advice.

But she didn't give any. She remained silent, in fact, until he finally peeled his hands away to look at her. "You're not going to tell me what to do?"

"Honey, this is something you're going to have to work out for yourself."

"What if I can't?"

"When it comes to figuring out love, you are no less qualified than the rest of us. Which means you might screw things up—or everything could work out beautifully. There's no right way to do love. It's custom-made, not off-the-rack. People need to tailor it to their particular needs."

Although she was obviously being careful not to give him false confidence, he found her words reassuring. Other people struggled with this too—even people who were smart and capable, like Jeremy. And many of those people succeeded, even if, like Nevin, they'd completely lacked competence to begin with.

A few tables away, the cat ladies were loudly arguing over whether a raw diet for felines was beneficial enough to be worth the hassle and expense. Over in the corner, Drew and Travis had their heads bent over a piece of paper on the table, maybe Drew's playlist for next Tuesday. A group of high-school girls sat at the next table, discussing a project for their history class. The prime window spot was taken by a newer regular, a guy named Mauricio who'd recently quit his job to spend more time caring for his preschool-aged daughter. She was a serious kid who liked to draw; right now she was digging into a plastic box full of crayon stubs.

P-Town was Parker's home too, and it always would be. No matter where he went, or with whom.

Rhoda reached across to take his hands in hers. "I do have a suggestion about Wes, if you'd like to hear it. It has nothing to do with romance."

"Lay it on me."

"I know he's doing well selling his larger pieces, but do you think he'd be interested in selling some smaller pieces here? I have people ask me every day if that shelf is for sale." She pointed at her Hanukkah gift, which hung on the wall behind the counter. "When I tell them no way, they ask where they can buy something similar."

"Huh. I can ask him."

"Good. He won't make as much as he does on his big furniture, but I bet he can turn out a fair number of small pieces quickly, and his profit margin will likely be larger. I've had people offer me eight hundred dollars for that shelf!"

"And you turned them down?"

She tsked at him. "No amount of money will get me to part with that."

A bunch of people all entered the shop at once, forming a long line at the register. Parker gave Rhoda's hands a quick squeeze, then let go and stood. "Back to the grindstone," he said with a wink.

"I THINK she's getting serious about Bob."

On Parker's phone screen, the corner of Wes's mouth hitched up. "And how do you feel about that?"

"Hopeful. She's great on her own, but I think she'll be happier with a partner."

"That could be a motto for a lot of people."

Wes was sitting under the tarp. Behind him Parker could make out something bulky on the workbench. Part of a dresser, maybe. Wes wore his Bigfoot jacket and the hat Parker had bought him, and the scars on his face were healing nicely, just two red lines without any residual puffiness. Parker tried to gauge whether Wes was happy, miserable, or somewhere in between, but it was hard to tell. He wasn't a guy who showed much emotion.

"I've been spending a lot of time thinking about you," said Parker.

"Is that good?"

"Yeah." Parker lay back against his pillow. Although he had a comfortable bed, it wasn't as nice as Wes's. "Do you think I'm qualified to make decisions about love?"

Wes chuckled. "I don't think I'm qualified to tell. Why?"

"Just something my mom said the other day." He rubbed his chin, which needed a shave. "Hey, Wes, would you agree that a person could get a reasonable table at IKEA?"

"Um, sure."

"I mean, an IKEA table can look good. And it'll hold a bowl of cereal and glass of OJ just fine."

"I'm sure it will," Wes said. "But if you need a new table I'll make you one."

"No, I'm good. Okay, so an IKEA dining table will run you, what? Maybe four hundred bucks tops?" That wasn't entirely a wild guess; he'd shopped there with more than one roommate in the past.

"I guess."

"And how much do yours cost?"

Wes appeared to think for a moment. "I think Miri sold the last one for sixteen grand."

Parker almost choked. "Really? Holy shit. So tell me. Why would somebody buy your table for a shit-ton of money when they can get one at IKEA for a few hundred bucks?"

"Good question. Mine will last a lifetime—generations, if it's well cared for. Mine's handcrafted instead of mass-produced. I think some people like to know that time and care went directly into their individual piece. And mine's unique. Nobody in the world will ever have that same table—which also means certain buyers are more likely to find one that uniquely fits them. IKEA tables might be adequate, but mine could be ideal."

Parker had been nodding while Wes spoke, and now Wes paused and looked at him quizzically. "I'm guessing there's a point to this?"

"It's a metaphor. Sometimes the perfect thing is unique—not like anybody else's perfect thing. And maybe a person shouldn't force himself into an IKEA life if what he really needs is a Wes Anker custom piece."

"I don't understand your metaphor."

Parker smiled. "I'm not sure I do either. Give me some time to think about it." It was weird, but saying it out loud to Wes helped anchor the idea in his brain. Parker couldn't fully grasp that idea, not yet. But he believed it was possible.

Anyway, time to shift the conversation before he lost Wes completely. "Are you still planning your workshop?"

"Yeah. Got some cost estimates. I've been replenishing my savings after missing so much work, but I'll get there sooner or later."

"Rhoda has a plan that could make it sooner." Parker shared Rhoda's idea for Wes to sell smaller pieces at P-Town, and Wes listened with apparent interest.

"But why would she do that?" Wes asked after Parker finished. "She runs a coffeehouse, not a furniture store."

"True, but she sells paintings all the time. P-Town makes a good place to display stuff, plus people seem to get into a spending mood after they've filled up with mochas and almond-peach scones."

Wes's gaze turned inward as if he were deep in thought. "Maybe...," he murmured.

"It wouldn't be a replacement for the big pieces you make. A supplement. Sort of a palate cleanser in between larger projects? And dude, you have enough hardware bits and bobs to make about a thousand little things."

"Hmm." Wes stood. "Want to visit your friends?"

"Yeah."

The two of them chatted while Wes walked to the pond. Then he turned the phone around so Parker could see the ducks paddling around. "Hi, ducks!" Parker called. They didn't answer, but that was okay. Maybe waterfowl didn't like to FaceTime.

After a minute or so, Wes appeared back on screen. "Thank Rhoda for the offer. I'll give it serious consideration."

"Good. I love you, Wes. And not in an IKEA way."

"Me too. Even when I don't understand you."

AFTERWARD PARKER told everyone he heard Morrison drive past on Belmont, even though the door was shut against the early March chill and Lena Horne was crooning over the sound system. Nobody believed him except John, who was eccentric in his own right, and Wes, when he later heard the story. Although Wes might have only been humoring him. But Parker *did* hear Morrison, and he froze as he counted out change to one of Jeremy's park rangers.

"Uh, sorry," Parker said, handing over the bills. "Dina will have your latte ready in a sec."

The ranger dropped the coins into the tip jar. "Thanks."

Wes must be bringing more of his small treasures, which was what Rhoda called them. Exquisite little jewelry boxes, fanciful phone recharging stands, exotic-looking plant stands. His first vanful sold almost as quickly as Rhoda could put the pieces out, and even after Wes insisted she take a commission, she was able to send him an impressive payment. Rhoda was thrilled, Wes was richer, and Parker was happy because Wes had spent the night after delivering his first batch. They'd snuggled in Parker's captain's bed, trying to keep their lovemaking quiet.

Parker hoped Wes would stay over again tonight. And maybe tomorrow too? Parker had tomorrow off, and they could make a day of it. A few hours in a Powell's bookstore, perhaps, followed by a walk through Forest Park and a nice dinner out. That might be enough to keep him from pining for a while. But it probably wouldn't last until he finally finished getting his head straight.

When Wes entered P-Town a few minutes later, Parker ran over and swooped him into a kiss. It got most of the customers clapping and cheering and made Wes drop the paper grocery bag he'd been carrying.

"Hi," Wes said when he was again steady on his feet.

"Hi yourself." Parker felt like a kid on his birthday—and boy, did he want to unwrap this present.

Wes simply stood there, head tilted a little, as if he were trying to discern a secret message in Parker's face. Then he nodded, apparently to himself. "We have things to discuss."

Parker's heart beat faster. "Good things?"

"I hope. But I have something else to take care of first." Wes picked up his bag and strode to the table where Rhoda sat with Jeremy, Nevin, and Qay. Parker trailed along.

Of course everyone at the table had been watching Wes since he'd entered—they probably clapped at the kiss—and now they all greeted him. "I hope you have more treasures," Rhoda said.

"Yep. I'll get 'em in a bit." Then, to everyone's surprise, he addressed Nevin. "I need to say this."

"Yeah?" Nevin stood up with his legs slightly spread and his arms crossed.

"Thank you."

Seeing Nevin speechless was a rare thing indeed, but there he was. Gaping.

So Wes continued. "You saved my life. And then you drove Parker to see me and got us both everything we needed to get by for a few days. I know you did these things because Parker's your friend, but I'm deeply grateful. Parker is really fortunate to have you in his life."

After Nevin blinked a few times, his shoulders slumped. "Fuck," he growled. Then he gave Wes a quick hard hug followed by a punch to his shoulder. The one that hadn't been shot.

Wes was grinning like a loon. "I brought you a little present," he said, handing over the bag.

Nevin took it carefully, as if it might contain live cobras. But after he reached inside, all he pulled out was a large, nonvenomous wicker basket. He set the basket on the table and began pulling out items: A small plaster version of the Grants Pass Caveman statue. A large pump bottle of a cleaning product called Ballwash and coordinating bottle of something called Sack Spray. Those items made everyone at the table hoot with laughter while Nevin attempted to scowl. Yet when he held the final item, a bottle of whiskey, even Nevin whistled his appreciation. "Expensive stuff," he said.

"I thought you'd be someone who appreciates it."

Nevin gave him a warm, genuine smile without a hint of snark or leer. "Let's pour some together, sometime soon."

"I'd like that," Wes said.

And Parker didn't bawl, which he counted as a major win.

"Excuse me," Wes said. "Parker and I need a few minutes."

Rhoda clearly tried to hide a smile behind her hand, but Parker could see it in her eyes. What did that mean? Did she have suspicions about what Wes wanted to discuss? Parker himself had no clue.

Eager to get it straight from Wes, Parker grabbed his arm and dragged him out onto the sidewalk. It wasn't raining, and neither of them would freeze if this didn't take too long.

"This is where we first saw each other," Wes observed.

"Yeah. That was a hell of a day for both of us. Yet not nearly the most traumatic one that month."

Wes lifted his chin. "Are you sorry it happened?"

"I'm really sad that Logan was murdered. I wish to God those fuckwads hadn't hurt you. But I'm not sorry at all about the rest. Meeting you is the best thing that's ever happened to me."

"Ditto." Wes looked down and scraped his foot along the sidewalk, clearly collecting his thoughts. His hair had grown out, and although it wasn't nearly long enough yet for a ponytail, there was plenty for Parker to run his fingers through. It would be soft and would smell of wood and pine sap and coffee. Parker could drown in that scent.

Finally Wes caught Parker's gaze again. "I've been thinking about your analogy. The IKEA one. I think I understand. And I'm offering you an epiphany in exchange—one I had just last night."

"I'd like to hear it."

"Okay." Deep breath. "You told me that you just float around. But that's not exactly true. Yes, you move around a lot. Sometimes without much planning."

"Any planning," Parker interjected.

"Whatever. But wherever you float to, you always end up back here—in Portland. At P-Town."

"'Cause I'm too useless to cut the cord."

"No! That's not it at all. You float *because* of the cord. You're a free spirit, Parker, the kind of unique, wonderful soul who doesn't fit in any preset slots. And you have the confidence to be that person—to be true to who you are—because you know you can always return home. Here's *my* analogy: you're like an acrobat, leaping and spinning high in the air, knowing that net is there below you. And who'd want to be an office drone when he can be an acrobat?"

Parker let those words sink in while traffic rumbled down the street and two of the cat ladies appeared around the corner. They waved at Parker before entering P-Town.

An acrobat. It sounded ridiculous at first, but the more Parker thought about it, the better sense it made. He'd never been truly unhappy with his directionless life—only with the sense that he was a disappointment to Rhoda and the world at large. But what if he wasn't disappointing anyone? After all, Rhoda never nagged him to do something more specific with his life, and it wasn't as if she was reticent about expressing her opinions.

"I think I like floating," Parker said quietly.

"Yes!" Wes gave him a fast embrace. "Maybe someday you'll decide to settle on the ground for a while, and maybe not. As long as you're being authentic to yourself, it doesn't matter."

Parker nodded. He felt shaky, almost in shock, and yet also wonderfully free. As if he really might float up into the sky at any moment. He clutched Wes's arm just in case. He didn't want to fly away right now.

"The other thing you need to know, Parker, is that however far you float, you're always right there when people need you. You're Rhoda's right hand—without you, she'd never give herself a break. You didn't let Logan's death just slip away unnoticed. And when I needed you in the hospital and after, you never left my side."

"Because I love you," Parker whispered.

"I know." Wes's eyes appeared suspiciously moist, but he was smiling. "And there's more to the epiphany. See, I'm your opposite. I've rooted myself firmly in place because I'm afraid if I let myself fly a little, I'll lose everything."

"You haven't had a net," Parker said solemnly.

"Exactly. I *want* to do more, I really do. I want to go places and… experiment a little. But I've been too chickenshit. I mean, look at me! I live in a bus that can't drive anywhere, and isn't that an even better metaphor than your Swedish tables?"

Wes's voice had risen enough to make passersby stare, but neither he nor Parker cared. Parker grasped Wes's other arm and looked steadily into his eyes. "What if you had a net? What if I was your net?"

"Then I think I could do anything."

They hugged again, this one so long and fierce that it was hard to breathe. And they each sobbed a little into the other's shoulder yet laughed at the same time. Parker *could* fly—and he could bring Wes along with him. And when they felt like it, they could touch down together.

They stood outside for a while, never quite breaking contact. They made some promises and a few plans. And even though Parker had begun to shiver, deep inside, he was toasty warm.

"Let's go in," Wes finally said, holding Parker's hand.

They must have been quite a sight as they marched to Rhoda's table. Puffy eyes. Runny noses. Grins so wide their heads almost fell off.

Everyone at the table waited silently. Even Rhoda.

"Hey, Mom?" Well, that was the most pathetic attempt ever at nonchalance. "Can someone cover my shifts for… the foreseeable future?"

Only when your boss was also your mother would a question like that bring a smile in response. "Do you have plans, Gonzo?"

"Wes and I are going to do some traveling. Road trip."

"Where to?"

They hadn't decided that part, so Parker looked at Wes. And Wes smiled brightly enough to illuminate the entire city. "We're going to Wyoming."

Epilogue

New Orleans, Louisiana
October 2019

Parker lay back on the mattress, rubbed his stomach, and groaned. "Oh my God. I ate way too much. I'm going to die." It was, however, a rather excellent way to go.

Wes was sitting at the motel room's wobbly little table, gloating over the bag of treasures he'd accumulated that day. "I thought two dinners was a great idea, actually."

"Two dinners, three bourbon punches, and, oh my God, bananas Foster."

"I thought you liked bananas," Wes said, waggling his eyebrows suggestively.

"*I* get to make the stupid double entendres." Parker considered throwing a pillow at Wes but decided it would take too much effort.

He watched as Wes, humming contentedly, took an item out of his bag and held it under the light. It was a piece of ironwork that, according to Wes, had probably been part of a fireplace screen. Round, about the size of a dessert plate, it was made to look like a spiderweb, complete with a fat spider in the middle. Wes would surely use it to create something amazing. It was a good thing they were leaving town in the morning, before Wes had a chance to empty every architectural salvage store in Louisiana. Morrison was already packed nearly full with his finds, large and small.

Oh, but to see the joy on Wes's face! Not just over his purchases, but every time he had a new experience. Like when he first caught sight of the Mississippi. When they took a tour of the old cemetery. When they strolled around town, rubbernecking at the mansions. When they walked up Bourbon Street, pausing in doorways to listen to the music flowing out.

Tomorrow they'd begin the long drive back to Oregon. They'd take a more southerly route this time, crossing Texas and New Mexico before cutting north. And they already had their next trip planned: a late-winter cruise to Mexico. Wes had to get his passport first, and they needed to sell more furniture to bulk up the bank account, but that was fine. Parker was looking forward to some quiet months in Rogue Valley. He planned to watch Wes work, do most of the cooking and cleaning, and update Wes's fledgling website.

He might put more thought into a vague idea that had been rolling around in his skull lately.

Wes's grandfather's old house had stood empty for years, making Wes a little sad every time they passed it. If Wes and Parker could rent or buy it for an affordable price, it might make a nice home for a nonprofit group. The region's only LGBTQ+ resource center had closed its doors the previous year—maybe it was time to open a new one. Bright Hope could have a Rogue Valley location staffed by Parker. And in the evenings he and Wes would have their music and their books. And their bed.

"You have that gleam in your eyes," Wes said.

"Do I?"

"I thought you were too full to move. I thought you were dying."

"I've recovered. It's a miracle. So put away your toys and join me instead." Parker patted the mattress beside him.

Wes had just opened his mouth to answer when Parker's phone made a familiar tone. He sighed theatrically.

"Go on," Wes said. "Read it. She hasn't texted you in over a week."

"No, but she tagged me on Facebook two days ago."

"Doesn't count."

Wes had turned into Rhoda's biggest ally. Which might have happened anyway, but back in March, when they returned from Wyoming, Rhoda asked Wes to call her Mom, and that sealed the deal. And how could Parker begrudge any of it when Wes was so thrilled to have someone to call Mom?

Gonzo r u there?

Sigh. *Hi Mom.*

U boys having a good time?

Not at the moment—at least not as good as Parker had been planning. For one thing, they still had their clothes on.

NOLA is fantastic. We love it.

Good. Will u b here for Thanksgiving?

Ugh. As if there hadn't been enough turkey-day disasters already.

Wouldn't miss it, he texted.

Can u stay for the weekend & maybe several days after? Keep an eye on P-Town?

Sure. Planning another trip to Vegas?

It took a couple of minutes for her reply, probably because she was at work and something needed her attention. *Hawaii.*

Ooh. Swanky! He added a palm-tree emoji.

A honeymoon should b swanky, don't u think?

Parker's whoop of delight brought Wes out of his chair and to the bed, where he peered over Parker's shoulder. When he read Rhoda's last text, he laughed and clapped Parker's back.

Congrats, Mom. We're so happy for u. This time he sent a string of emojis: the congratulations horn, clapping hands, a piece of cake, and a bunch of hearts.

"That's very eloquent," Wes intoned.

You 2 will have to arrange tuxes. We'll discuss when you get home. And maybe u should talk to the rabbi. This one does a beautiful ceremony. Doesn't care if you're diff religions & same gender.

"Oh my God," Parker moaned. "I knew this was coming. She can't help herself."

Wes was staring at him. "Are you that opposed to the idea?"

"No." Parker reached over to lightly stroke Wes's cheek. "Not opposed. Is that a proposal?"

"I guess it is. Is that a yes?"

"I guess it is."

Parker dropped the phone and gathered Wes in for a kiss.

He'd respond to Rhoda later. And on the drive home, he and Wes could work out some wedding plans of their own. Oh my God—he was going to be a married man! He'd need to warn Wes that getting hitched wouldn't stop Rhoda. Next she'd be hinting about grandkids.

But for now Wes was in his bed, in his arms, in his heart, in his soul. For now both of them were exactly where they wanted to be.

KIM FIELDING is pleased every time someone calls her eclectic. Her books span a variety of genres, but all include authentic voices and unconventional heroes. She's a Rainbow Award and SARA Emma Merritt winner, a LAMBDA finalist, and a two-time Foreword INDIE finalist. She has migrated back and forth across the western two-thirds of the United States and currently lives in California, where she long ago ran out of bookshelf space. A university professor who dreams of being able to travel and write full-time, she also dreams of having two teenagers who occasionally get off their phones, a husband who isn't obsessed with football, and a cat who doesn't wake her up at 4:00 a.m. Some dreams are more easily obtained than others.

Blogs: kfieldingwrites.com and www.goodreads.com/author/show/4105707.Kim_Fielding/blog
Facebook: www.facebook.com/KFieldingWrites
Email: kim@kfieldingwrites.com
Twitter: @KFieldingWrites

LOVE CAN'T CONQUER

KIM FIELDING

A Love Can't Novel

Bullied as a child in small-town Kansas, Jeremy Cox ultimately escaped to Portland, Oregon. Now in his forties, he's an urban park ranger who does his best to rescue runaways and other street people. His ex-boyfriend, Donny—lost to drinking and drugs six years earlier—appears on his doorstep and inadvertently drags Jeremy into danger. As if dealing with Donny's issues doesn't cause enough turmoil, Jeremy meets a fascinating but enigmatic man who carries more than his fair share of problems.

Qayin Hill has almost nothing but skeletons in his closet and demons in his head. A former addict who struggles with anxiety and depression, Qay doesn't know which of his secrets to reveal to Jeremy—or how to react when Jeremy wants to save him from himself.

Despite the pasts that continue to haunt them, Jeremy and Qay find passion, friendship, and a tentative hope for the future. Now they need to decide whether love is truly a powerful thing or if, despite the old adage, love can't conquer all.

www.dreamspinnerpress.com

LOVE IS HEARTLESS

A LOVE CAN'T NOVEL

KIM FIELDING

A Love Can't Novel

Small but mighty—that could be Detective Nevin Ng's motto. Now a dedicated member of the Portland Police Bureau, he didn't let a tough start in life stop him from protecting those in need. He doesn't take crap from anyone, and he doesn't do relationships. Until he responds to the severe beating of a senior citizen and meets the victim's wealthy, bow-tied landlord.

Property manager and developer Colin Westwood grew up with all the things Nevin never had, like plenty of money and a supportive, loving family. Too supportive, perhaps, since his childhood illness has left his parents unwilling to admit he's a strong, grown man. Colin does do relationships, but they never work out. Now he's thinking maybe he won't just go with the flow. Maybe it's time to try something more exciting. But being a witness to a terrible crime—or two—was more than he bargained for.

Despite their differences, Colin and Nevin discover that the sparks fly when they're together. But sparks are short-lived, dampened by the advent of brutal crimes, and Colin and Nevin have seemingly little in common. The question is whether they have the heart to build something lasting.

www.dreamspinnerpress.com

FOR MORE OF THE BEST GAY ROMANCE

DREAMSPINNER PRESS
dreamspinnerpress.com

Made in the USA
Coppell, TX
19 April 2025

48465110R00125